A VENDETTA
OF THE HILLS

By

WILLIS GEORGE EMERSON

First published in 1917

𝔇𝔢𝔡𝔦𝔠𝔞𝔱𝔢𝔡

TO MY WIFE

BONNIE O'NEAL EMERSON

Our enchanting years of pleasure, dear, are speeding all too fast,
As our ever-fleeting joys become blest mem'ries of the past.
Heaven's blessings, glad and golden, strew with bliss the paths of life
When a sweetheart, fond and cheery,
Has her "hubby" for her dearie,
And her "hubby" has a sweetheart for his wife.

—The Author.

January 18, 1917.

WILLIS GEORGE EMERSON

Willis George Emerson was born in 1856, and spent his early education at Knox College, Illinois, USA. He later attended *Northern Ohio University*, after which he was admitted to the bar in 1886. Emerson quickly lost interest in the legal profession however, and moved to Kansas where he became heavily involved in politics; actively campaigning on behalf of the Republican Party in both the 1888 and 1900 elections.

Emerson is best known as a prominent American novelist though, and is famed for his evocative tales of the Mid-West. Among his better-known novels are *Buell Hampton* (1902), *The Builders* (1906), *Smoky God vs. Voyage in the Inner World* (1908), *The Treasure of Hidden Valley* (1915) and *The Man Who Discovered Himself* (1919). *Smoky God vs. Voyage in the Inner World* is particularly notable for its unusual plotline; the protagonist discovers an Eden like civilisation in in the centre of the earth, where a scientifically advanced race of long-lived giants is discovered worshipping a 'smoky God' – the interior sun. This was the first literary work to bring Emerson widespread acclaim.

A man of many talents and interests, Emerson also worked as a newspaperman, lawyer, politician and promoter, forming the North American Copper Company in Wyoming. Emerson is also credited with founding the town of Grand Encampment, a municipality in Carbon County, Wyoming. With Emerson's Copper Company based there, it became a booming centre of copper mining and smelting. A sixteen-mile tramway was built to carry copper ore from the mountains into the town for smelting; a tramway which was, at the time, the longest in the world.

He died on 11 December, 1918.

The Jail Delivery—Page 181

CONTENTS

ILLUSTRATIONS

Chapter I

Guadalupe

IT was a June morning in mid-California.

The sun was just rising over the rim of the horizon, dissipating the purple haze of dawn and bathing in golden sunshine a great valley spread out like a parchment scroll. It was a rural scene of magnificent grandeur—encircling mountains, rolling foothills, and then the vast expanse of plain dotted here and there with clumps of trees and clothed with luxuriant grasses.

Thousands of cattle were bestirring themselves from their slumbers—some sniffing the air and bellowing lowly, others pawing the earth in an indifferent way, and all moving slowly toward one or other of the mountain streams that wound serpent-like through the valley, as if they deemed it proper to begin the day with a morning libation.

To the south, commanding a narrow pass that pierced the Tehachapi mountain range, stood old Fort Tejon, dismantled now and partly in ruins, picturesque if no longer formidable—a romantic relic of old frontier fighting days. In the fore-

(1)

ground of the crumbling adobe walls, sheltered under giant oaks, was a trading store and post-office combined.

Within this building half a dozen men were in earnest conversation, swapping yarns even at that early hour. Perhaps they, too, like the cattle, had felt the call for their "morning's morning."

A young army officer, Lieutenant Chester Munson, was telling of a rough experience he had had a few days before with a mountain lion in one of the near-by rugged canyons.

The story was interrupted by a sound of galloping hoofs.

"Here's Dick Willoughby," someone announced.

The rider brought his mustang to a panting stop, threw the bridle rein over its head, and, leaping lightly from his saddle, entered the store.

Dick Willoughby was a tall, athletic, square-jawed, grey-eyed young fellow who looked determinedly purposeful. He was originally an architect from New York City, but during the last five years had become an adopted son of the West—had made the sacrifice, or rather gone through the improving metamorphosis, of assimilation.

"Good morning, Ches, old boy," he shouted to the lieutenant.

The latter returned the salutation with a friendly nod.

"The camp was lonely without you last night, Dick," he said. "Who is the fair senorita that keeps you away?"

"That's all right," replied Willoughby, smiling. "I will tell you later." Then after a genial all-round greeting for the others present, he eagerly exclaimed: "Boys, she is coming."

"What! Guadalupe?" shouted everyone in chorus of surprise.

"Yes, Guadalupe is headed this way. I spied her on the mountain trail an hour ago, and thanks to my field glasses, was able to determine the moving speck was none other than the old squaw herself. She is just beyond yon clump of trees and will be here shortly."

"I am wonderin' if she's got her apron filled again with them there gold nuggets," remarked Tom Baker inquiringly, while a smile flitted over his grey-bearded countenance. "That squaw is a regular free-gold placer proposition."

"She would have been held up before now in the old days, eh, sheriff?" laughed one of the cowboys. Tom Baker had been sheriff for a long term of years in early times, and, although no longer in office, the title had still clung to him.

"By gad!" exclaimed Jack Rover, another cowboy, and a gentlemanly young fellow in manner and appearance. "She's not going to get back to her hiding-place this time, nor to that will-o'the-wisp placer gold mine of hers unless she shows me."

"That will do for you," said Dick Willoughby with an admonishing look. "Don't you forget that Guadalupe, although an old Indian squaw, is also a human being. There is going to be no violence if I can prevent it."

"Well," laughed Jack, pushing his hat back as if to acknowledge that he had been checkmated, "you're my boss on the cattle ranch, and I'll have to take your tip, I guess."

"I say, Dick," asked the other cowboy, "did you see anything of the white wolf?"

"Do you mean the real wolf?" interjected Jack Rover, "or the bandit, Don Manuel?"

Willoughby was looking along the road and took no notice.

"I guess both are real," mused Tom Baker, grimly smiling, and a general laugh followed.

"Well, I for one will subscribe to that," exclaimed Buck Ashley, storekeeper, postmaster, bartender, and all-round *generalissimo* of the trading establishment. "If Don Manuel is not a wolf in human form, and a bigger outlaw than Joaquin Murietta ever thought of being, why you may take my head for a football."

"But he's dead, ain't he?" asked the cowboy who had introduced the subject of the white wolf.

"Just one thing that I want to emphasize good and plenty to you fellers," said Tom Baker, "and that is—"

"Here she comes!" interrupted Dick Willoughby.

A hush fell over the group as the bent, aged figure of an Indian woman was seen approaching the store. Her features were hidden by a shawl that closely muffled her head and shoulders.

Buck Ashley saluted Guadalupe with a "How?" The squaw answered with the same abrupt salutation, shuffled up to the counter and said brokenly, "Coffee—sugar—tea—rice." With her left hand she had gathered up the lower portion of her calico apron and held it pouch fashion. She thrust her right hand into the pocket so formed, and bringing forth a handful of gold nuggets, laid them on the counter. Some were the size of peas, and others as large as hulled hickory nuts. •Not a word was spoken by the onlookers, who were wild-eyed in their astonishment. Soon interest rose to high tension.

Buck Ashley tied up a large package of sugar and pushed it toward the bent form of his customer; then resting his hand on the counter, he looked fixedly at the squaw and said, "More gold."

Again she thrust her hand into the apron pocket and brought out another handful of nuggets, whereupon Ashley proceeded to tie up a large package of coffee. This done, he repeated the request for more gold. Old Guadalupe added another handful of nuggets to those already on the counter, and Ashley tied up a package of rice.

The squaw looked up at the storekeeper for a moment and then said, "Tea."

Buck Ashley's laconic response was "More gold," and immediately another handful of nuggets was brought forth, whereupon a fourth package was deposited on the counter.

Old Guadalupe stowed the parcels in her apron on top of any remaining gold nuggets she might have brought. Then she turned and walked limpingly away, through the low brushwood toward a little grove of gnarled and twisted sycamores close to the ruined fort.

When she had gone Buck Ashley observed, "No use following her—not a damn bit of use in the world! She'll make camp out there under the trees until some time tonight, and then vanish like a shadow into the dark."

While speaking, Ashley had been gathering up the gold.

"I say, Buck," observed Dick Willoughby, winking at his friend Lieutenant Munson, "it is my private opinion that that bandit, the White Wolf, has nothing on you."

Tom Baker laughingly chimed in: "If I am any judge, and I allow as how I am, Buck here would make that pound-of-flesh Shylock feller look like thirty cents Mex."

Ashley smiled greedily, but in a satisfied way, as he said with unruffled calm: "Guess I'd better weigh them nuggets and see how much the old squaw's groceries cost her."

"The treacherous Indian and the honest paleface," laughed Dick Willoughby in a half-rebuking tone.

Buck Ashley bridled up. His voice rang with deep feeling.

"Boys," he said, "you think I'm a Shylock, a robber, a devil I expect, and everything that's bad. I don't talk much about myself, but just so you'll not think too blamed hard of me, I'll ask you a question. Supposen when you was only about fifteen years old, you stood by, tied hand

and foot, and saw a lot of redskins scalp and kill your father and mother and two little sisters, and then rob your dead father of over ten thousand dollars in gold, run off the family stock, and take you to their camp to burn at the stake as a sort of incidental diversion at one of their pow-wow dances; and supposen you performed a miracle and got away and took an oath to kill and rob every derned Indian you might see throughout the remaining days of your life—what, then, if I reformed and gave up the killin' and stuck to robbin', would you blame me?"

During this tragic recital of his wrongs the old storekeeper had become noticeably excited.

Dick Willoughby got up from the cracker-box where he had been resting, and advancing with hand extended, said: "Buck, what you have told us presents the whole matter in a new light. Shake!"

"Thanks," replied the storekeeper as he turned away to wipe a mist from his eyes.

Then quickly facing about, he called out in his usual gruff, hale and hearty manner: "Say, boys, what'll you all have? This round is on the house."

They drank in silence. A fragment of Buck Ashley's history had cleared away a good deal of previous misunderstanding.

Chapter II

Charmed Lives

THE spell of restraint that resulted from Buck Ashley's story was at last broken by the cowboy, Jack Rover.

"Look here, Dick," he exclaimed, "I'll give a month's salary if you will let me take a chance and follow old Guadalupe. I've simply got to find out and locate that sand-bar in some mountain stream from which she brings in all this gold. This is the third time I've seen our friend Buck Ashley collect a grocery bill from the old squaw, and the whole business, gold nuggets and all, is getting on my nerves. Why, I dreamed about it for a week last time I saw her forking out whole handfuls of gold."

"Very well," replied Willoughby, "if you want to take the chance, Jack, go ahead. But it is a mad project which will end in my expressing your remains back East or else planting you in the cemetery on the hill. It's up to you to make your choice before you tackle the job. You certainly know what happened to four or five others who attempted to follow the old squaw. Each mother's son of them was buried the next day."

"Oh, that's ancient history," Jack retorted.

"Not such very ancient hist'ry," remarked Tom Baker. "I myself saw young Bill McNab drilled through the heart with a bullet that seemed to come from nowhere. After that I'll allow I wasn't filled up with too much curiosity as to where Guadalupe hiked over the mountains."

"There was a regular sharp-shootin' outfit," concurred Buck Ashley.

"And there wasn't a sheriff in the country would have led a posse into that damned ambush," Tom went on. "There wasn't a sportin' chance along that narrow ledge round which Guadalupe always disappeared. And with all them outlaws in the mountains!"

"But the outlaws have been wiped out years ago," persisted Jack Rover.

"Mebbe," said Tom Baker, sententiously.

"You forget the White Wolf," added Buck Ashley.

"Which white wolf?" asked Jack. "I put that question before but got no answer."

"Both," replied Tom. "To begin with I don't believe that Don Manuel is dead at all. That was only a newspaper story. You may take it from me that the bandit won't pass in his checks till he gets old Ben Thurston. I'm allowin' as how Ben Thurston would quick enough give a thousand head of his fattest beeves just to rest easy in his mind on that score. He'll find out, sure enough, some day."

"Yes, when the White Wolf finds him," interjected the storekeeper with a terse emphasis.

"What's that old feud anyway?" queried Lieutenant Munson. "Tell me, Tom."

"Oh, it is an old story," the sheriff answered. "I thought everybody knew about it, but of course you're a newcomer. Well, you see," he continued, clearing his throat and expectorating a copious and accurately aimed pit-tew of tobacco juice toward a knot-hole in the floor, "the White Wolf's father, Don Antonio de Valencia, a reg'lar high-toned grandee from Spain, had settled in these here parts away back longer than anyone could remember. He claimed this whole stretch of country from horizon to horizon. Then came the Americans, among them a government surveyor named Thurston. He had a pull at Washington and managed to get a legal grant to the San Antonio property. Of course the old Spaniard had no real title—his was just a sort of squatter's claim. But they do say as how he had lived in this here valley more than half a century, so it was mighty hard luck to lose the land. And the boy Manuel never would admit the Thurstons had any right to call it theirs."

"Don Manuel had a younger sister," interposed Buck Ashley. "Rosetta, a beautiful girl—looked like a morning-glory. Gad! but she sure had a purty face. You remember, Tom, don't you?"

"Oh, yes," replied Tom Baker, "it's not likely I should forget the poor girl. It was 'cause of her the quarrel became a bitter blood feud—the Vendetta of the Hills, as we got to calling it. You see," he went on, resuming the thread of his story, "old man Thurston's son, Ben, the present owner of the rancho, was in his younger days a gay Lothario scamp, and he came from the East to his new home in California loaded down with a college education and a mighty intimate knowledge of the ways of the world that decent folks don't talk about, much less practice. He had not been here a month until he commenced makin' love to little Senorita Rosetta. Before the second sheep-shearin' time came around, she was—well, in a delicate condition. To save himself and, as he thought, cover up the disgrace—you see he was engaged to a rich Eastern girl of prominent family—why, the young scoundrel conceived the hellish plot of lurin' little Rosetta to Comanche Point one dark night. And when he got her there he threw her over the cliff—at least that's the way the story goes. Guess Don Manuel was about twenty-five years old at that time, and Ben Thurston two or three years his junior. Well, the disgrace killed Rosetta's father and mother. They died of grief and shame soon after the affair, almost on the same day, and Don Manuel buried them together in the old churchyard on the hill by the side of his murdered sister. And it was there and then, they say, that he took an oath to kill Ben Thurston. That was mor'n thirty years ago and the feud has been on ever since, and all us old-timers know hell will be poppin' 'round here one of these days."

"But nobody ever sees the White Wolf, Don Manuel," added Buck Ashley. "That's the extr'ornery part of it."

"Oh, you yourself are likely to see him one of these dark nights, Buck," laughed Jack Rover, as he winked at the other boys. "A storekeeper that'll work night and day stacking up money year in and year out is liable to have a call sooner or later from the bandit and his friends."

"Oh, hell!" was the laconic response of Buck Ashley. "Guess I sure can take care of myself."

"But Don Manuel may not be alive," suggested the young lieutenant.

"He's alive right enough, make no mistake," said Tom Baker, "although I'll allow I don't know a single soul who has actually seen him personally for more'n twenty years. He is a kind o' shadowy cuss. Everybody knows him by his old-time deeds of high-way robbin' and all-round murderin' for golden loot. I heard of a feller last year who claims to have seen the White Wolf when he was makin' that last big stage delivery over by Tulare Lake. He was masked, and had all the passengers out on the roadside with their hands thrown up over their heads while he was takin' their valuables away from them."

"It's a dead cinch," Buck Ashley observed, "that whenever there was a hold-up or a robbery, or a murder in cold blood for money, why everybody knew that the White Wolf was again in the hills and playin' his cut-throat game for pelf and plunder, or mebbe just for revenge against the gringos, whom he hated like hell. Sometimes he was not heard of in these parts for two or three years, and then he showed up more blood-thirsty than ever. His hand was agin every man, and it looked like as every man's hand was agin him."

"I've been told," said Dick Willoughby, "that when the White Wolf was a boy he saved the life of the old highwayman, Joaquin Murietta."

"Yes, them are facts," replied Tom Baker. "Leastways I've heard say so. They claim that he saved Murietta's life from a posse of deputies one night, and altho' the White Wolf was only a boy at that time, yet a heap of people think he's the only livin' soul who knows the whereabouts and location of the secret cavern where Joaquin Murietta planted his loot, amountin', they say, to millions of dollars in gold and jewels and valuables of all kinds. The retreat always proved a safe one for the murderin' gang, and now they're gone no one even to this day can find the place. It's somewhere on San Antonio Rancho, but where? The White Wolf kept his secret well."

"If old Pierre Luzon ever gets out of San Quentin," remarked the storekeeper, "I guess he could tell. But he's up for life. He was nabbed in that same Tulare Lake affair 'bout which Tom had been talkin'."

"Yes," said the sheriff, "two others were shot dead before they got back to the mountains. The White Wolf and Pierre were ridin' alone when the Frenchie's horse stumbled. They picked him up insensible, a broken leg and concussion

of the brain, and he was the only one of the
gang who ever went to jail."

"God 'lmighty," exclaimed Buck, "old Pierre
used to sit around in this here store day after day,
smokin' an old foreign-lookin' pipe, and hardly
speakin' a word. He used to pretend he knew no
English. We never once suspected that he was
one of Don Manuel's bunch—always thought of
him as an old sheepherder, a bit off his nut, who
had saved a few dollars and was takin' things
easy. And hell, all the time he was the White
Wolf's look-out man, makin' note of everything
and passin' the word o' warnin' when there was
talk of the sheriff gettin' busy."

"I'll allow Pierre Luzon fooled me proper,"
concurred Tom Baker. "However, he got what
was comin' to him all right, a life sentence, though
he ought to have been hanged. Well, perhaps it
is only the White Wolf and Pierre Luzon who now
know the cave where Joaquin Murietta cached
his treasure."

"And Guadalupe perhaps as well," remarked
Buck Ashley.

"Yes, perhaps Guadalupe also," assented the
sheriff. "But the White Wolf keeps guard over
her."

"That's the real White Wolf this time," laughed

Dick Willoughby, with a nod toward the young lieutenant, who had been listening intently to the tale of weird romance.

"The real White Wolf?" replied Munson, enquiringly. "You've got me all tangled up. What do you mean?"

"Don't you know how Don Manuel came by his name of the White Wolf?" asked the sheriff.

"No, all this folk lore is new to me."

"Why, gosh all hemlock! He is named because of a darn big white wolf that has been seen at different times in this here country for a hundred years."

"Wolves don't live so long," protested the lieutenant incredulously.

"Well, this one does," retorted Tom, curtly. "Leastwise he's been seen from time to time since ever I can remember. In the old days they named the White Wolf Rancho after this monster animal. It has a charmed life. No one can kill this big fellow, altho' lots of shots have been fired at him. And the same was true of Don Manuel de Valencia. He escaped so often that folks believed his life a charmed one. And so they called him the White Wolf."

"I saw the white wolf once myself," said Buck Ashley, "the real white wolf that even now, as

Tom says, guards old Guadalupe and makes it best for young fellows like you, Jack Rover, to leave the squaw alone when she makes back for her hidin' place in the mountains. I'll never forget that morning, although it's more or less twenty years ago. The great shaggy brute was following Guadalupe along the trail like a Newfoundland dog. In those days I was out on the hills roundin' up some mavericks. One of the calves broke from the herd and scampered along a trail that led directly in front of the old squaw. And say, boys, would you believe it? From less than half a mile away I saw with my own eyes that monster devil of a white wolf—white as the driven snow—make one terrific mad leap and grab that yearlin' by the neck. Guadalupe spotted me and disappeared, and the white wolf trotted after her round the bend, carryin' the dead calf in its jaws as a cat carries a mouse."

"Did you not shoot at the wolf?" excitedly asked Lieutenant Munson.

"Shoot, hell! What would have been the use? Didn't you hear what Tom Baker said? White wolves have charmed lives whether they go on two legs or four."

CHAPTER III

Feminine Attractions

TOM BAKER, the sheriff, cleared his throat. "You fellers, I'm assoomin', are all boys. I have been loafin' 'round in this man's land for forty years. I was here the day Don Manuel had been buryin' his old father and mother from the little Mission Church, less than a quarter of a mile from where we are settin'. He was standin' right in front of this store when young Ben Thurston and two of his ranch hands rode up. If ever I saw real bravery it was that mornin'. Don't take much bravery to do some things heroic when you have your artillery handy, but it requires the real stuff when you're gunless.

"Young Thurston spoke to his companions and they drew their guns and kept them leveled at Don Manuel as their boss dismounted.

"Don Manuel was one of the handsomest young fellers I ever laid my two eyes on. He walked straight up to Thurston, and notwithstandin' the two loaded pieces of artillery was pintin' straight at him said:

" 'Ben Thurston, you are the man who killed my sister.'

" 'You are a damned liar!' retorted Thurston.

" 'Yes, you killed her,' went on Don Manuel. 'I found this button in her dead hand, and right there, by God! is where it came from. Look at your coat. Your life shall pay for this dastardly murder. If I had my gun I would settle the matter now, notwithstandin' that today I have been burying my beloved father and mother.'

"When young Thurston heard about there bein' no gun, he snatched the tell-tale button from his accuser's hand, swung himself into his saddle, laughed mockingly, and with his quirt struck Don Manuel across the face; then he wheeled round his pony and rode away with his bodyguards in a cloud of dust.

"God! I will never forget it. Don Manuel stood there, as white as a piece of paper, and never moved for a whole minute. The quirt had drawn the blood from his face in one long streak. At last he turned away with a resolve in his eyes —one of them there terrible resolves that change the life of a man, and went back to the little church to finish the last sad rites to his people. It's my opinion Don Manuel, from that very hour, turned bandit in his heart and took oath to murder all the gringos in California.

"As I said before, that was thirty years back, and mebbe a little more, and I have never seen him since. But we all heard of him good and plenty. He certainly left a red trail."

A silence followed. Presently Buck Ashley in the way of explanation, said:

"That tombstone on his sister's grave was put up one night. Nobody saw it done, but everyone knows, of course, it was the work of Don Manuel. It has just one word—'Hermana'—chiseled on the cross of white marble. That's the Mexican for 'sister,' guess you all know. So the name Rosetta is only remembered by old-stagers here, like Tom Baker and me. And we ain't forgotten her pretty face either. Poor little girl!"

"A doggoned shame," muttered the sheriff, meditatively, his eyes cast down.

"How about the law?" asked Lieutenant Munson.

"The law!" exclaimed Baker, raising his eyes and flashing a look of withering contempt. "What kind o' law was there in those days and in these parts? A gun was usually both judge and jury. Besides, with the only bit of evidence gone, how could Don Manuel prove anything agin a rich young feller like Ben Thurston?"

"But if he was laying for him all the time, how is it that the White Wolf never got his man all through those thirty years?"

"Because Ben Thurston lit out—he was too derned scared to live on the rancho any longer. But that's another story."

"Let's have it, sheriff."

"Well, it's a longish yarn, and p'raps you fellers are about tired of hearing me."

No one protested; there was rather a movement of settling down in pleased expectancy of something worth listening to. So Tom Baker continued:

"Ben Thurston had one warnin', good and plenty, and he didn't wait around for a second one. After Don Manuel's threat, he seldom left his home, and a little later went back East again. It wasn't till more'n a year that he showed up agin at the rancho. This time he brought with him his Eastern bride, a fine slap-dash young woman who could ride a horse and handle a team in good shape. But we could all see that she wasn't too happy, for Ben Thurston started in to drink heavily, and she was ashamed of him and showed it."

"Guess it was to drown his conscience and keep from thinkin' about Rosetta," interjected Buck Ashley.

"Like as not," assented Tom. "Well, anyhow, he hadn't been here very long afore Don Manuel got him—yes, got him fair and square, although he managed to save his neck at the last moment. There was card-playin' and drinkin' one night at the rancho—Thurston had got a bunch o' gay young dogs down from San Francisco. Mrs. Thurston had left the room, and was sittin' out alone in the moonlight on the verandah. Suddenly she heard a sound that made her sit up and listen—the clatter o' twenty pairs o' gallopin' hoofs a-comin' straight for the house. She must ha' known something about the vendetta, for she rushed in terror to her husband and gave him warnin'. He escaped by a back door, and a minute later the place was surrounded. The shootin' came first from some of the ranch hands, who had tumbled out of the bunk house and were spyin' around corners. They said later that the hold-up party numbered more'n twenty, some of them masked with handkerchiefs tied around their faces, but others bold as brass and not carin' a dang who saw 'em. Among these last was Don Manuel. But Pierre Luzon was a downy duck, for no one spotted him, although later on we came to know that he played the principal part that night, next to the leader of the gang.

"Well, after the shootin'-scrap became general, there was a pretty scare in the ranch house—one of the card-players dropped, and the others were hiding under tables, when Don Manuel appeared and asked for Ben Thurston. His wife, mighty brave, denied that he was there—he had left that afternoon for Visalia to buy some cattle, she boldly declared. Don Manuel, always the true gentleman, mark ye, was for believin' her when Pierre, his face masked, came in from the verandah and in a low voice passed some words to his chief. Mrs. Thurston knew in a moment that her bluff was goin' to be called, and, while the outlaws were confabbin', darted from the room.

"But Pierre was just as quick out by the verandah, and before she got to the door o' the woolshed beyond the horse corral, he was there to block her passage. It was Pierre who had caught a glimpse of the fugitive sneakin' into this out-building, and now he knew for certain that Thurston was hiding among the bags o' wool inside. But a cornered man is a dangerous animal, and it might mean a good few lives if the door was opened and any attempt made to rush the place

"The gang was soon buzzin' all around; the woman, now almost in hysterics, was hustled aside, and a few bundles of loose hay was being

dumped into the shed through an open window.
A match did the rest. Within three minutes the
door opened and Thurston came staggerin' out
through thick clouds of smoke. Pierre grabbed
him and had a noose around his neck in double-
quick time.

"The shootin' was over before this, and some of
the ranch hands were lookin' on from a little
distance, for now everyone knew that it was only
the boss that the night-riders were after. So
more'n one was able afterwards to tell the story—
how the young wife threw herself at Don Manuel's
feet, and with sobs and tears pleaded for mercy.
And by the living God she won out even after
the rope, with her husband at the end of it, had
been swung over the limb of a near-by sycamore.

"The White Wolf stood stock-still for perhaps
a minute, weighin' things like, his arms folded
across his breast. Then he raised the weepin'
woman, and, turnin' to Thurston, now half-dead
with fear, laid hold of him by the shoulder and
shook him as a terrier shakes a rat. Then with
his other hand he flung the noose from around
his neck. 'Take your miserable life, then, this
time'—that's what Don Manuel said. 'Take it,
but the day will come when we shall meet again,
man to man, with no woman's tears to save you.'

And he pushed Thurston away contemptuously, topplin' him over like a ninepin, and a minute later rode off at the head of his men."

The narrator paused, and there was a general murmur of repressed excitement.

"My word, that's a peach of a story," exclaimed Jack Rover.

"He certainly was a chivalrous fellow, this old-time Don Manuel," remarked the lieutenant.

"And don't you see," said the sheriff, "that when a man acted like that and spoke like that, his words must come true? Don't tell me that Don Manuel today is dead while Ben Thurston is still alive. But he has taken mighty good care of himself ever since that day. He an' his wife skipped East the very next morning, and I'm told they never stopped till they got to Europe. Nobody knows where exactly they lived during the time that followed, but news came through years later that the wife had died, somewhere in the south of England, leaving a son behind. That's young Marshall who has come West with his dad now—the young man's first visit and his father's last one, I reckon, if he sells the ranch, as I'm told he's trying to do."

"But I say, boys," observed Jack Rover, "what do you suppose the White Wolf did with all the

gold he took away from the people? It's said that
in one stage robbery he got over fifty thousand
dollars of the yellow stuff."

"Hid it," replied Buck Ashley, "with Joaquin
Murietta's hoarded gold. For it's sure as sure can
be that Don Manuel came to know the secret o'
the bandits' cave where Murietta used to store
his loot. The only thing anybody else knows is
that it is around here somewheres."

"But they do say," observed one of the cowboys, "whatever Sheriff Baker may think, and you,
too, Buck, that Don Manuel is sure 'nuff dead.
Most folks herabouts believe that the White Wolf
has gone to his long restin' place, sort a j'ined
forces with old Joaquin Murietta. The Tulare
Lake affair was, I guess, his last raid."

"He ain't dead," muttered Tom, determinedly,
while Buck Ashley also shook his head in repu-
diation of the cowboy's theory.

"Well, I happen to know," observed Dick Willoughby, "that Mr. Thurston has run down the
story of the White Wolf's death in that Seattle
saloon brawl pretty thoroughly, and he is of the
opinion that the big-featured articles in the San
Francisco and Los Angeles papers were correct—
that the dead man's identity was absolutely
established."

"That's how he'd wish it to be, at all events," said Buck Ashley. "But even now, when Ben Thurston ventures to come home to the rancho, he brings with him a great big hulking body-guard—Leach Sharkey, I'm told is the fellow's name. That don't look much like believin' the White Wolf to be dead and the vendetta played out, does it? You can see it in his hang-dog face that it isn't any real pleasure for him to be around in these parts. He ain't once paid me a visit at the store. Guess he thinks his hide'll last longer by stickin' close to home. You owe your job o' runnin' his cattle, Dick Willoughby, to the fact that he's still plumb scared."

"Oh, well, I am in his employ," said Dick loyally, "and I'm inclined to give him the benefit of the doubt as regards these ugly rumors and idle stories. He has always been on the square with me. But perhaps he'll stick to the rancho, now he believes the White Wolf to be dead."

"He may believe it, but, as Buck says, why then the bodyguard?" commented the sheriff as he relighted his pipe.

"Yes." replied Dick Willoughby, "but I believe he is thinking of letting Leach Sharkey go. Personally I would be willing to wager that Don Manuel, whom no one has seen since that last raid on the stage coach, is dead and sleeping with his sires."

"Well, dead or alive," exclaimed Jack Rover, "I don't care a hang for the White Wolf and his buried treasure. But what I would like to know is the exact location of that rippling mountain stream, the identical sandbar where the old squaw Guadalupe gathers up her pocket change with which to buy groceries. That would be a heap better than any blooming cave. Them's my sentiments."

As he said this he threw some silver on the bar and invited everybody to lubricate.

"Just nominate your poison, boys, and let's drink to my finding old Guadalupe's gold mine."

They all laughed good-naturedly, and Lieutenant Munson declared that he thought he would put in the balance of his furlough days prospecting. "You know," he explained in an aside to the storekeeper while the latter was preparing the drinks, "I am only here to visit my old college pal, Dick Willoughby, and incidentally see the place where my father was a soldier in the early California days. He was stationed several years in Fort Tejon."

"That was before my time," said Buck Ashley.

"The soldiers had abandoned the old fort when I came first into these parts."

Meanwhile Dick Willoughby was clinking glasses with Jack Rover.

"There are some mighty pretty little senoritas hereabouts," said Dick, "good American blood mixed with Spanish blood, you know, and all that. If a fellow could only find the right one—understand, I say the right one, Jack—he wouldn't be losing any time in chasing after the old squaw's secret gold mine or the White Wolf's buried millions."

Jack Rover laughed outright.

"I say, Dick, what are you reddening up about? Gee, if I had as fine a lead as you have staked out, I'd feel the same way. Ain't that right, Buck?"

Buck Ashley winked at Jack Rover and said: "If you mean who I think you mean, you sure are righter than right. I speak wide open and unrestrained when I give it as my opinion that Miss Merle Farnsworth is the finest specimen of young womanhood that I ever set eyes on, and I have seen some girls East as well as West. Take it from me, she is a jewel, she is a regular beauty rose. Yes," he went on, "and too damned good for that young Thurston whelp, who hangs around tryin' to act smart whenever she and that old duenna chaperon

of hers comes here to trade. I'll simply boot him
out of the store one of these days."

Dick Willoughby smiled in a satisfied way as
he moved toward the door.

"Well, hold on, Dick," called out Jack Rover,
"don't be in such a dangnation hurry. I'll ride
with you in a minute. I've just got this to say to
you, Buck Ashley, that I like you better than
ever for what you've said about Marshall Thurston. Even though I'm working for the Thurston
outfit, I'm free to express my opinion that that
young feller is about the meanest specimen of
low-down humanity I've ever struck."

"It's a case of the second decadency, I suppose,"
remarked Munson. "The worthless profligate
spawn of the rich old roué, Ben Thurston."

"Such a drunken pup," continued Rover,
"aint' good enough for a half-breed Indian, much
less for the likes of the young ladies of La Siesta.
Gee, if I thought there was one chance in a
thousand for me with either of them, why good-
bye to that placer gold mine ambition that's
eating my vitals, or to the planted millions of the
White Wolf."

As he spoke the last words, he followed Dick
Willoughby into the open. Dick was standing
by his pony.

. "You're superlatively in earnest, aren't you?" he said as he laughed good-naturedly at the cowboy.

"You bet your life I'm in earnest," replied Jack. "And if you don't get busy with that love affair of yours, well, take it from me, you had better look out, for somebody will be picking the peach right from under your very nose. Well, so long, Dick; I've changed my mind; I'll not ride with you. I'll see to that bit of fence repairing up on the range. And who knows but I may find a sand-bar and a riffle sparkling with yellow gold?"

He laughed like a big overgrown boy as he touched the rowel to his pony and galloped away across the valley.

CHAPTER IV

Back to the Soil

"JACK ROVER is a great boy," said Dick Willoughby to Lieutenant Munson as the two rode off at a leisurely pace toward the group of ranch buildings peeping through a clump of trees at the edge of the foothills.

"A type of Western character," replied Munson, "that in a way is quite new to me. And yet, do you know, I rather like this Western atmosphere."

"Like it!" exclaimed Dick. "Why, man, it is *the* atmosphere in which to live, move and have one's being."

They both laughed at his enthusiasm.

"Really," continued Dick, soberly, "I would not live another year in New York City for all the property fronting on the Circle, the coming centre of old Gotham. Out here a man is a man for what he is worth. You grow bigger, you think broader thoughts, you are not confined to following precedents or taking orders from the man higher up."

"Oh, I know," replied Munson, "or at least I

am beginning to understand something of what you mean. I have only been here ten days and I am already feeling loath to return to my post."

"Ches," exclaimed Dick, turning abruptly and facing his companion, "give it all up, old fellow, and come and live in this glorious country—California! There's music in the very name. It is the land of sunshine, of fruits and flowers, and of pretty girls into the bargain."

"You keep telling me of the pretty girls, but when am I to see them?" questioned Munson. "If you have any real senoritas who will cause a fellow to forsake his Eastern home and send in his resignation to army headquarters, let me get a peep at them."

Again they both laughed, this time at the challenge in Munson's words.

"All right," said Dick, "you shall see them. And, by the way, don't you remember that this is the very day we have arranged to call on Mrs. Darlington at the Rancho La Siesta? It is a beautiful place, this little rancho, and Mrs. Darlington you will find to be a most admirable woman. But just wait until you see Grace Darlington."

"How about Miss Farnsworth?"

"Not for you, old man," replied the other

quickly, reddening at the temples. "Not as long as my name is Dick Willoughby—providing, you understand, always providing that I shall prove successful in my wooing."

"Is it as bad as that, Dick?"

"Well,"—his laughing tone was only a mask to deeper feelings—"I cannot deny that I am pretty hard hit."

"My, but you do whet my impatience," said the lieutenant. "And I am about as anxious to be paying that afternoon call as I am to have my breakfast. I don't know how you feel, Dick, but I'm as hungry as a lean coyote." He paused a moment, then asked in a musing tone: "How far away is this wonderful La Siesta Rancho?"

"Oh, only about twenty miles."

"Twenty miles! You speak of miles out here in the same way as we speak of city blocks back in New York. Surely it must be quite a farm."

"Quite a farm? I should say! You musn't confound our Californian ranchos with Eastern farms, old man. Why, this rancho of San Antonio covers over four hundred square miles of territory."

"You astonish me."

"La Siesta Rancho adjoins the great San Antonio possession and contains comparatively

few acres, just under three thousand. But it
surely is a beautiful little place, fixed up like a
nobleman's park in the old world. And then
the ladies—"

"Aha, the ladies," repeated Munson, doffing his
hat in courtly fashion and smiling audaciously.

Dick touched the flank of his pony with his
spur, and for a few miles they rode on at a quicker
pace and in silence. Soon they were approaching
the ranch buildings. On the outer edge was a
little cottage, covered with vines and surrounded
by fruit trees, the place which Dick Willoughby,
the cattle foreman, had called "home" for the past
five years.

After turning their horses into a corral, they
passed by way of a broad verandah into a big
room, roughly but comfortably furnished. Some
logs were smouldering in the fireplace, and quickly
started into a bright blaze when Dick kicked
them together. The warmth was grateful, for
while out of doors everything was now bathed in
genial sunshine, here the morning air was still
keen.

A Chinaman appeared from the back quarters,
and smiled expectantly.

"Breakfast, Sing Ling," called out Dick, "and
just as quick as you can serve it."

Sing Ling departed as noiselessly as he had come.

"These are certainly great quarters," observed Munson, settling himself in a big Old Mission rocker and glancing around.

The walls, curiously enough, were pretty well covered with pen-and-ink sketches and designs of buildings that might have adorned an architect's office, while there was a partly completed landscape painting in oils standing on a rudely fashioned easel.

"And you've certainly stuck to the old line of work, Dick," the lieutenant went on.

"Of course one must have something to think about when he is all alone in a new country," replied Willoughby. "But most of that stuff I did in my first year here," he added, following the other's survey of the walls.

"You still paint, however," remarked Munson, his eyes resting on the unfinished canvas.

"Or try to," was the laughing response.

"Oh, that's a modest way of putting it. Do you know, old man," Munson went on, "since I came here I have often thought what a marvelous change has been wrought in you—what a transplanting has taken place? You were a chronic New Yorker, except for that one year you spent in the Latin Quarter of gay Paree. You thought then you were going to make a great painter. And, by gad, I almost believe so myself," he added, bending forward to make a more critical scrutiny of the work on the easel. "By jove, that's really fine, Dick."

"I'm afraid that's flattery, Chester, my boy," responded Willoughby. "However, it sounds good to hear you say so. A word of appreciation is what all hearts hunger for. Personally I even believe in a moderate amount of flattery. Its psychic influence is more potent in arousing and causing the heart to throb with ambition than all the stimulants, drugs or reasoning in the world. Indeed, without a certain amount of flattery one becomes ambitionless, languid, and perishes; whereas the unexpected caress or kindly words of praise from loved ones, just or unjust, adds more strength to the good right arm of the bread-winner than all the beef in Christendom, and makes the sunshine seem brighter and earth's every breeze a south wind blowing across beds of violets."

"A bit of a poet, too, I see," smiled Munson.

Willoughby made no reply. He had crossed over to the open door and was looking out on the valley that stretched away for miles—great oak trees in the foreground, with cattle-dotted pasture lands beyond.   Waving his hand toward the vast expanse, he said:

"Just look at that for a picture, and see how tame a man-made gallery is as compared with this great art gallery of Nature.   Do you know, Ches, I despise New York?   There was a time, when I first came here, that I felt I should die of ennui, yearning for the Great White Way once again. But I have outgrown all that.   I know now, thank God, there's nothing to it.   Here a man can fill his lungs with pure air, and at the same time feast his soul all day long with beautiful things."

There followed a brief interval of silence. Munson had risen and joined his comrade at the door.   Both were gazing over the glorious sun-lit sweep of territory rimmed by the distant, pine-clad hills.   In the heart of Dick Willoughby was supreme contentment, in that of Chester Munson a vague longing to get away from red-tape army routine and breathe the exhilarating and inspiring freedom of life in the open.

"Blakeflast," bleated a soft voice behind them, and turning round they found the suave, smiling Chinaman with hand outstretched toward the smoking viands upon the table.   Sentiment was instantly forgotten in favor of lamb chops grilled to a turn, a great fluffled omelette with fine herbs that would have done credit to a Parisian chef, and coffee that was veritable nectar.

At last appetite was satisfied. The lieutenant had produced his cigar case, Dick was filling his briar-root pipe with tobacco from the humidor. The latter spoke:

"Say, Ches, we were talking about New York. Do you want me to give you a toast on that modern Babylon?"

"Sure, old man, go ahead! You know I haven't lost my interest in old Gotham, by any manner of means. It may be a modern Babylon. But to me it is none the less the greatest of American cities."

"That's just the trouble," said Dick, seriously. "It is too great. There identities are swallowed up. Individualism cannot survive. It is all one great composite."

"Well, let us hear the toast."

Dick raised his cup of coffee and said: "Very well, here it is; here is my opinion of New York:

> 'Vulgar in manners; overfed,
> Over-dressed and under-bred;
> Heartless, godless, hell's delight,
> Rude by day and lewd by night.
> Bedwarfed the man, enlarged the brute;
> Ruled by boss and prostitute.
> Purple robed and pauper clad;
> Raving, rotten, money mad;

La Siesta — Page 44

A squirming herd in Mammon's mesh;
A wilderness of human flesh;
Crazed by avarice, lust and rum—
New York! thy name's delirium.' "

"Great Heavens, old man," exclaimed Munson, when Dick had finished, "you are severe, to say the least."

Willoughby laughed good-naturedly as he passed the match box to his friend.

"Not severe, only truthful," he said. "You see, in New York no man dares think for himself. Everything is controlled by a machine-appointed chairman, secretary and committee, and you must hear the resolutions read before you know the doctrine you are perforce to advocate."

Then he lit his pipe and rose from the table.

"Now, I have a lot of things to attend to, old fellow," he resumed. "Make yourself comfortable. Here's a bunch of Eastern newspapers— oh, I read them regularly, haven't got rid of that bad habit yet. I'll tell Sing Ling to have lunch ready on the stroke of noon. Then we'll be in good time to start out for the Rancho La Siesta. So long!"

Chapter V

At La Siesta

SOON after one o'clock Dick Willoughby and Chester Munson were again in the saddle. They galloped along the foothills for some time in silence. But coming to the boulder-strewn wash of a mountain stream, they had perforce to rein their horses to a walk. Conversation was now possible.

"Dick, will you give me a job as a cowboy if I quit the army?" asked Munson abruptly.

"Surest thing you know," replied Dick. "But why try to kid me like that?"

"Oh," laughed the other, "I am not jesting."

"Well, by gad, if you feel that way already, the chances are you will write out your resignation when you get back to the shack tonight."

"You mean by that—"

"I mean," said Dick, smiling benignly at his friend, "that when you have once seen Grace Darlington you will feel like browsing on the California range until you have learned to throw a riata."

"Oh, it is not the thought of any mere girl that will influence my decision. I feel like getting back to Nature—back to the soil—back to a life of untrammeled freedom."

"Back to unspoiled womanhood," added Dick sententiously.

"Well, you've certainly got my curiosity aroused over these young ladies at La Siesta. How much farther do we have to go?"

"Within an hour, sir, within the hour, my lord, shall you see the lady fair. But remember," Dick went on banteringly, "that you are not to practise any riata-throwing on Miss Merle Farnsworth."

"I understand. But we won't fall out over her. You may have your beautiful brunette. I have always been partial to blondes."

"In the plural number," grinned Dick. "But Grace Darlington will dim the light of all your previous flames. She is the most perfect blonde you have ever yet encountered."

"You are certainly enthusiastic—for a disinterested party."

"Well, you'll say the same thing, Ches, my boy, when you see her."

It was not yet four o'clock when they approached the Rancho La Siesta. The house was of a style quite unusual in California—a miniature castle that might have been planned by some European architect of renown. It stood amid noble oak trees, old and gnarled and of gigantic size, but not too numerous to hide the architectural features of the building. To the rear the trees grew more thickly till they finally merged into one great forest that covered the lower ridge of the mountain beyond. Far up, just within the timber line, could be seen the red-tiled roof of a house which Dick told his friend was the home of a Mr. Ricardo Robles. Beneath the forest, the gently undulating lands sloped away to a considerable stream that dashed down from one of the mountain canyons and debouched into the great valley.

"Whew!" exclaimed Munson admiringly, as they rode up and turned their horses over to an attendant. "Some swell architecture around here! Is this your work, Dick?"

"Oh, no!" replied Willoughby. "I had nothing to do with it. But I do like the architectural lines of Mrs. Darlington's home. She's English and has English tastes, and transplanted ideas are not always successful in a new country. But in this case the building just seems to fit the scenery. It has always delighted me."

"It is certainly beautiful," concurred Munson

as they walked along a winding graveled pathway
that climbed the gentle slope and led to the portico
of the mansion.

Around them were gay beds of flowers dotting
the greensward. Almost hiding the columns of
the portico were climbing roses, one bush of the
purest white, the other of deep crimson.

As they passed under the porch roof, a handsome and well-preserved lady of middle age
appeared at the top of the steps with a welcoming
smile. She descended to give them gracious
greeting.

"How glad I am to see you, Mr. Willoughby.
No one could be more welcome at La Siesta."

"Thank you," said Dick with marked chivalry.
"Mrs. Darlington, permit me to present my friend,
Lieutenant Munson."

The introduction over, they ascended the steps
together, and passed into a spacious courtyard,
with broad verandahs running all around and a
fountain playing in the centre. The hostess con-
ducted her visitors to a cosy corner, screened by
glass panels from the open air and furnished with
rich Persian rugs, divans, cushions, tapestries,
carved ebony tabarets, all in oriental fashion.
When they were comfortably settled, she opened
the conversation.

"Lieutenant, the young ladies of La Siesta are most impatient to meet you. Mr. Willoughby has told us so much about you and yet has been so very dilatory—yes, really you have, Mr. Willoughby—in bringing you over, that we have put down several black marks against his name."

"Oh, thank you," stammered the young officer, reddening. "I quite agree with you about Willoughby, for I have been pleading with him to present me from the very first day of my arrival."

Turning to Mrs. Darlington, Dick laughingly protested: "My dear Mrs. Darlington, that is the first whopper you have heard from my esteemed friend. You have yet to learn that he always speaks in the superlative degree."

At this moment Grace Darlington stepped through one of the French windows. As she stood hesitating for a moment, Chester Munson there and then agreed with all the preliminary praise Dick Willoughby had bestowed. She was certainly a vision of loveliness, with a wealth of golden hair and eyes of sapphire blue; petite, her figure plump but beautifully molded, her cheeks aglow with the red roses of health and youth and happiness.

"My daughter Grace," announced Mrs. Darlington, rising and formally introducing the lieutenant to her as she joined the group.

Again Munson blushed and stammered. Dick was chuckling; he saw that the gallant son of battle, with a penchant for blonde beauties, had succumbed to the first glance from Grace Darlington's eyes.

"Delighted to meet you, Lieutenant Munson," she declared with frank friendliness as they shook hands.

"Where's Merle?" asked Dick almost before Grace had time to turn to him.

"There now, Mr. Impatience," she replied, shaking her finger teasingly at him, "Merle will be here in her own good time. She's busy with Bob just now."

"Who the dickens is Bob?" asked Dick, visibly disconcerted.

"Oh, her new Irish terrier," laughed Grace, her voice ringing with mischievous merriment. "And such a beauty!"

Dick breathed again. The lieutenant had recovered his composure; it was his turn now to bestow a sardonic smile upon his comrade.

"We'll have afternoon tea," suggested Mrs. Darlington. "And of course you two young men will stay for dinner."

Both uttered a simultaneous protest—they were only in riding clothes. But Mrs. Darlington made short work of the argument, and touched a push-button by her side. A maid responded, the extra covers for dinner were ordered, and meanwhile tea was to be sent on to the verandah. Pleasant small talk succeeded, the lieutenant being called upon for his first impressions of California.

Of a sudden Grace exclaimed in a voice, half of joy, half of surprise:

"Why, here comes Mr. Robles!"

Advancing along the verandah, hat in hand, was a man of striking presence and dignity, perhaps fifty years of age. His jet black hair was streaked with gray, the full beard almost verging on whiteness. Olive complexion and brown eyes, together with the courtly manner of his salutation, indicated the thoroughbred Castilian.

He bowed and raised to his lips the hand of his hostess. To Grace he paid the same deference. Next he turned to Dick Willoughby and extended his hand.

"I have met Mr. Willoughby. I am pleased, sir, to see you again."

Then his eyes rested on Lieutenant Munson, and Mrs. Darlington presented the young army officer.

"And where, I pray, is Miss Merle?" Mr. Robles finally asked, glancing around.

"That's what I want to know," blurted out Dick. Then he reddened just a little.

The older man looked kindly at Dick, and smilingly said: "The audacity of youth."

"Yes," put in Grace, "the audacity and the impatience as well."

But just at that moment there floated from the recesses of the home the fragment of a song: "I dreamt I dwelt in marble halls, with vassals and serfs at my side."

"Ah, here comes the recreant now," exclaimed Mrs. Darlington.

The song stopped abruptly, and a moment later Merle Farnsworth appeared. She went first of all to Mr. Robles and greeted him warmly, giving him both her hands, which he kissed in his princely fashion. For Willoughby she had a pleasant smile, and for his friend, the lieutenant, a kindly welcome to California.

The tea tray had meanwhile arrived, and soon both the young ladies were busy attending to their guests. While he sipped his tea, Munson completed his inspection of Merle Farnsworth—dispassionately, for the brunette type of beauty had never yet made his pulses beat faster. But he could none the less admire. She was a stately girl, taller than Grace Darlington, with fine, regular features and brown eyes that matched the dark heavy braids of her hair. Her manner was alert and vivacious, yet there was the quiet dignity of gentle breeding even in her smile.

After half an hour of general conversation, Mr. Robles arose to take his leave, notwithstanding Mrs. Darlington's pressing invitation that he should remain and join the dinner party.

"My home is not far away," he said when shaking hands with Munson, "up in the woods yonder. Perhaps you may have seen it as you came along the road."

"Yes," observed Dick, "I pointed it out to the lieutenant."

"Well, both you gentlemen are cordially invited to pay me a visit any time you are riding through this part of the country. Although I live far away from the busy world, and am a recluse by choice, I have some things that may interest you—pictures, old manuscripts and books of the Spanish days."

"Pictures?" interposed Dick, inquiringly.

"Yes, a few that I picked up during several visits to Europe."

"If people only knew it," remarked Mrs. Darlington, "Mr. Robles has perhaps one of the finest private picture galleries in America."

"Then I'm certainly coming to see you," said Dick, eagerly.

"Me or my pictures?" asked Mr. Robles with a quizzical smile.

"Both," and the young fellow showed he meant it by a cordial hand grip.

"You will pass our door, Mr. Willoughby?" exclaimed Merle in half-laughing reproachfulness. "You will dare to give the go-by to La Siesta?"

"Well, art is art," replied Dick sturdily, although he did not trust himself to look at Merle while he answered.

"But perhaps the young ladies will show you the way through the oak forest," suggested Mr. Robles.

"That would be great," said Lieutenant Munson, with his eyes fixed on Grace Darlington.

"Delightful," she blushingly assented.

"Well, arrange it among yourselves. For the present, *adios*." And with a sweeping bow the senor took his departure.

A stroll through the gardens and orchards, dinner and sprightly conversation, an hour of piano-playing and singing to follow—altogether a delightful evening was spent. The nearly full moon had risen before the young men found themselves on the homeward trail.

As side by side they rode down into the valley, Munson said:

"Dick, boy, there's no use talking. You have introduced me to some perfectly charming people today—they're wonderful."

"What did I tell you?" asked Dick.

"You surely did not tell me the half," replied the other. "I think Grace Darlington is the prettiest girl I have ever seen."

"Guess you'll be writing out your resignation and sending it to army headquarters," laughed Dick. "*Quien sabe?*"

The lieutenant made no reply, and quickening their pace, they pushed on in silence.

At last they were nearing home—passing round the last spur of the mountain. The moon was now riding high overhead, bathing the whole landscape in bright effulgence. Willoughby brought his pony to a walk, and Munson, coming up behind, soon joined him.

"How do you like riding by the light of the California moon?" asked Willoughby.

"Really, Dick, you call even the moon a California moon, as if the same moon didn't shine in New York City or in Paris."

"Not in the same way," said Dick soberly. "The truth is, the moon really looks larger and brighter here, and the stars, too, are more brilliant. Haven't you noticed it?"

"I have noticed that the atmosphere is exceedingly clear," replied Munson, and, as if to verify his observation, he cast a glance up to the rock-ribbed flank of the mountain above the belt of timber.

"Good God, what's that?" he added breathlessly grasping the arm of his friend.

Instinctively both halted their horses as they continued to gaze.

The bent form of the old Indian squaw Guadalupe was unmistakable as she toiled slowly along a narrow ledge on the face of the precipice. But following close behind her was a vague, shadowy figure—the figure of some four-footed beast, bigger than a big dog.

"The white wolf!" gasped Dick.

"Is it real, or is it a spectre?" whispered Munson.

Just then a scudding cloud momentarily obscured the moon, and when the full light again shone forth, both woman and wolf had vanished.

The young men looked into each other's eyes in awe and wonderment.

CHAPTER VI

The Quarrel

THE following days were busy ones on San Antonio Rancho. Dick Willoughby was constantly in the saddle, looking after his subordinates, watching the line fences, and generally keeping track of the vast herds. Lieutenant Munson was becoming acclimated. He not only accompanied Willoughby on many of his rides, but had also paid several visits to La Siesta, and one afternoon in particular had enjoyed immensely a successful trout fishing expedition with the young ladies along the mountain stream that flowed through the property.

One morning there was great excitement at San Antonio headquarters. Ben Thurston returned from a visit he had been paying to Los Angeles, and with him floated in a circumstantial story that the rancho had been really sold. As usual, he was attended by the plain-clothes detective whom he retained as bodyguard. Leach Sharkey was a big, hulking fellow, more than six feet in height, with a tousled shock of reddish hair, a stubby red mustache, and teeth that showed even when his face was in repose. Bulging hip pockets indicated the brace of heavy revolvers which he invariably carried.

Within an hour of Mr. Thurston's coming, Dick Willoughby, as foreman, was summoned to an interview at the ranch house. The owner received him alone in his office.

Ben Thurston was a squat, solidly built man, and despite his life of idle luxury, carried his fifty odd years well. He was sullen and taciturn in manner, but brusque and imperious when he did choose to speak. Two features were markedly characteristic—the chin was weak and the eyes had the restless, alert look of one who constantly lived in an atmosphere of fear and suspicion.

Thurston opened the conversation without any preliminaries.

"Willoughby, I want an accurate count of all the cattle and horses on the ranch; and especially I require a fair idea as to the number of fatted beeves—those ready for the market, you understand."

"Very well," replied Dick, "your orders shall be carried out as expeditiously as possible, but it will require a few days to complete the work."

"How many days?"

"If I make use of all the force it may take a week—perhaps a little longer."

"All right, use all the help you can get. I must have these figures promptly. There is a Los Angeles syndicate who are after an option on the rancho. They are counting on buying me out—lock, stock and barrel." Ben Thurston smiled, squinted his shifty eyes and blew his nose vigorously.

"It always makes me laugh," he added pompously, "to have these fellows come around this great principality of mine and try to buy me out."

Just then someone outside flitted past the window, and, quick as lightning, Thurston turned and exclaimed in a startled tone: "Who was that?"

"That was Jack Rover," replied Dick, "one of our cowboys."

"Oh," and the frightened look in the eyes subsided.

"Tomorrow then," Dick went on, returning to their former topic of conversation, "we'll begin a round-up of the stock at this end of the range. I'll put the boys on the job right now."

"I'll join you tomorrow myself."

"All right, Mr. Thurston."

"What time?"

"At any time agreeable to you."

"Well, say eight o'clock in the morning. You see," he continued, "I want to get through with this damned business in a hurry and start back East. I have friends who are waiting for me. Of course I will have to stay here until the representatives of this syndicate come up from Los Angeles, but I will make short work of them, believe me."

This time Ben Thurston laughed outright and rubbed his hands together in a satisfied way. For once he seemed inclined to be communicative, and, turning to Willoughby, resumed:

"Do you know, I have collected over three hundred thousand dollars, first and last, selling options on this San Antonio Rancho? It is quite a joke. They all fall down. They make a first payment of twenty-five or fifty thousand dollars, and then," throwing up both his hands and shrugging his shoulders, "their payments cease and I am just that much ahead of the game."

Willoughby listened in frigid silence; there was not even the flicker of a responsive smile on his face.

Thurston, eyeing him for a moment, looked disconcerted. He drew himself up stiffly in his chair. His voice assumed its usual gruff tone.

"That's all; get to work then," he said curtly as he lifted some papers to show that the interview was at an end.

The first round-up was held some twenty miles southwest of the ranch house, at the base of the foothills across the valley from La Siesta. Ben Thurston, attended closely by his bodyguard, was there, his shifting eyes scanning each new face. Not fewer than ten thousand head of cattle were milling about, pawing the earth and bellowing in low tones of irritation at being herded together and held away from their accustomed haunts of juicy grasses.

From a knoll at a little distance Lieutenant Munson, seated on a fine riding pony, watched the great performance, which to him was more wonderful than any hippodrome show or military parade. He was so engrossed with the spectacle that he did not hear the patter of approaching hoofs.

"Good morning, Senor Lieutenant," came a lady's voice in cheery greeting.

Turning quickly in his saddle he saw Grace Darlington and Merle Farnsworth on their ponies, which had been brought to a sudden halt close behind him.

"Really, Mr. Munson," said Grace Darlington, "one would think you were so completely lost in contemplation of a mob of cattle that you had no eyes for your friends."

Chester bowed and raised his hat as he replied with a bright smile:

"It is certainly a great scene, isn't it? But you are none the less welcome. Indeed when one is witnessing something unusual, it always adds to the interest to have the companionship of friends."

"Very prettily put," observed Merle Farnsworth. "Fortunately the place selected for the round-up this year isn't very far from La Siesta, so we rode across the valley."

"Have you anything in New York," asked Grace, "to compare with this?"

"Indeed we have not," replied the lieutenant with conviction. "I am beginning to think that the West is a pretty good place in which to live. By the way," he went on, taking a newspaper clipping from his pocket, "here is something that our mutual friend, Dick, gave me, and said I should read once a day for a month, and then—well, then, he says I will never go East again, but remain in this great picture country. Shall I read it?"

"Oh, do, by all means," said the girls in unison.

"Well, here goes! 'Every idea we have in the East is run with a convention. We cannot think without a chairman. Our whims have secretaries; our fads have by-laws. Literature is a club. Philosophy is a society. Our reforms are mass meetings. We cannot mourn our mighty dead without some great chairman and a half hundred vice-presidents. We remember our novelists and poets with trustees, while the immortality of a dead genius is looked after by a standing committee. Charity is an association, and theology at best only a set of resolutions.'"

"What do you think of that?" he asked, laughing. "Isn't that an awful slam on the East?"

"It is rather severe," smiled Merle. "But you know, Mr. Willoughby has become a thorough Westerner. The lure of the hills and the valleys has taken complete possession of him."

"And yet he remains unspoiled." exclaimed the lieutenant. "But are you aware he is trying to tamper with my old allegiance to the East?"

"Indeed," asked Grace, "in what way?"

"He wants me to resign my commission and take pot luck with him, as he terms it."

"You couldn't do better," exclaimed Grace enthusiastically.

While this conversation was going on, an exciting incident was taking place only a short distance away. Young Marshall Thurston had come with his father to the round-up, and was riding about watching the operations. Chancing to pass near, Dick Willoughby overheard him use an insulting epithet in regard to Miss Farnsworth —the young man was evidently peeved that the ladies had not sought him out instead of Munson, and it was obvious, too, that he had been drinking even at that early hour in the morning.

Swiftly wheeling, Dick rode up to him with a look of anger so intense that even the cowboys who knew him were taken aback.

"You foul-mouthed beast!" he hissed, as he pushed his quirt into the slanderer's face. "Just let me overhear you make a rude remark again about Miss Farnsworth and I will hammer the life out of you. You are nothing better than a drunken hobo, not fit to associate with ladies."

The outburst was so sudden that young Thurston was cowed and attempted no reply. But as Willoughby rode off he sent after him a look of sullen and resentful hatred. Two or three of the cowboys, who really were good friends of Dick Willoughby, but were nevertheless not above fawning for the favor of the heir to the great rancho, indicated that they were on Marshall's side.

"Guess two can play at the hammering game," remarked one.

"He don't come any of his rough-house business over you, Marshall, while I'm around," affirmed another, pugnaciously.

But the young man, still without uttering a word, turned gloomily away and started his pony in the direction of home.

"Guess he feels like another drink," grinned an irreverent youth.

"Hell," exclaimed an elderly man, the blacksmith at the rancho, "if the Thurston family don't beat the band for quarrels and bloody feuds!"

But just then a bunch of cattle broke from the main herd and the group of cowboys dispersed in a galloping scamper.

Munson and the young ladies, engrossed in their light conversation, knew nothing of this unpleasant episode. They were now discussing the date of the projected visit to the home of Mr. Ricardo Robles among the oaks above La Siesta. It was decided to fix it for the first Sunday after the cattle muster was completed, when Dick Willoughby would be free to make one of the party.

"But hold a moment," exclaimed the lieutenant suddenly, "unless I'm to be court-martialled for absence without leave, I must take the train East next Saturday, or—or—"

His eyes fixed on Grace, he hesitated to complete the alternative.

"Or what?" she inquired.

"Follow Dick's advice and send in my resignation." As he spoke he thrust a hand into his breast pocket and drew forth a letter, sealed, addressed and stamped, all ready for the mail. "I really can't quite make up my mind," he added, dubiously.

"Let me help you," said Grace with a gay smile as she extended her hand for the letter.

"How?" he asked.

"I'll mail your resignation for you. We shall be riding home by La Siesta postoffice."

"Oh, Grace!" murmured Merle in timid protest. "Think of the responsibility you are taking."

"A woman's mission in life is to encourage men to do the proper thing," replied Grace with roguish defiance. "Our friend here is enamored of the West, and the West is the very best place for him. I'll post your letter, lieutenant."

He placed it between her fingers, doffed his hat, and bowed gallantly.

"Be it so. Let the gods—or should I say, a
fair goddess?—decide."

"Thanks for the compliment," cried Grace,
with a pretty flush on her face. "Good-bye, then,
for the present. Get ready for Sunday's picnic
among the oaks. Come along, Merle, my dear."

And with a touch of the quirt she started her
pony into a canter.

"Great guns, but she's worth while," exclaimed
Munson as he gazed after the retreating figures.

CHAPTER VII

Old Bandit Days

ON the evening of the day that followed the big round-up of cattle, Dick Willoughby and Chester Munson rode over to the store. As they cantered along, both men were pre-occupied with their thoughts.

Dick was not worrying over his sharp passage of words with his employer's son, for he knew that his services at the present time were quite indispensable, more especially if the rancho was to be sold to the best advantage. The owner had spoken lightly of the negotiations, and had chuckled in a sinister way about the money he had frequently made over unexercised options. But this time it was a Los Angeles syndicate that was seeking the property, composed of men whose financial reputation and keen business ability Willoughby knew well. For he had learned their names after his interview with Ben Thurston, and he felt certain that this particular group of capitalists would have entered into no serious negotiations without having both the cash and the intention to put the deal through. Therefore he scented a change of ownership in the rancho, and consequently, perhaps, the necessity for his looking around to find employment elsewhere. He hated to think of leaving a place that he had come to look on as home and parting from all the friends he had made throughout the countryside. Unconsciously to himself, the greatest tie of all was proximity to La Siesta and to Merle Farnsworth. But Dick was not thinking of Merle just then—he was merely turning things over generally in his mind as he rode across the valley.

Munson also was cogitating the change in his own outlook that had been brought about by the mailing of the letter of resignation to army headquarters. He was recalling the many years he had striven to reach the lieutenancy now voluntarily surrendered—of his youthful zeal and ambition for an army career which had been powerless to withstand the witching call of the West. And although Grace Darlington's act of putting the letter in the post had been only the last feather to tip an evenly balanced scale, he could not but feel that thereby this beautiful girl of the West had entered into his life and into all his future plans, hopes, and aspirations. The thought gave him joy; he was more pleased than ever that the decisive step had at last been taken.

Arriving at the store, they found old Tom Baker seated on a dry goods box, while Buck Ashley leaned against the counter, waiting for the stage coach and the mails. Already two or three others were beginning to congregate under the trees, in readiness for the distribution of letters and newspapers.

"Hello, Dick," called out the sheriff, "I heard of your scrap yesterday morning with that young ne'er-do-well, Marshall Thurston. My God, I'm glad you gave him hell."

"Please don't speak about it," replied Willoughby quietly. "That was my affair and mine alone. I guess we can find some more agreeable topic."

"Wal," drawled Buck Ashley, "Tom here was just a-tellin' me a yarn that'll interest both you boys a heap, or the lieutenant at all events, for he's new to these parts and don't know the local hist'ry yet. Of course I've heard the story before, but not all the pertic'lars the way Tom can tell 'em. And its a dangnation good story. So start from the beginnin' again, Tom."

Thus addressed, the sheriff, after taking a bite from his tobacco plug, began:

"The yarn has to do with the old-time bandit Joaquin Murietta, about whom we were speakin' the other mornin'. Well, the way it all happened was this: On a neighboring ranch, over Ventura way, beyond the Lagunita Rancho, owned at that time by Senor Olivas, a rich cattle dealer comes down from 'Frisco to buy a bunch of beeves. The stock had all been driven up on a mesa near the Olivas ranch house, and for several days the herders had been cuttin' out the cows and the young calves from the steers, 'cause this feller was only goin' to buy the steers.

"The great herd was bellerin' and pawin' in a big cloud of dust, through which the vaqueros—cowboys, you know, lieutenant—could be seen ridin' round and round. Of course roundin' up cattle is always more or less excitin' work, but this rich chap had come down from 'Frisco with his saddle bags bulgin' out with gold, and this sorta added a mighty sight to the interest of the doin's. Part of the bargain was that the deal was to be for spot cash, all in gold, too, mind you, and it was arranged that the buyer and Senor Olivas were to take their stations at one side of the narrow gate, and every time a steer was driven through that gate a twenty-dollar gold

piece was to be tossed into a big bag which Senor
Olivas was holdin'.

"They do say as how the work continued all
day, from early mornin' until dark, afore the last
blamed steer passed that 'ere gate, and they claim
that there was eighty thousand dollars in the
Senor's bag as pay for the day's drive. They
say, too, that Joaquin Murietta, disguised, was
one of the vaqueros doin' the drivin'. Anyway
that very night old Olivas was waked up mighty
abruptly by feelin' the cold nose of a revolver
shoved against his own nose.

"Well, the long and short of it all was that
Senor Olivas and his wife were both gagged and
bound hand and foot, while Murietta ransacked
the house, found the strong box and carried away
every blamed gold coin that Olivas had received
for the sale of his steers. The outlaw succeeded
in makin' his escape into the Tehachapi mountains with his cut-throat gang, and they found a
hidin' place in the robbers' cave that is somewhere
hereabouts on the San Antonio Rancho. It sure
was as slick a piece of rascality as was ever pulled
off in the old lawless days."

"Well," observed Buck Ashley, as he shook his
head reflectively, "I'm assoomin' some of the
cowboy fellers around here will find that cave one

of these days. I've put in a good many Sundays huntin' for it myself."

Just then there was the sound of horses' hoofs outside, and a moment later Jack Rover strolled into the store. Over his shoulder was slung the big leather bag for the rancho mails.

"Hallo, everybody," was his greeting. "I'm ahead of time Buck, but the stage will be here in five minutes. I saw its dust above the ridge. I hear, lieutenant," he went on, "you're going to stick to the West and be one of us."

"Quit the army?" exclaimed Tom Baker in surprise.

"That is so," replied Munson. "California has fairly got hold of me, and I intend to make my home in the West."

"Then you just stick here, young man," said the sheriff, rising to his feet and extending his hand. "California is the pick of the States, and our valley the pick of California. Don't you forget it. We're proud to welcome you as a new resident."

"That's what I say, too," concurred Buck Ashley, cordially.

Munson smiled. "Well, I don't know if you can put me in the resident class all at once," he observed, diffidently. "Guess I've got to join

the cowboy brigade first, if Dick and Jack here
will break me in."

"Sure thing," assented Jack Rover. "You're
a good rider now—for an army man."

"An ex-army man," corrected Willoughby,
laughing.

"It strikes me we should put you in as postmaster, Munson," suggested the sheriff, a sly
gleam of mischief in his eye. "Buck Ashley here
is growin' old."

"Yes, but not too old to hold down his job till
your tombstone's in the cemetery, Tom Baker,"
retorted the storekeeper, with a grin. "No man
takes the Tejon postmastership while I'm alive,"
he added defiantly.

"I'm forewarned and won't apply for your job,
Buck," laughed Munson. "But here comes the
stage, so show your spryness, old fellow, by getting
us our mail."

Chapter VIII

A Letter from San Quentin

BUCK ASHLEY had retired into the partitioned-off section of the store that formed the postoffice, and was busy stamping and sorting out the mail. The scattered loiterers outside crowded into the building expectantly, and the local parliament was in session. Amid the buzz of conversation Willoughby could not but hear his own name mentioned, coupled with that of Marshall Thurston. He understood quite well that all manner of gossip was flying around in regard to the quarrel at the round-up. But he remained stoically indifferent, shut his ears, and leaning against the counter busied himself with an old *Saturday Evening Post* that had been lying there.

At last the wicket was shoved up with a bang, and those present began to move toward the little aperture through which Buck Ashley proceeded to hand out correspondence and newspapers. One by one the throng melted away. Jack Rover was examining the big bunch of mail for San

Antonio Rancho as he stowed it into the letter bag. · Munson was opening and gleaning the contents of two or three letters that had come to him from New York. Dick Willoughby continued his reading, unconcerned; Jack would pass over any correspondence for him. Old Tom Baker had not risen from his accustomed seat on an empty box; he had few correspondents, and the mail did not worry him, although he invariably assisted with his presence at its distribution.

These four were now the only ones in the store besides Buck Ashley, who still remained behind the partition. At last the postmaster appeared, holding in his hand an open letter. His face showed great agitation as he glanced around to take stock of those who might be present.

"Say, boys," he whispered in a mysterious manner, as he held up the letter, "this is the most dangnation extr'ornery thing that has ever happened to me. You're just the bunch of fellers I'd like to consult. Close the door, Tom."

"What's up, Buck?" asked the sheriff as he rose to comply. "You look as if you had the ague shakes."

"No ague in this here land of California," laughed Jack Rover. "Is it a proposal of marriage you've been getting, Buck?"

"A derned heap better'n that. God 'lmighty, boys, this may mean millions for all of us. Shoot the bolt, Tom; I'll hand out no more groceries tonight. Come close together, all of you. You read the letter aloud, Dick. My hand's a-tremblin', and I can't get the Frenchie's lingo just right."

"The Frenchie?" echoed Tom Baker in puzzled surprise.

"It's a letter from Pierre Luzon," explained Buck.

"Good God!" The sheriff was now as deeply stirred as his old crony.

"The bandit scout you were telling us about the other morning?" exclaimed Jack Rover, also fired with excitement.

"I thought that fellow was in San Quentin for life." remarked Munson, composedly.

"Wal, and ain't this letter from San Quentin?" retorted Buck. "See the headin'! But Dick'll read it aloud. I feel clean knocked out." And the old man sank back on his chair behind the counter.

The four others were now clustered around Dick Willoughby. The latter, deputized to do the reading, had nonchalantly taken the epistle from Buck Ashley's trembling hand. While the others were speaking he had bestowed a preliminary glance, and from his lips there escaped a murmur of surprise.

"Great Caesar!" As he uttered the ejaculation Dick sat up, keenly alert.

"Well, what's it all about?" inquired Munson, by this time the only cool man in the bunch.

"Read, read!" cried the storekeeper hoarsely.

Dick Willoughby began:

"*Mr. Buck Ashley, Storekeeper,*
  Tejon, California.

"If God in His goodness permits this letter to come to your hands, remember it is from old Pierre, the Frenchman, who used to be about your store sometimes a half a day at a time, smoking his pipe. You never knew much about me or where I lived. But I will tell you.

"I am an old man now—very old. I was born in the South of France, came to this country in the '40's and entered into the service of Joaquin Murietta, who was one great man, but a big bandit. Peace to his soul! Well, he was good to me, and I was faithful to him, taking care of the cave, the big grotto, the cavern among the Tehachapi mountains where he many times hid from the sheriff's posse, and also, where he brought all his gold to stack up and keep from everybody.

"You also know Don Manuel, him whom the people call White Wolf. Well, once when a boy, Don Manuel he save Murietta's life from the sheriff by helping him to escape from one close place. Murietta was very grateful, and one day he bring the boy to the grotto cave, and there I see him and like him very much. That was while Murietta still lived.

"Afterward when the little boy grow up and was one man, and turned bitter against the gringos because they wrong his sister, Senorita Rosetta, and his old father and mother die of grief, he say to me, 'I will become a bandit like Joaquin Murietta.' He came to the cavern one night and tell me and say, 'You be my servant.' So I say, 'All right,' because Don Manuel one brave man.

"So that night of the great stage robbery over near Lake of Tulare, I hold horses. That's all I do, but all the same they put me in this horrid prison, and here I am. The other two men, Felix Vasquez and Fox Cassidy, were shot by the posse and I have been told by a Portugee in the jail here about the White Wolf being killed away north in Seattle, and he is no more.

"Don Manuel de Valencia, he was one great man. Peace to his soul!

"I am alone. I want to get away from this terrible prison. I have promised one of my guards—a good Frenchman who comes from my town in France—$5,000 in gold if he can secretly get this letter into postoffice to you and get me away from this living hell. You do this and I show you the cavern. Nobody knows where it is but me.

"Come and get me, please, my good Mr. Ashley, come, and may the spirit of the Virgin Mary reward you. All I say here is truth. You come get me and I show you the secret grotto. I show you the great stacks of gold hidden by Joaquin Murietta and Don Manuel. Also the sand-bar in the hidden stream where Guadalupe gathered up much gold.

"I beg and pray you to keep what I say in this letter secret. I am old and weak and sick. Come and get me.

"Obedient servant,

"PIERRE LUZON."

"Ain't that just one hell of a letter, boys?" exclaimed Buck Ashley.

"Gospel truth, every word," cried Tom Baker, emphatically.

"It certainly reads like the truth," concurred Munson.

"Then what are we going to do about it?" asked Jack Rover.

Dick Willoughby spoke now with the quiet and quick decision that marks the leader of men:

"What we will do is this. We five are partners in this secret, and, if Buck is willing, we'll play the game together for all it is worth. To begin with, we'll put up one hundred dollars apiece to send Tom Baker to Sacramento. He will try to get a pardon or a parole for Pierre Luzon."

"That can be managed," assented the sheriff. "I've got a political pull, you know, boys."

"Well," continued Dick, "we'll bring old Pierre here and we'll get from him the information he promises about the secret grotto."

"Not forgetting Guadalupe's placer mine," interjected Jack Rover.

"Everything will be attended to in its turn," replied Dick. "One thing at a time, and the first thing to be done is to get the Frenchman out of San Quentin. When can you start, Tom?"

"The day after tomorrow."

"Well, we'll have the cash ready for you by tomorrow night. You must bring Pierre Luzon here without anyone else besides ourselves knowing his name or getting next to him."

"I'll fix up a cot for him in my own room behind the store," suggested Buck Ashley.

"That's a good plan," assented Dick. "When the Frenchman's here, it will be time then to discuss our next move. Meanwhile, it's an honorable promise of secrecy all round, and to begin with I give my word."

While speaking the last words, Dick solemnly raised his hand, and each man in turn followed his example as he gave the pledge required.

Chapter IX

Tia Teresa

TEN days had passed and the count of the stock on San Antonio Rancho had been completed, every canyon searched, the last wandering maverick roped and branded, the number of fat beeves accurately estimated. Three members of the Los Angeles syndicate had arrived in a big automobile and remained over night at the ranch house. Most of the time they had been closeted with Ben Thurston in his office, and had finally taken their departure without exchanging a word with anyone else on the rancho. Nobody knew whether the deal had gone through or not, but rumor said that, after some disagreement on the first day, terms had been arranged next morning.

Dick Willoughby, although he discussed the question with no one, made his own inferences. The very fact that the visitors had not made any inspection of the property proved that they already knew it thoroughly well. The counting of the cattle and horses had been the final factor in the negotiations, and the figures had enabled the deal to advance a further stage toward completion. Ben Thurston might fool himself about easy option money put up only to be forfeited, but Dick Willoughby was not fooled. The days of closer settlement in California had come, and these Los Angeles men were the most enterprising and skilful subdividers in the West. They dealt only in big propositions, and after mopping up all the available tracts in the southern end of the State, were extending their operations northward. This vast so-called "Spanish grant," an empire in itself, had no doubt for several years been in their eye, and now they were prepared to handle the San Antonio Rancho with the lavish expenditure it deserved and required to transform the great sweep of cattle range—rich agricultural land, as the luxuriant native grasses showed— into smiling orchards and alfalfa farms, each provided with the irrigation water which intelligent conservation would ensure in abundance.

Dick knew in his heart that the era of transformation had at last come, that the roaming herds were to be pushed back into regions more remote, that homes and schoolhouses and garden cities would soon be dotting the landscape, that the passing of Ben Thurston, the cattle king, and of his hard-riding, devil-may-care vaqueros was at hand.

Yet Thurston spoke no word—in fact, he seemed to be more grouchy and taciturn than ever. Not even his son Marshall was in his confidence, for the young man was seldom with his father, preferring to spend his time in the drinking saloons and dance halls of Bakersfield, where the activity of oil-developing operations attracted all sorts and conditions of men, among whom the dissipated decadent had readily found friends to his liking.

Ben Thurston who had gone the pace himself in his early days, did not seek to interfere with his son's pursuit of pleasures, but he had very promptly squelched any interference from Marshall with his own business operations. On the evening of the quarrel with Dick Willoughby at the round-up, Marshall had attempted to tell his father about the affair and suggest Dick's dismissal. But the old man had at once silenced him by saying: "Why, damn you! I brought you out to this country to enjoy yourself and not to get into trouble. So far as Willoughby is concerned, I can't afford to quarrel with him. He is my foreman, and I am right in the midst of a big business transaction. So just you mind your own business, my boy, and leave him alone."

Accordingly, Marshall Thurston, a coward at heart, had not sought to pursue the feud single-handed, and Dick had seen but little of him during the rest of the mustering work. When they did happen to meet, it was a case of a black scowl of hate from the one and a contemptuous smile of indifference from the other. And so the days had passed until the task was finished.

It was the Sunday morning that had been fixed for the visit to the home of Mr. Ricardo Robles, when the cattle foreman could at last conscientiously take a day of recreation. With the first break of dawn he and Munson were in the saddle, for they had been invited to breakfast at La Siesta before starting with the young ladies on the ride through the oak forest.

The visitors arrived early, but not too early for their hostesses. Grace and Merle were waiting to welcome them in the portico, looking more charming than ever in their neat riding suits of khaki.

"We saw you cross the bridge," declared Grace, "and mother has gone in to order breakfast to be served. You must be hungry after your early start."

"Oh, Sing Ling didn't let us go without a cup of coffee," laughed Dick. "But I fancy we'll do full justice, all right, to the bountiful fare of La Siesta."

It proved to be a delightful meal in every way, the viands seasoned with gay repartee and laughter. A full hour had sped before Dick recalled the real object of the day's excursion.

"We usually walk to Mr. Robles' place," remarked Merle. "It is only a mile or so by the short cuts up the hill, but by the winding road it is very much longer. So we ordered our ponies."

"I see," smiled Munson, "to prolong the pleasure of our foursome among the oaks."

"Not at all, sir," retorted Grace. "The climb on foot is a stiff one, and we knew that you must be out of condition from the lazy life you are living."

"I am only waiting for Willoughby to give me a cowboy's job," replied the ex-lieutenant.

"I don't know if there will be any cowboy jobs going," observed Willoughby. "It's my belief that San Antonio Rancho is sold and is going to be broken up into small holdings."

"Oh, what a pity!" exclaimed Merle.

"From one point of view, perhaps," answered Dick. "But from a hundred other points of view, what a blessing! There will be a dozen happy homes for every steer the range now feeds!"

"But La Siesta will remain just as it is," cried Grace.

"That will be all right," replied Dick, gallantly, "It's already a happy home."

The ladies smiled pleasantly.

"Then this will mean the elimination of Mr. Ben Thurston," observed Mrs. Darlington.

"The greatest blessing of all," declared Merle, clapping her hands. "You see, I am already converted to the change, Mr. Willoughby," she added merrily.

"But what about my job?" asked Munson in mock dolefulness.

"Consult Mr. Robles," laughed Grace. "He may take pity on you, and find you a place as handy man on his estate."

In merry mood they all sallied forth. The saddle horses were waiting, and standing beside them was an elderly Spanish woman.

"Tia Teresa, Mr. Munson," said Mrs. Darlington by way of introduction.

Munson had often enough heard the name, and in answer to an inquiry, Willoughby had told him that the old dame had been the personal attendant of the two young ladies ever since they could remember. Tia or Aunt Teresa was now more a friend of the family than a servant of the house, and, taking her hand in salutation, Munson treated her with the affable courtesy that was her due.

"I am glad to make your acquaintance," he said, raising his hat.

Tia Teresa looked pleased. Despite her seventy years, she was a buxom and splendidly preserved woman, and there was still the flash of youthfulness in her big dark eyes.

"You will look after my little girls," she said, as she gathered together the folds of her black lace mantilla. "By rights I should be coming with you, too," she added, in the manner of a true Spanish duenna.

"You forget that we are home again—in free America," laughed Merle as she settled herself in the saddle.

"Too free, I sometimes think," rejoined Tia Teresa. "But there is safety in four," she added, turning with a smile to Mrs. Darlington.

And as the young folks rode away she waved them a pleasant *adios.*

Chapter X

The Home of the Recluse

AT a gentle pace they wound their way through the forest of magnificent old oaks. As for Munson, riding by Grace Darlington's side, the miles were the shortest he had ever before traversed. It seemed only a few minutes before the red tiled roof and towers of a house built in the California Mission style were gleaming through the trees only a short distance ahead.

Great oaken doors closed the arched gateway, but at the clatter of hoofs and the sound of voices, a little peep-hole wicket was withdrawn. The inspection by unseen eyes apparently was satisfactory, for a moment later a postern was opened, and two men, Mexicans obviously by their garb and deferential manner, emerged to take and lead away the horses. Within the patio stood Senor Robles, his usually grave face lighted by a smile of cordial welcome.

"Let me tell you, young men," he said while shaking hands, "that while Grace and Merle are quite at home here, you are the very first strangers who have passed through my portals."

"Strangers no longer then," said Dick, good-naturedly.

"Precisely," replied Mr. Robles, "or you would not be here. But I foresee that all of us are going to be very close friends. Isn't that so, Grace, my dear?"

"I'm sure I cannot say," replied Grace, with a smile of demure innocence toward Mr. Munson. Then she turned to Mr. Robles with a roguish twinkle in her eye. "But I've news for you. Mr. Munson has resigned from the army and is looking for a job."

"Both facts are already known to me," answered Robles, smiling.

"Oh," exclaimed Grace, "one can never surprise you, Mr. Robles. Although you live the life of a hermit, you seem to be always the first to learn everything that is going on."

"A hermit, my dear, need not necessarily be out of touch with the world," replied Robles, playfully pinching her ear. "And now, Mr. Willoughby, you came specially to see my pictures. Lead the way, Merle. Gentlemen, I say again—welcome to my mountain home."

They lingered awhile in the patio to admire the

marble columns of the cloister that ran all around, the playing fountains at each of the four corners, with groups of symbolical statuary, the wealth of beautiful shrubs and flowers. On the side opposite to the gateway rose a tall tower, fashioned like the campanile of an Old Mission and crowned with bright red tiles.

"We shall ascend there later on," remarked Mr. Robles, following Dick's upward glance.

Then they passed through the wide-opened French window into the living rooms.

The first was a great apartment that occupied one entire side of the building. In the centre was a large globe of the world. Here and there were glass cases displaying manuscripts and illuminated missals. Along the walls were finely-carved bookcases filled with several thousands of volumes.

"When you have the leisure you can come and browse here," said the host, addressing both young men. "Meanwhile you may care to look at the bronzes and statuary"—this with a sweep of the hand that indicated the art treasures distributed about the apartment.

On the side of the house beneath the tower were the dining room and the billiard and smoking room. Passing through these, the visitors came

Guadalupe and the White Wolf—Page 53

to the picture gallery, a room corresponding in
size to the library.   Here were hung treasures
of the painter's art, masterpieces signed by names
that are immortal.   These, as their owner again
explained, had been acquired by him during
several prolonged visits to Europe.

"Count this just as a preliminary survey, Mr.
Willoughby," he said finally.   "Then come again.
There are guest chambers on either side of the
gateway, and one of these will always be at your
disposal when I am at home.   I extend the same
invitation to you, Mr. Munson."

"My word, but you may feel honored," exclaimed Grace, in unconcealed amazement.

"When I open my gates, I open my heart as
well," said Mr. Robles, with a courtly little bow
to his new friends.

Next they ascended the tower.   Its first floor,
above the living rooms, was a delightful den
filled with curios of all kinds.   From this sprang
a winding iron staircase, up which Mr. Robles
led the way.

The upper chamber, extending on all sides some
distance beyond the supporting tower, proved
larger than might have been expected.   Its one
conspicuous article of furniture was a great terres-
trial telescope.   The sliding panels of glass which

formed a complete window all around the room showed that the instrument could be used without obstruction in any direction.

Here a Mexican boy was on duty. When the visitors entered, his hand was resting on the telescope. A bright red sash around his waist imparted a touch of picturesqueness to his costume. He was perhaps only twelve or thirteen years of age, but wonderfully keen and alert-looking for his years. At a glance from his master, the youngster took his departure, closing the door behind him.

"Gentlemen," remarked Mr. Robles, when they were again alone, "perhaps before I brought you here I should have exacted the promise I am now going to ask you to make. Grace and Merle know that I am a recluse and wish to live undisturbed by curiosity-mongers or tittle-tattlers. I want nobody but the friends I deliberately choose to know about my habits of living or the contents of my home. Only in this way can I hope to be left alone. Therefore, please give me your word, Mr. Willoughby and Lieutenant Munson, that you will not speak with any outsider about the things I am showing you today."

The promise was instantly given and sealed by a hearty hand clasp.

"Now," resumed the host in lighter tone,

"perhaps you would like to view the landscape. I may explain that I had this observatory, as I call it, specially built and equipped so that I could sweep the valley from end to end. For example, I saw you two young men riding along the road this morning," he went on, with a smile. "I saw one of you alight, about twelve miles from here—it was you, lieutenant—and tighten the girths of your saddle."

"Great Scott!" murmured Munson, in half-incredulous surprise.

"Test the glass for yourself," continued Robles, as, placing one eye at the lens, he adjusted the instrument. "Look"—and he stepped back, motioning Munson to approach.

Munson peeped through the long tube and there came from his lips a cry of mingled delight and amazement.

"Dick, Dick, there's the store as large as life— Buck Ashley standing at the door and lighting a cigar. Geewhizz, and it must be twenty miles away."

He rose erect and made room for Dick. The latter gazed in silence for a few moments. When he turned to Mr. Robles he said:

"It's really wonderful—it is the most wonderful glass I ever looked through."

There was the glimmer of an exultant smile on the face of Ricardo Robles.

"I saw you at the round-up across the valley the other day," he remarked. "You were much nearer to me than is the store. And while I do not invite any confidence, Mr. Willoughby, you certainly engaged in a very spirited conversation, to say the least, with young Marshall Thurston. Indeed, I half expected to see you come to blows."

"What was that?" asked Merle in some trepidation.

Willoughby had reddened.

"Nothing of consequence," he responded, almost curtly. "I had to tell the young cub to mind his own business. That was all."

"You certainly have the whole valley under observation," remarked Munson, considerately diverting the conversation.

"Yes," assented Mr. Robles, with an almost grim smile of satisfaction. "The telescope teaches one not merely to observe, but to reason from the facts observed. Tia Teresa evidently thought that she should have come along today to play duenna, eh, Merle?"

"You don't say you guessed that?" exclaimed Merle in great astonishment.

"Guessed it! I knew it when she raised her protesting finger."

"You are a magician, Mr. Robles," cried Grace.

"No, only a logician," was the sententious rejoinder.

"Please let me peep at our garden," asked Merle. "I wonder if mother is among her roses."

Without a word Robles swung round the instrument on its pivot and changed the focus.

"That's about right," he said, stepping back. "There is no one out of doors at present. Move the glass slightly and you can see over the entire garden."

Each girl in turn made a prolonged scrutiny; they were enchanted with the clearness and marvellous detail of the picture.

"Henceforth we'll have to be on our best behavior, Dick," laughed Munson, as they turned toward the winding stairway. "We've got to remember Mr. Robles has a constant eye on us."

"Perhaps I've had you under observation quite a while," laughed the senor, tapping the young fellow on the shoulder.

Then he threw open the door, and, with a slight bow and extended hand, motioned to his visitors to descend. At the foot of the narrow, winding staircase they found the Mexican youth standing on guard. He bowed low as the ladies passed, and when Mr. Robles followed last of all, saluted, and then immediately returned to the chamber above, again without a single word of instruction from his master. Munson and Willoughby exchanged meaning looks; obviously a well-disciplined outlook was kept from the observatory all the time, as if from the conning-tower of a battleship.

Again the party was in the patio. Mr. Robles turned to Willoughby.

"I hope Grace and Merle have explained to you that at present I do not entertain. My own fare is of the simplest."

"Mother is to have luncheon ready at one," interposed Grace. "I caught the broiled trout myself this morning."

"You caught them ready broiled, eh?" laughed Munson.

"Oh, you know what I mean," rejoined Grace, with a pretty little *moue*.

"Broiled trout!" exclaimed Dick, appreciatively. "Then I think we'll be hurrying down the hill, senor." He had recognized with intuitive courtesy that the interview was at an end.

"Is he not delightful?" asked Merle, as their horses started off at a walk. "And you would never guess how sweet and kind he can be."

"I don't doubt it," assented Willoughby. "A polished gentleman, but a man of mystery, isn't he?"

"Not when you come to know him. A recluse always has his little idiosyncrasies." As she spoke, she set her pony at a canter down the gentle incline.

After luncheon, Dick found himself tête-à-tête with Mrs. Darlington in the music room. The mystery attaching to the personality of the recluse was still uppermost in his mind. But for the present the music claimed his attention.

Merle had seated herself at the grand piano and was softly fingering the keys, striking a chord here and there, until finally she drifted into Chopin's Fifth Nocturne. There was something almost divine in her interpretation. The music fairly rippled from her deft fingers, as they glided on from one beautiful cadence to another until at last, note by note, as if sobbing a reluctant adieu, the melody died away.

Both the visitors were generous in their tributes of congratulation.

"Thank you," said Merle, as she arose from the piano and proceeded to unfasten the clasps of a violin case.

"What now?" exclaimed Munson.

"Oh, I am not the performer; I am merely the accompanist," and she held out a beautiful old violin to Grace. As Merle sounded a key on the piano, Grace touched the strings of the Stradivarius. When all was ready she tenderly caressed the violin with her chin, and, her bow sweeping across the instrument, Beethoven's Moonlight Sonata trembled from the strings, in soft and plaintive melody, filling the room with echoing and re-echoing notes of sweetness, while Merle's accompanying notes lent support, in blending harmony, to the rich cadences.

"Splendid! magnificent!" exclaimed the young men in unison.

Munson was now called upon to sing, and Dick felt himself at full liberty to converse with Mrs. Darlington. He broached the subject that had been occupying his thoughts.

"What is known of Senor Ricardo Robles?" he enquired. "Have you been long acquainted?"

"Oh, I have known him for many, many years," replied Mrs. Darlington. "We used to be next door neighbors in Los Angeles. That was twenty years ago. Then we returned to England—Mr. Darlington had fallen heir to the family estates. Mr. Robles used to visit us off and on. He is, as you have seen, very fond of Grace"—she paused a moment, then went on—"and of my adopted daughter Merle as well.   Merle, you know, was the child of my dearest girl friend who died a year after her baby was born."

"Yes, Merle has told me this."

"Well, six years ago my dear husband died, and it was Mr. Robles who persuaded me to return to California.   He selected this beautiful ranch for us, near to his own home.   And we have all been so happy here at La Siesta."

"Mr. Robles is certainly a wonderful man, with all those art treasures around him."

"He has princely tastes and princely wealth as well—this you will have seen for yourself today. He travels a great deal abroad, sometimes for a whole year at a time, and then returns quietly to his hermitage.   He has taken a great fancy to you, Mr. Willoughby.   You are lucky in gaining the friendship of such a man."

"I think I'll like him, too—when I know him better," replied Willoughby, with cautious reserve.

Chapter XI

A Rejected Suitor

IN Dick Willoughby's presence Marshall Thurston contented himself with sullen looks. But beyond his sight and hearing he spoke truculently of what he was going to do some day to get level with "the hired hand who had had the infernal insolence to call him down in public." So all the little world on the rancho knew, or at least believed, that a bitter feud was in progress.

Two or three of the cowboys fostered young Marshall's feelings of animosity, partly out of sheer devilment, partly because they deemed it good policy to keep in the good graces of the heir to the rancho. Moreover, so long as old Ben Thurston knew nothing about it, they were always willing to break a bottle with the dissipated spendthrift, not only because good liquor was not to be despised at any time, but also for the sake of the amusement afforded by Marshall, in his cups, with his stories of fast life in New York and his apparently inexhaustible fund of highly spiced anecdotes. Even his braggart threats against Willoughby had an element of fun.

"Why don't you cut him out with the girl?" one of his boon companions had suggested on an occasion of this kind.

"By gad, I will," Marshall had responded with vehemence. "You just watch me."

Thenceforward this thought was uppermost in his alcohol-sodden brain.

Marshall Thurston had met Mrs. Darlington and her daughter on several occasions, but, although he had been formally introduced, he had never been invited to call at La Siesta. Nor up to the present had he felt any inducement to take the initiative. Like clings to like, and these people were not of his kind—in the presence of pure and refined womanhood the human toad becomes uncomfortably conscious of his own loathsomeness.

But now there was a valid reason to egg him on. He would show Dick Willoughby who was who on the San Antonio Rancho. If the heir to all those broad acres chose to pay court to Merle Farnsworth, the girl would only be too glad to jump at him and his millions. He would tell her, too, that Willoughby was going to be fired and that the fellow was not worth a moment's consideration.

Such was his mood one afternoon when, his motor car being in the repair shop, he had not made his usual trip to Bakersfield. "Yes, he would ride over that very day to La Siesta;" and he proceeded to fortify the resolve by opening a bottle of champagne in the solitary seclusion of his den. After gulping down the wine he felt brave enough to face the devil himself. Yet, when mounted on his horse, he still evinced sufficient discretion to make a wide detour lest Willoughby should catch sight of him and divine his intentions.

As he rode along young Thurston nursed his wrath to keep it warm. At the same time the desire to possess the girl for her own sake began to inflame his imagination. Unscrupulous passion had been bred in the very bone of this worthless degenerate. Just as his father, Ben Thurston, had thirty years before trampled on the virtue of the young Spanish beauty, Senorita Rosetta, the sister of Don Manuel, so now was the son hatching in his brain a foul plot of spoliation.

"I'll get even with Willoughby, by God, in the very way that will hurt his pride the most. Women!—pshaw, they're all alike. And she's a peacherino all right—those flashing dark eyes— she sure looks good to me." This was now the tenor of his musing as his pony cantered up the slope to La Siesta.

He advanced on foot to the portico with a swagger and a smile, and there, as luck would have it, he found Merle seated in a rocker, reading, and alone. She rose with quiet courtesy and returned his greeting.

"I am sorry," she said, "mother is not at home. She and my sister Grace have driven over to the dairy. We have a model dairy, you know, on La Siesta," she went on, anxious to make conversation that would not prove embarrassing. For already she divined some particular object in the young man's visit, knowing as she did that he and Willoughby had recently exchanged angry words.

"Won't you show me your famous rose gardens?" asked Thurston, boldly.

"With pleasure," she replied, assenting with a sweet smile of politeness, although there was sore reluctance in her heart, as she stepped from under the portico.

But, unknown to herself, she did not go unattended, for as Merle and her visitor passed round the house and through the shrubberies there glided after them the figure of a woman, clothed in black, wearing over her head and shoulders a Spanish mantilla. It was Tia Teresa, the ever watchful duenna.

The roses of La Siesta, as Marshall Thurston had said, were indeed famous. Here were all the finest varieties, growing in the perfection to which only care and scientific skill applied under ideal climatic conditions can attain. Merle was glad to point out the different blooms and give them their names—the topic was certainly an innocuous one, and she smiled at the thought as they strolled along. She was vaguely wondering, too, whether Dick Willoughby would approve even this slight measure of courtesy toward the visitor to her home. Although she had as yet not the remotest conception that the quarrel at the round-up had been in any way connected with her name, she knew that the two young men were at daggers drawn, and toward Dick there was the instinctive loyalty in her heart that prompted her to count his enemies as her enemies, his friends as her friends.

The young girl was too unversed in the ways of the world to notice that Marshall Thurston was under the influence of wine. He was too experienced a toper to show any signs of unsteadiness on his feet, but all the same there was undoubted tipsiness in his leering side-glances and occasional slurring of his words. Of this Merle in her maidenly innocence was supremely unconscious, nor did she dream that the very sparkle of her eyes was completing the intoxication of wine fumes.

Once she cast a look up the hill and asked herself whether the wizard of the red-tiled tower had his spy-glass on La Siesta and was even then quietly surveying the scene in the gardens. The thought made her uncomfortable; she felt sure that her kind friend, Mr. Robles, would not look with favor on her condescending to show even the slightest attention to one whose evil ways of living were notorious.

Suddenly she came to a halt, close beside a little clump of oleander trees laden with rich blossoms.

"I am sorry I must leave you now," she said, quite abruptly.

"Leave me?" stammered Thurston. "What for?"

"I have other things to attend to," she replied.

"Oh, I say, Miss Farnsworth"—the inebriate as he spoke made a gesture of appeal—"I hope you are not angry with me. If that scalawag of a fellow Willoughby told you I said anything disrespectful of you the other day, he is a derned liar—that's what he is, a derned liar, and a poor penniless beggar as well, whom my father's going to fire off the ranch."

Merle stood speechless. She stepped back when Thurston advanced with outstretched hands.

"The truth of the whole matter is," he rambled on, with growing incoherence, "I am madly in love with you myself. That's what I am, and I'm going to have you, too." And he grabbed her fiercely and attempted to draw her to him.

Merle screamed both in fear and in repulsion as she tried to push him away.

Just then, from among the oleanders, rushed Tia Teresa. The old duenna came like a cyclone. Her eyes blazed with anger. Grasping the young libertine by the collar of his coat, she pulled him madly from the now half-fainting girl. Then, whirling him around, she rushed him, with the strength and ferocity of a tigress defending her whelps, down the gravelled path and flung him bodily over the low retaining wall along the embankment that separated the rose gardens from the public road. She spat upon his prostrate figure below and rained down on him a torrent of imprecations in the Spanish tongue.

It was all over in one brief minute. When young Thurston picked himself up, it was to see the aged fury half-leading, half-carrying Merle away in the direction of the house.

"The hell cat," he murmured.

Then he brushed the dirt from his coat and straightened out his tumbled appearance as best he could. His horse was tied to the gate post a hundred yards along the road. He slunk toward it, climbed into the saddle, and rode slowly away in the falling twilight. He had been thoroughly sobered by the incident, yet continued somewhat dazed, for his horse was headed toward the woods and hills and not in the direction of home.

CHAPTER XII

The Sped Bullet

MEANWHILE events had been happening in the conning tower high up among the hills. The Mexican boy on duty had observed the lone rider approaching the gateway at La Siesta, and for a brief few moments had put the figure under observation by the telescope. He had then sprung alertly erect and pressed a button on the wall. Mr. Robles had quickly responded to the summons, and it was he who had had his eye to the lens during the scene in the rose garden which had terminated in the ignominious expulsion of young Thurston at the hands of the infuriated duenna.

When the recluse at last withdrew his gaze, his hands were clenched and he stood absolutely rigid in the tenseness of his indignation. He had seen Merle's insultor ride toward the hills and Merle herself taken indoors under Tia Teresa's protecting care. For almost a minute the storm of rage held him, then he relaxed and his look changed to one of terrible determination. He seized a rifle that was hanging on one of the walls and swiftly departed.

At the arched gateway he spoke a few words to the two retainers on guard, and when he passed through the postern one of them, also equipped with a rifle, followed. Taking a cross-cut from the high road, together they descended the wooded hillside.

In a little canyon just below the forest Dick Willoughby was rounding up a bunch of vagrant steers. He was alone, riding at a walking pace, driving a dozen or more beasts in front of him, and keeping an eye among the brushwood searching for more.

On the roadway through the woods Marshall Thurston ambled along. He was a poor and awkward rider at all times, the discreetly-veiled jest of the nimble cowboys, to whom reins, saddle, and spurs were all as second nature. Now, when he imagined himself free from observation, he did not take pains to display even a semblance of horsemanship and, with bridle dropped, steadied himself by a grip on the saddle horn.

In her bedroom Merle had soon recovered from her distress of mind. Dashing the tears from her eyes, she had enjoined Tia Teresa to say nothing to anyone about the unpleasant incident. Mrs.

Darlington would be angered and would certainly tell Mr. Robles, while if the story ever reached Dick's ears there could be no saying what further trouble might not ensue—a horse-whipping at least, with jeopardy to Dick's position at the rancho and embitterment of an already dangerous quarrel. So Tia Teresa, to complete the comforting process, had assented to secrecy.

On the pathway down through the forest the Mexican, now in advance, uttered a low "hist," halted, and held out a warning hand toward his master. The gaze of both was now fixed in the same direction. Below them could be seen the figure of the horseman coming around a bend in the roadway. The Mexican raised his rifle to the shoulder, but the hand of Robles detained him. The time was not yet—the distance was too great in view of the obstructing timber.

Robles turned away and rested an arm against a tree trunk. His eyes were downcast; for the moment his mind was far away. He saw once again the little cemetery on the hill, with the marble cross inscribed "Hermana," and the other gravestone at the head of the twin mounds that marked the resting place of his parents whose hearts had been broken by Rosetta's tragic end. The fingers of the man who had long years ago sworn the vendetta worked nervously, closing and unclosing themselves.

The rider was nearer now, in a higher loop of the road where the trees were more scattered than below. Merle, drowsy from the reaction of her emotions, had dropped off asleep on her sofa. Tia Teresa had returned to the portico, to make sure that the interloper had taken himself off for good and would not return. In the little canyon Dick Willoughby was quietly riding behind his accumulating drove of cattle.

Suddenly a shot from among the woods rang through the air. Tia Teresa heard it, and after the start of first surprise, into her eyes came the light of swift comprehension and her whole face was illumed by fierce vindictive joy. "At last, at last," she murmured, "vengeance begins." And in the fervor of her triumph she threw up her extended arms, as if to give benediction to a righteous deed.

Dick also heard the sharp detonation which his experienced ear knew at once to be from a rifle, not from the shot-gun that some sportsman after quail or rabbits might have been using. He betrayed no great surprise—just the unspoken word "curious" hovered on his lips as, halting his horse, he turned in his saddle to glance upward in the direction whence the sound had come. Then after a moment he wheeled the pony round, and, abandoning his drove for the present, ascended at a leisurely pace the narrow pathway which he knew communicated with the winding highroad above.

When the bullet had reached its fated billet, Marshall Thurston's fingers were still gripping the saddle horn. And right there the missile of death struck, glancing upward from the metal crown and piercing the victim right through the heart. Not a cry—just an outflung arm, a swaying figure slipping down onto the roadway, and a terrified riderless horse pivoting quickly round on its haunches, then galloping madly for home.

Dick, glancing upward through the timber, caught a glimpse of the fleeing steed, and he touched his own pony with the spur so that it, too, darted forward.

Farther along the road Tia Teresa heard the clatter of the hoofs and saw the animal in its swift stride disappear in the direction of the rancho. She knew now for certain that her surmise was correct, and the first flush of triumph on her face settled down into an expression of grim satisfaction. "It served him right in any case," she muttered. "It was just what the young villain

deserved." Then she re-entered the house and
passed upstairs. Her young mistress was placidly
asleep, smiling in her dreams. The duenna
nodded her head in a satisfied sort of way; Merle
would learn the news at the proper time, and would
not meanwhile be agitated by wild conjectures.
So she tiptoed from the room, and was soon
busied with domestic duties as if nothing had
happened.

Dick, emerging on foot from the last steep
ascent of the canyon, promptly swung himself
again into the saddle and started at a loping
canter up the winding roadway through the
woods. After rounding the first corner he spied
the huddled figure on the ground. Before he
turned the body over he knew that the man was
dead. But when the dead face looked up at his,
it was with a terrible shock of surprise that he
recognized Marshall Thurston.

Dick stood for a few moments, gazing around
in utter bewilderment. One hand of the dead
man was shattered and bloody, while a big
splurge of red on the shirt showed where the
bullet had completed its work. Murder—palp-
able murder! But who could have done this deed?
Who had any valid motive to rid the world of
this stray piece of humanity—and in such cold-

blooded manner, not in the heat of some angry quarrel, but by a deliberate act of assassination in a place so lonely as these pine-clad hills? Dick sat him down by the roadside and pondered these questions.

There was no real pity in his heart. Young Thurston had been utterly bad—not big-brained enough to belong to the social dregs, but just equally worthless scum, the more repellent because it made itself visible all the time. He would pass almost without a tear except from the father whose own record had been so foully besmeared that there could be scant sympathy even for him in the hour of his bereavement.

Dick just wondered and wondered. For the time being he had quite forgotten that old legend —the Vendetta of the Hills.

CHAPTER XIII

Accused

AROUND the horse corral at the San Antonio
Rancho some half-dozen cowboys were
squatted on their heels, cowboy-fashion,
swapping the news of the day. They had ridden
in from various points of the compass, and two
or three of their horses, those of the latest comers,
still stood saddled outside the enclosure, the
reins dropped loosely over their heads, which
for the trained cow-pony is just as effective an
anchorage as any stake and rope.

Two or three cigarettes were a-light, and the
"makings" were passing from hand to hand among
those not yet engaged in the leisurely blowing of
smoke rings. The topic of conversation was the
rumored sale of the ranch, which some declared
to be assuredly impending, while others dismissed
the possibility of such a big deal going through
as the merest moonshine.

Jack Rover was among those who had no
illusions as to the future.

"Believe me, fellers," he was remarking, "it's

no false alarm this time. The old rancho is as good as sold, the stock is a-going to be shipped out, the farmers is a-coming in, and in a few months' time we'll all be hunting jobs if there's any more cow-punching jobs left in this blamed new topsy-turvy world. And that's the straight goods—hell!''

Just as this terse and vigorous summation of the whole dispute found utterance, all eyes were turned in a particular direction. It was young Thurston's riderless steed that had attracted attention as it swept toward its accustomed quarters in the corral.

"It's Marshall's horse," observed one of the boys.

"Off again, on again, gone again, Flannigan," laughed another—an adaptation of a popular story that evoked a general grin.

But one youth had sprung to his feet, and skilfully caught the bridle of the panting animal as it passed him.

"Whoa, beauty!"

The others had not stirred. The involuntary dismounting of the young boss was too familiar an episode to provoke anything more than a laugh tinctured with mild satisfaction—"No Easterner can ride a Western broncho, anyhow."

"Pass your baccy, Bob," came a voice from the ring. But the cowboy holding the riderless horse now brought them all to instant attention.

"By God, he's been shot! There's blood on the horn, and here's the rip of the bullet."

Everyone was on their feet now, and the situation was being eagerly discussed while the saddle was undergoing confirmatory inspection.

"Something's happened, boys," exclaimed the big husky fellow addressed as Bob, conclusively, if somewhat obviously. "And I guess we'd better investigate."

As he spoke he swung himself into his saddle— he had been one of the late arrivals and his horse was all ready for the road or the range.

"Up toward the hills then," remarked another, indicating the direction whence the riderless horse had come. And a moment later he, too, was astride his broncho.

"I'll borrow your pony, Ted," cried out Jack Rover as he jumped astride a third mustang.

And a moment later all three riders were pelting along the road leading to La Siesta. There was no difficulty whatever in picking up the long galloping strides on the dusty highway, and the speed of the trackers depended only on the swiftness and endurance of their mounts.

Meanwhile the boy who had caught Marshall's horse had disencumbered it of saddle and bridle, and turned it into the corral with a kindly pat on its heaving flank.

"Guess I'll report to the boss," he called out, as he picked up the saddle and moved away toward the ranch home.

"Look out for yourself," shouted one of the group. "Old Thurston will be madder than hell."

But it was terror, selfish terror, not anger nor grief, that came into Ben Thurston's eyes when he saw the saddle horn smeared with fresh blood and scarred by a bullet.

"My God, and I believed Don Manuel was dead," he whispered in a hoarse voice to Leach Sharkey.

The two had been, as usual, in close companionship; Sharkey reading a weekly newspaper, while the employer he was paid to protect, restlessly, as was his wont, paced the room.

"Disappeared and dead ain't exactly the same thing," replied the sleuth as he critically examined the saddle. "And there may be another explanation to this. What about Dick Willoughby?"

"Yes, yes, Dick Willoughby," eagerly assented the trembling man.

"You saw them quarreling the other day—they hate each other like poison," continued

Sharkey. "Where's Dick Willoughby now?" he
enquired, with a swift glance at the cowboy.

"Good Lord, that's just where he is—searching
the canyons below the forest for mavericks," was
the reply.

Sharkey smiled blandly; the informant looked
disappointed, yet confident.

"I couldn't have believed that of Dick," he
added, regretfully.

"Well, clear out now," said Sharkey. "Mr.
Thurston and I will want to be alone. You say
Jack Rover and two others have gone out to search?
Well, we can't do more till they bring us in some
news. Let us know at once when they return."

Ben Thurston had collapsed onto a chair, then
raised himself, and was leaning eagerly forward
now. He met Sharkey's glance of hardly concealed contempt.

"That's right," he murmured, "It has been
Dick Willoughby's work. I knew Don Manuel
was dead."

"And what about your boy?" asked the sleuth
curtly.

"Oh, yes, poor Marshall! I forgot about him.
But perhaps he's only wounded. We'll send to
Bakersfield for a doctor." And he half rose from
his seat.

"You'll just wait patiently here," replied Sharkey, as he pushed Thurston back into his chair. "All that is possible for the present is being done."

And the rôles were now reversed—it was the bodyguard who slowly and meditatively paced the room.

Meanwhile Dick Willoughby had ceased from his ruminations, and was beginning to take practical steps for getting Marshall's body home. He had no thought of coroner's regulations that a corpse should be left undisturbed till the proper official investigation had been made. He had got his riata ready, and was just going to sling the body across his saddle and tie it there, when the rhythmic thud of clattering hoofs smote upon his ear. Thank God! Help was coming. There would be others to assist him in his gruesome task. So Dick patiently waited while the sound grew nearer and nearer, until at last the three cowboys dashed round the bend.

"I heard the rifle shot," Dick explained, "and rode up from the canyon below to have a look. I found him here, huddled up just as you see him by the side of the road."

"Who the devil did this?" asked Jack Rover, contemplating the corpse.

"God only knows," replied Dick. "You take him on your saddle, Bob," he added, addressing the big cowboy, whose horse was a full hand taller than the other ponies and more stalwart in proportion.

And so the cortege was formed, Jack Rover leading the way, with Bob and the body following and Dick Willoughby bringing up the rear.

The sun was low when at last they gained the rancho. They made their way quietly round to the bunk house and quite tenderly swathed the mortal remains of the young boss in a blanket, before carrying it to his father's home.

At the sound of approaching footsteps old Ben Thurston, with Leach Sharkey close on his heels, emerged onto the verandah. There was no need to announce the death of his son—the ominous bundle told its own sad tale. The ranch owner stared at it, horrified, inarticulate from a conflict of emotions, the hunted look of terror again in his eyes. Leach Sharkey took up the work of interrogation.

"How did it happen?" He was addressing Jack Rover, who chanced to stand next to him after helping to deposit the body on a bench that stood conveniently against the wall.

"Dick Willoughby heard the shot up among

the woods, and found him lying dead on the road."

Sharkey advanced a pace or two and confronted Dick.

"Who fired the shot?"

"How should I know?" retorted Dick, reddening slightly from the brusqueness of the enquiry.

"I reckon I can tell," cried Sharkey. And with a swift, experienced movement he grabbed Dick by both arms and clicked a pair of handcuffs on his wrists before anyone, Dick least of all, had fathomed his intention.

Dick Willoughby was a square-shouldered, powerful fellow, but the great husky bodyguard, Leach Sharkey, towered above him. In the first flush of anger and surprise Dick struggled to break the shackles of ignominy. But the sleuth grabbed him by both shoulders with a grip that rendered its recipient absolutely powerless.

"Go easy, young man."

Dick's muscles relaxed, and Sharkey was content to release his hold.

"Go easy. If you have any answer to make to the charge of murdering that boy, you'll have the chance all in good time."

"What right have you to arrest me?" demanded Dick, somewhat recovering his poise.

"Oh, I've a special constable's star all right,"

replied Sharkey, throwing open his coat and displaying, close to his armpit, the badge of the office he had claimed.

"Guess that's good enough for you and all others here. And now take my advice, Willoughby. You'll come quietly with me to Bakersfield. I've no special grudge against you, but have my obvious duty to perform. You threatened young Marshall more than once in all our hearing, and it will be up to you to prove yourself guiltless of his death. You bring round Mr. Thurston's automobile, Rover. We start right now."

Everything had happened so rapidly that none of the cowboys, had they so desired, could have protested or interfered. Meanwhile the news had spread, for others among the ranch hands were coming up and crowding toward the verandah rails. General sympathy was obviously with Dick. Several of the onlookers advanced and shook his manacled hands. "All right, Mr. Willoughby," "You'll be home again tomorrow," "Buck up, it's a ridiculous charge"—these were among their expressions of encouragement. Dick just smiled his thanks—a wan, wistful smile. He now had himself under perfect control—even his resentment toward Sharkey had been allowed to evaporate.

"Very well," he said quietly, addressing the sleuth. "I'll give you no trouble, Sharkey. Let us get away from here as quickly as possible."

Just then Lieutenant Munson came hurriedly onto the scene. For a moment he looked thunderstruck when he saw the handcuffs around Dick's wrists.

"Great Scott, Dick! What's the meaning of this?" Then without waiting for a reply he turned to the sleuth.

"I've just heard about young Thurston's death, but you're surely not going to mix up Dick Willoughby's name with it, Mr. Sharkey? You must know that he would have nothing to do with such a cowardly crime."

"He can prove all that at the proper time and place," was the cool, determined rejoinder.

"Don't interfere, Munson," interposed Dick. "Mr. Sharkey considers that he is doing his duty. That's an end to all argument. I'll have no difficulty in obtaining my release once we get to Bakersfield."

"And the lieutenant can come along with us if he likes," observed the sleuth, conciliated by his prisoner's sensible view of things. "As Mr. Willoughby's best friend, you can see that everything's done right, Mr. Munson."

"But why these handcuffs?"

"I know my own business," replied the sleuth, with returning severity, as he touched the constable's star on his breast. "And as a soldier you should know the wisdom of letting it go at that, sir."

Munson turned to Mr. Thurston. All through the colloquy the ranch-owner had spoken not a word. He had dropped onto the bench beside the still swathed body of his son, and was sitting there with bowed head and stolidly fixed eyes.

"You are no party to this accusation, Mr. Thurston?" the lieutenant enquired. "I am sorry for the blow that has fallen on you. But you can't seriously believe that Dick Willoughby's the man who fired that shot." As he spoke he pointed at the dead rigid form.

Thurston raised his eyes. There was a dull glare of fury in them, a savage snarl on his parted lips.

"Mind your own business, young man. He killed my boy, and by God he'll hang for it."

While speaking he rose to his feet, holding forth a denouncing arm toward Willoughby

"Yes, he'll hang for it," he growled again with savage determination, turning round to the open door.

With a gesture to the cowboys standing nearest,

he bade them carry the body within. He stood aside to let them pass with their burden, then followed and slammed the door behind him with an angry bang.

Despite the tragedy of it all, a little smile went round the group of onlookers. It meant to say that that was just Ben Thurston all over—irascible and vindictive. But some faces looked grave.

"May go mighty hard with Willoughby," murmured one voice, that of the old grey-headed man, the blacksmith at the rancho for twenty years or more. "I wouldn't like to feel the weight of the old devil's hand."

But just then the automobile came round the house, piloted by Jack Rover. Sharkey began to make his dispositions for the journey.

"Do you want to take anything with you, Willoughby?" he asked in a considerate manner.

"Nothing," was the prompt reply.

"Well then, you'll ride with me on the front seat. Lieutenant, you can share the tonneau with Mr. Thurston." There was a slight grin on the sleuth's face as he signified the arrangement.

"Mr. Thurston?" queried Munson, taken somewhat aback. "Does he come, too?"

"Sure," replied Sharkey. "Who's going to make the charge, I'd like to know? Willoughby,

I just need your promise that you won't move
from this verandah till I return."

Dick nodded assent. "You have my word,"
he said with quiet dignity.

"Then I'll be back in a minute," added the
sleuth, his hand on the door knob.

Ben Thurston was standing alone in the centre
of the living room, the body with its bearers
having passed to an inner apartment. His arms
were folded across his breast in an attitude of
deep dejection. But it was with the scared look
of a hunted beast that he started away at the
touch of Leach Sharkey's hand upon his shoulder.

The sleuth smiled understandingly.

"You don't want to be left here all alone, do
you?"

"No, no. For God's sake, no. I had forgotten that."

"Then you've got to come with me to Bakersfield. In any case you will be wanted to swear
the information. And you can also make arrangements for the funeral. So get your hat and overcoat. We are all ready outside."

"Yes, yes, I'm coming," faltered Thurston.
"Wait for me, Sharkey," he added, as with nervous
fingers he detached his overcoat from a rack
on the wall.

And a few minutes later the automobile, with Sharkey at the wheel, the handcuffed prisoner by his side, and Thurston and the lieutenant seated frigidly apart in opposite corners of the tonneau, was spinning through the gathering dusk of evening on its way to the county town of Bakersfield.

Chapter XIV

Entanglements

FROM the observatory high up among the hills, Mr. Robles had witnessed the arrest and the departure of the prisoner. He had understood every move just as if he had been present on the verandah down below and had heard each spoken word.

As he stood erect, his hand still rested on the telescope. For a few moments he pondered, then murmured to himself as he turned to leave the room: "A bad complication! I must break the news tonight to Merle. Poor little girl!"

But it was two hours later before he wended his way down through the moonlit forest in the direction of La Siesta.

There dinner was over. No word of untoward happenings had as yet come from the outside world to disturb the tranquillity of the little household. In the drawing room Merle was at the piano, while Grace, close by, was curled on a sofa reading the latest novel. At some distance from the young girls was Mrs. Darlington, occupied intermittently over a piece of embroidery.

She was seated in semi-darkness, only her hands and her work illumed by the soft pink radiance of a shaded lamp resting on a little table by her side. In the evening costume of the chatelaine of La Siesta was the suggestion of old lace and old-time lavender—the old lace at her bosom and around her neck, the subtle fragrance of lavender exhaled from her garments that gave to her a sort of personal atmosphere.   And as she sat musingly, with the skeins of silk passing through her fingers, she might have formed a picture of some Penelope seated at the loom of pensive memory.

The music from the piano was in harmony with both her mood and her attitude—the soft dreamy melodies of Mendelssohn's "Songs without Words" to which she was vaguely listening while busy with her thoughts and her stitches.

Downstairs amid the oriental luxuriousness of the cosy corner sat Tia Teresa, waiting in the dark to intercept the visitor of whose coming she had been apprized by a secret messenger. And at last Ricardo Robles came, with the noiseless footfall that was characteristic of the man and imparted to him an air of mystery. He was standing by the old duenna's side before she had realized his presence.

"I wanted a few words with you first of all, Tia Teresa," he murmured, as she grasped his hand in both her own and affectionately kissed it. "Something has happened."

"I know what has happened, Don Manuel," she whispered. "The young man deserved his fate, for I am sure you saw what occurred in the rose garden during the afternoon. For one of his breed to have dared even to touch my little girl!" She hissed the words venomously, then added in calmer tone: "So all is well. He brought down his doom upon his own head, and vengeance for Rosetta begins."

Robles pressed her hand as he disengaged his own from her almost fiercely caressing touch.

"I nursed you both," continued the duenna in a low impassioned voice. "Your people were my people, you children were my very life, and your revenge has come to be my own. So I rejoice that the young ruffian died."

He had seated himself by her side on the divan.

"We shall say no more then about that," he responded. "In some ways I am sorry over the day's work. At times I find it difficult to reconcile my firmness with my softness."

"But you cannot forget that you are no longer the owner of your father's lands and flocks, and are virtually childless besides." She breathed the words with intense repressed fury, intensified as she added: "And all through the accursed gringo who wrecked our happy lives—Rosetta's, yours, your beloved parents' as well. While that abominable wretch lives, the vendetta can never end."

For a moment Robles remained silent. Then he spoke resolutely:

"I know it, Tia Teresa. Today my work only begins. Rest assured that it will be carried to the bitter finish. For this I have waited all through those long years. But I wanted to tell you of another matter—to warn you of a very serious complication. Dick Willoughby has been arrested for the slaying of Marshall Thurston."

The duenna sat bolt upright in shocked surprise.

"Oh, my! What will this mean?" she murmured.

"Terrible grief for my little girl—possibly much suffering for him until I choose to take the responsibility upon myself."

"You must not do that."

"No. Not yet, at all events. Or the victory will be his—my enemy's."

He mused again. She, too, remained silent. At last he broke the spell.

"But I have already devised measures for his safety. Now I must go upstairs. They have heard nothing yet?"

"Not a word."

"Then I must tell them of the mysterious shooting in the woods, and at the same time reassure Merle that her lover is in no real danger."

"And Mrs. Darlington?" asked Tia Teresa. "How much is she to know?"

"Nothing! The vendetta is for us Spaniards. It is ours and ours alone. No one knows of my vow but you and I. Let it remain so. *Adios*, my dear friend."

In the darkness he stooped and kissed her on both cheeks. For a moment she clung to him, but he gently liberated himself from her embrace. He moved toward the stairway, and Tia Teresa followed him cautiously up to the drawing room door, outside of which she remained. Knowing that she was there, he left the door ajar. The soft music was still playing, but suddenly ceased when Robles advanced into the apartment.

"My word, but this is an unexpected pleasure," exclaimed Merle, as she came from the piano with outstretched hands.

He took them both in his own, and bestowed on her a grave but kindly smile. He also nodded to Grace, who had dropped her book and risen in courteous greeting.

"But you look sad and serious," Merle went on, with quick intuition that his coming at this late hour meant something more than a mere neighborly visit.

"Something sad and serious has happened," he replied.

Mrs. Darlington had advanced from her lamp-lit table.

"What?" she enquired eagerly. "Somehow I had a sense of impending trouble all day long."

"Young Thurston of the rancho has met with an accident."

"Dead?" gasped Merle, her hands clasped against her bosom.

"Yes, dead, I am afraid. He was mysteriously shot this afternoon when riding through the pine woods."

Merle was stricken dumb. Grace glided to her side and listened in silent expectancy.

"Shot! By whom?" asked Mrs. Darlington.

"That I cannot tell," gravely replied Robles. Then he smiled faintly. "But an amazingly stupid blunder has been made. By some combination of circumstances suspicion is being fastened on our dear friend Dick Willoughby."

"Dick!" exclaimed Merle. "Who dares to suggest such a thing?" she added indignantly.

"I infer that Mr. Thurston is his accuser," replied Robles.

"The two young men quarreled," murmured Mrs. Darlington, in a voice of deep agitation.

"Mother!" cried Merle reprovingly. "Even to think for one moment that Dick, whatever the provocation, could have done such a thing! He is absolutely innocent, Mr. Robles," she went on decisively, again turning to their visitor.

"Of course he is innocent—absolutely innocent. No one knows that better than myself." And he gave an enigmatic smile as he spoke the words of reassuring confidence.

"Where is Mr. Willoughby now?" queried Grace.

"He has been compelled to go to Bakersfield."

"To Bakersfield?" exclaimed Merle, half wonderingly.

"There to prove his innocence," replied Robles.

But Mrs. Darlington had probed the real significance of his words.

"You don't mean to say that they have—arrested him?"

Robles nodded gravely. "That's how the law

acts. A man under suspicion must be taken into custody—he must be charged so that he can refute the shameful calumny."

Merle had dropped into a settee—white and speechless. Her lips trembled. Then she burst into a passion of weeping, burying her face against an arm flung across the upholstery.

Mrs. Darlington moved forward quickly to comfort the sobbing girl.

"Oh, don't take on like this, my dear child. The arrest was a mere formality. He will be immediately set at liberty."

Merle raised her tear-stained face. She spoke in gulping sobs.

"But, mother, I never told you—I shrank from telling any of you. While you and Grace were away this afternoon, Marshall Thurston called and wanted to make love to me—he even dared to try to kiss me. Tia Teresa flung him out of the rose garden. It was I who made Tia Teresa promise to say nothing about it to anyone. I feared trouble. And, oh, trouble, terrible trouble, has already come." Again she bowed her head and continued weeping, but quietly weeping now. Grace was bending over her, patting her shoulder in soothing sympathy.

Mrs. Darlington's eyes met those of Robles.

"This may prove serious," she said softly, that Merle might not overhear.

"It is decidedly unfortunate," replied Robles; "an unfortunate complication that may, of course, strengthen the suspicion against Willoughby and so render it more difficult for us to help him."

Merle sprang to her feet, and with a hand dashed away her tears.

"Suspicion!" she exclaimed. "There can be not one moment's suspicion." And she gazed up into Robles' face in ardent appeal.

"Of course not, my dear, among us—among all those who know Dick Willoughby. But there is the harshly judging world to reckon with besides. They may say that this discloses a motive for the crime."

"However, Merle has just told us," commented Mrs. Darlington, "that only she and Tia Teresa know anything about this unhappy episode in the rose garden. Mr. Willoughby has not been here at all today."

"But I happen to know that he was not far away this afternoon—that he was rounding up some cattle in the near-by canyons. Malice may suggest that he was a witness of Thurston's insolent behavior."

"Then we should all keep silent on the subject."

"Which might be compromising in the long run, my dear Mrs. Darlington. Altogether it is a difficult situation."

Merle had been hardly listening to this conversation. She had been thinking, and with thinking had regained her composure. Her mind was quickly made up as to the line of prompt action that must be taken. She spoke quite calmly now.

"He is in prison. You have not spoken the word, Mr. Robles, but I know the truth all the same. We shall go to him tonight."

"Not tonight, my dear," replied Robles, with gentle firmness. "But tomorrow morning, certainly, I would suggest that you drive over to Bakersfield. He will appreciate your kindness in paying him this prompt visit, and you can at the same time convey to him my message of absolute belief in his innocence."

"You will not come, too?"

"I can do more for him, Merle, by not going to Bakersfield for the present. Do not forget that for reasons of my own I live in seclusion. My name must be mentioned to no one but Mr. Willoughby. Trust me, all three of you, and leave me to work quietly alone and by my own

*Grace Darlington Carries Lieutenant Munson's Letter of
Resignation to the Postoffice — Page 63*

methods. There, I give my promise. The captive will be set free within a short time. My hand on that, and you know that I never break my word."

There was a joyous smile of confidence on his face as he spoke the words. Merle took the extended hand gratefully, trustfully, and pressed it to her lips. Robles went on:

"My advice is—try to sleep tonight. Tomorrow, or within a few brief tomorrows, all will be well. Good night."

Tia Teresa followed him from the open door down into the outer hall.

"You heard everything," he said as he paused to speak a final word of parting. "Comfort her, but at the same time guard our secret closer than ever. Not one hair of Willoughby's head will be touched—make her know that for certain. And everything will come right in a very little time."

"My poor little girl," he murmured to himself as he strode down the silent tree-shadowed avenue.

CHAPTER XV

Behind the Bars

DICK WILLOUGHBY had been lodged in the county jail at Bakersfield, duly charged by Ben Thurston as the murderer of his son. To his surprise, and indeed to his dismay, the prisoner was informed that, the crime alleged being a capital one, no bail could be accepted. This was first of all a blow to Willoughby's pride. Here he was under the stigma of imprisonment, but with no possibility of redress. It was not the loss of comforts, the deprivation of personal liberty, the hardships to body and to soul, inseparable from such restraint, that he resented, so much as the semi-conviction of guilt implied by the durance vile to which he was to be subjected, although absolutely innocent of the deed of which he was accused.

However, after first chagrin came manly philosophy. The law might be right or wrong, wise or unwise, necessary or superfluous. But all the same it was the law of the state and had therefore to be obeyed. So, when the situation was finally reviewed, it was Lieutenant Munson who, when bidding his friend good-night, had been the angry man, fretting and fuming over such an abominable act of injustice, while the prisoner himself was tranquilly resigned to the ordeal through which he must pass and to which unkind fate was subjecting him for reasons that he was powerless to fathom.

"Good night, Ches, old man. You'll see me again in the morning. It's mighty kind of you to stay in town all night. But we can decide on the best lawyer to employ, and then you must hasten back to break the bad news at La Siesta."

Such had been Dick's quiet words when their colloquy had been broken up, and he had been ordered to the retirement of his prison cell. To enter that place was for Dick a horrible experience. But he accepted the experience calmly, bade the turnkey a cheerful good-night, and laid him down to sleep on the narrow mattress resting upon the hard bench, at peace with himself and the world, even with the bitter enemy who had all so unexpectedly appeared on his path.

Although Munson was back in the jail betimes next morning, he found Dick already conferring with a lawyer—the best and most honored in the .

town, as Munson knew the moment his name was mentioned.

"Let me introduce you to Mr. Bradley," said Dick, presenting him. "Some kind friend whose name he declines to reveal for the present, sent him a special message last night retaining his services for my defence."

"Mrs. Darlington, I bet," interjected the lieutenant.

"No, not Mrs. Darlington, let me assure you," rejoined the lawyer, "although undoubtedly she would be willing to do the same thing. But I am not permitted to say any more."

"And he has *carte blanche* for all expenses," smiled Dick. "Although I should not think there will be much money required to clear an innocent man," he added.

"Wait till you see," said the lawyer crisply. "We have to reckon with a malignant persecutor, I am already informed."

"Well, I've got a bit to my bank credit," Dick replied. "And we'll draw on that first before I accept the generosity of an unknown friend. It will be quite a saving here," he went on with a humorous twinkle in his eye as he glanced around. "Free board and lodging at the state's expense for a week at all events."

"Much longer than that, I am afraid," gravely remarked the lawyer. "You see, Mr. Munson, just before you arrived we were discussing the decidedly unfortunate coincidence that at the time the shooting occurred, Mr. Willoughby, by his own admission, was in the little canyon below the scene of the tragedy."

"Rounding up some cattle," observed Dick.

"Of course. But all the same, open to suspicion as being on the ground, and indeed being the first to reach the dead man's side."

"That should be proof of innocence," observed Munson.

"Or may be taken as evidence of well-reasoned audacity to throw accusers off the trail," retorted the attorney. "You see we have to look at everything, not from our own point of view, but from the other side. Now I want to learn something more about that quarrel between you and young Thurston at the cattle muster."

"He made an insulting remark about one of the young ladies from La Siesta," replied Dick. "I told him I would tan his hide if he ever did it again. That's all. But the last thing I want is that these ladies' names should be dragged into the case."

"But his remark and your reproof were overheard by others," commented the attorney.

"Oh, yes, by a bunch of ranch hands."

"Whose evidence will undoubtedly be called for the prosecution, necessitating, perhaps, the evidence of the young ladies on our side."

"By God, I won't stand for that," exclaimed Dick hotly. "I can defend myself without their being called to the witness stand. Think, Munson, of subjecting Merle or Grace to any such thing"—and his indignant face appealed to the lieutenant's.

"I saw nothing of the quarrel," observed Munson, addressing the lawyer, "although, of course, I heard something about it later on—not from Willoughby, however, for he has never once referred to the matter in conversation with me. But I say, Dick, old fellow, you know that Merle Farnsworth and Grace Darlington, too, will be only too proud and happy to stand up for you in a law court or anywhere else."

"That may be," replied Dick gloomily, "but I don't propose that they shall be made the objects of vulgar curiosity in a crowded court-room, or that their ears should ever hear the vile words that fell from that miserable degenerate who has at last met the fate he properly deserved."

"Well, it is a point that we shall have to consider carefully," spoke the lawyer as he rose to take his departure. "I have all the main facts of the case now, Mr. Willoughby. Of course I shall apply formally to the court for bail, but I know it is bound to be refused. I'll make all arrangements outside for your comfort here—meals, etc., and no doubt your friend, Mr. Munson, will bring you over clothing, toilet requisites, and the other little things you will require. I'll see you again later on today."

The lawyer was gone, and the two comrades were alone in the little room, stone-walled and bare of furniture except for a few chairs, where the consultation had been held. Beyond the open door stood a constable, just out of earshot. But he now took his stand within the room.

"Well, Munson, old chap," said Dick with cheerful alacrity, "you get back to the rancho in double-quick time. Then go on to La Siesta and tell Merle not to worry on my account. Tell her that I'm bright and happy, and just enjoying a good rest, and will be set at liberty within a week or so. But remember, she is not to come here. Good Lord, I never want her to see me in a place like this." And he glanced around forlornly, and in a measure ashamed.

But at the very moment there was a flutter along the corridor—the sound of voices, and

women's voices, too.   A moment later the superintendent of the jail appeared, bringing with
him Mrs. Darlington and Merle.   At the doorway he spoke to the officer on guard; the man
withdrew.

"Mr. Willoughby, here are some more friends,"
said the superintendent as he ushered in the
ladies.   "I am going to interpret the regulations
as leniently as possible—that's a matter which
can rest between ourselves.   I'll come back for
you, Mrs. Darlington, in half an hour."

Merle advanced toward Dick with outstretched
hand.   In her other hand was a fine bouquet of
roses.

"What a shame that you should be here," she
exclaimed.   "But I realize that the only thing to
do is to submit as cheerfully as possible to the
inevitable.   Mother and I came over to give you
our sympathy and proffer our help in every possible way.   Grace also sends her very kindest
regards, and I was bidden by Mr. Robles, whom
we saw last night, to assure you of his complete
belief in your innocence."

"Oh, I'm not afraid of any real friend thinking
me capable of a cowardly deed like that," replied
Willoughby.   "But it is nice to have these kind
messages, although I could have wished, Miss

Farnsworth, that you had not seen me amid such surroundings."

"Do you think that we would desert you in such a time of trouble as this?" replied Merle, as she sat down. "But seeing that our visit is to be restricted to half an hour, it is well that we should get to the important points without delay. I have been talking over a certain matter both with mother and Mr. Robles, and although I shrink from telling it, they have decided that you must know about the affair."

She then proceeded, in a low voice and with lips that trembled, to tell how young Thurston had forced his attentions on her just a little time before the shooting occurred and how Tia Teresa had rescued her from his clutches.

This was the first that Dick had heard of the incident and his face flushed with anger. But Merle quieted him at once. "You need not be angry now, Mr. Willoughby. It is all over. But your lawyer will want to consider what bearing this may possibly have upon the case."

"It can have no bearing at all," maintained Dick. "In the first place I didn't even know till now that Marshall had been visiting at La Siesta. And in the second place, just as I was saying to Munson a few minutes ago, I am determined that the names of you ladies shall not be dragged into this miserable affair.   Isn't that right, Mrs. Darlington?"

"In a measure.   But all the same we are ready to stand by you so as to establish your innocence with the least possible delay.   I heard this morning that Mr. Thurston is very bitter against you, keeps vowing vengeance, and announces that no money will be spared to bring the slayer of his son to retribution."

"Well, I hope he'll find him without loss of time," smiled Dick.   "That will be the quickest and easiest way to get me out of confinement.   But at this moment I have not the faintest idea on whom to fasten the charge.   Lots of the cowboys despised young Thurston, but none were really his enemies, and I don't know any one among the bunch who would have shot him in that dastardly, cold-blooded manner."

"Which makes the situation for you all the more disagreeable," commented Munson.   "You had been known to threaten him, and if there is no one else to whom suspicion can point, you may be kept here, Dick, for quite a time—for months, perhaps, until the case goes to trial."

Dick's face fell.   "For months!" he exclaimed. "Surely that would be an outrage."

"Oh, I wouldn't be too despondent," protested Merle. "Besides, Mr. Robles has pledged his word to me that you will be free in a very brief time."

"Then he may know who the culprit is," remarked Dick eagerly.

"No," interposed Mrs. Darlington. "He is like ourselves—quite in the dark. But you may rest assured that Mr. Robles will leave no stone unturned to solve the mystery and restore you to liberty, Mr. Willoughby, for I happen to know that he holds you in highest esteem."

"I'm glad of that," replied Dick. "Well, I want you to tell him from me how keen I am that you ladies shall be spared from all association with this case. You know that I am exercising great self-denial, Miss Farnsworth, when I say that you are never to come here again. This is no place for you."

"Pardon me," laughed Merle, "but we are interested in you and will excuse the hotel you have chosen to patronize. We brought these roses for you from La Siesta"—as she spoke she presented him with the beautiful blooms—"and if Lieutenant Munson will be kind enough to come out to our automobile he will find there some books, also a box of fruit and a few delicacies

which we hope will help to make your stay he
just a little more tolerable."

"You're kind indeed," murmured Dick grat
fully. "Don't worry about me," he added chee
fully, "I'll have a fine rest here, and will be ab
to catch up with my arrears of reading."

And in this philosophic frame of mind th
prisoner was left to begin his holiday.

Chapter XVI

Pierre Luzon Returns

IN the outside world the question on everybody's lips was—who had fired the fatal shot
among the pine woods? The young reprobate
had been thoroughly despised, but he had no known
enemies except Willoughby. So while Willoughby's
staunch friends could only reiterate the question
in vain perplexity, most people were inclined to
answer it with Dick's name. The angry quarrel
between the two young men was universally
known and had been subjected to sundry embellish-
ments—for example, the threatened horse-whipping had become an actual recorded event, and
so on. And even there were whispers about
rivalry in some love affair—that Marshall had had
his eye on one of the young ladies at La Siesta
where Dick for some time had been a constant
caller.

So among the cowboys on the ranch, the oil
drillers who frequented the Bakersfield saloons
and had often enough stood around while young
Thurston had set up the drinks, the newspaper-

reading public generally for whom all the facts had been set forth in elaborate detail—the universal concensus of opinion seemed to be that Dick Willoughby was the man.   Not that this verdict of popular opinion carried with it any real reprobation.   Everyone agreed that the worthless degenerate had met even a kindlier fate than he merited.   Had he lived, not all his father's millions could have long saved him either from the penitentiary or an asylum for the insane.

A week passed.   Thurston brooded in solitude, but at his bidding Leach Sharkey kept up active investigations with a view to nose out every bit of evidence that could tell against the accused man.   Sharkey worked, not from any special animosity against Willoughby, but from keen professional pride.

Dick accepted his confinement with manly fortitude.   It was one of those untoward happenings that come into some people's lives for no obvious reason, but he was calm in the confidence that everything would be made clear in a very short time.

Moreover he was clear to his own conscience, which was the main thing.   Next in importance was that Merle, Grace and Mrs. Darlington, Robles and Munson, all the friends whom he held in highest esteem, had never for one moment doubted him. In their unshaken friendship was sufficient reward for all the tribulations through which he was passing.

Meanwhile word had reached Buck Ashley that old Tom Baker was on his way home in company with Pierre Luzon, to whom the Governor of the State had at last granted parole. In view of Dick's imprisonment Munson had well-nigh lost all interest in the romance of the buried treasure. But it had been Dick himself who had insisted that his friend must attend to their joint interests during his period of enforced sequestration.

Thus it had come about that Munson found himself one evening at the store, awaiting with Jack Rover and Buck Ashley the arrival of the automobile in which the sheriff was bringing the liberated convict from San Quentin. In a brief letter Tom Baker had explained that he had decided on this manner of transportation both because of its ensuring privacy and also because Pierre Luzon was so enfeebled by age, sickness and prolonged confinement that he could not travel by train. "I've rigged up a stretcher," wrote Tom, "but the poor old Frenchie is as weak as a kitten, and we'll have to run slow."

Nine o'clock that night was the scheduled hour around which the automobile might be expected. Buck Ashley had the extra cot for the invalid all ready in his own bedroom at the rear of the store.

It was close on ten o'clock, however, before the headlight of the automobile showed across the valley on the high-road. Buck piled another big log on the fire in the sitting room. He saw that the doors were all carefully closed and the shades pulled down. Then he brought in from the bar a tray with glasses and a bottle of whisky.

"Kentucky bourbon—that was old Pierre Luzon's favorite lotion," he said as he set down the tray. "And I guess he'll be glad of a good stiff drink on a cold night like this."

At last the automobile entered the yard, and the invalid was carried in on the stretcher and propped up comfortably in a rocking chair near the cheerful blaze. His teeth were chattering from cold, and he gratefully gulped down the stiff glass of bourbon which Buck lost no time in proffering him.

"You see," explained Tom Baker, as he bustled around, "the Governor just grants paroles; he can't grant pardons. Some sort of a board has to pass on the pardons. But I got him out all

right, and that's the main thing. Eh, Pierre,
old man?"

The sheriff nodded with great friendliness to
his protégé. Luzon responded with a wan smile
that silently spoke his thankfulness. His face was
deathly pale, but there was wonderful snap and
vitality in the black bead-like eyes that roamed
around the room and searched each countenance.

Buck was now standing by the rocker. He
laid a hand familiarly on the Frenchman's
shoulder.

"You see, Pierre, old scout, I don't forget
you"—he pointed to the bottle on the table.
"Kentucky bourbon, the best I've got in the
house, and the very label you used to call for.
Now we've got to drink to your speedy recovery.
Fill up all round, boys. The drinks are on me
tonight."

"Hip, hip, hooray!" shouted Tom, as the glasses
tinkled.

"Hush!" exclaimed Buck, warningly. "We
don't want to bring any booze fighters prowlin'
around here tonight. You see, Pierre, we four are
in cahoots and understand each other. You
know Tom and myself—we ain't in need of any
guarantee. And you can trust Mr. Chester
Munson and Jack Rover here to the limit."

Luzon bowed acknowledgment of the informal introduction.

"It was we who put up the cash to get you out of San Quentin," continued Buck, as he dropped into a chair close beside Tom Baker.

"Together with Dick Willoughby," interjected Munson.

"Oh, yes, not forgettin' Dick," resumed the storekeeper, "as fine a young feller as ever walked on shoe leather. But, by God, he's in jail just now."

"Eh?" ejaculated the ex-convict, with a look of awakening, almost fraternal, interest.

Buck turned to the sheriff.

"Of course, Tom, you'll have read all about that terrible affair in the newspapers?"

The sheriff surreptitiously grabbed Buck's arm. He spoke in a confidential whisper.

"Drop that subject for the present. I've said nothin' about it to old Pierre in case it might upset him. I ain't dared to mention the name Thurston to him, for he shared the White Wolf's hatred of the breed." Then Tom gave a little cough and glanced across the fireplace at the Frenchman. "Just a little cowboy shootin' scrap, Pierre, in which our chum Dick Willoughby has got himself temporarily involved. But say, boys," he went on, casting his eyes toward Munson and Rover, "I just thanked the Lord it wasn't me as had to arrest Dick. Of course if I had still been sheriff I'd a done it—when I was a sworn-in officer, duty was duty all the time with me, as every damned horse-thief within a hundred miles knows. But to take an honest man into custody for shootin' a miserable human coyote like that young —"

"Well, we're not a-goin' to speak about him just now," interrupted Buck, bestowing a cautioning kick on the sheriff's shins.

Tom took the timely reminder.

"That would have gone sore against the grain," he said emphatically, as he reached for the whisky bottle and replenished his tumbler.

"Glad to be back?" asked Buck, beaming pleasantly on old Pierre.

The Frenchman lifted one thin hand and smiled.

"Here I will become once more strong," he murmured. "No place in ze world like ze dear old Tehachapi mountains."

"Wal, I see you've begun to let your beard grow again," continued Buck, pointing to the gray stubbled chin. "And when your hair comes along, too, you'll just be lookin' fine and dandy.

The same old Pierre that used to sit for hours at a time in the store."

He paused a moment, surveying the visitor.

"A leetle more whisky, please," murmured Pierre, as he watched the sheriff lay down his glass.

"All the whisky you want, old fellow," exclaimed Buck, with effusive hospitality. "By gunnies, you're entitled to a good few nips after all the long years you've been locked up. Ain't that so, boys?"

"I should say," declared Tom, fervently, wiping his lips with the back of his hand.

The Frenchman drank gratefully, and as he felt the warm alcoholic glow in his vitals, uttered a deep-drawn "Ah!" of appreciation.

"Tastes good, don't it?" observed Buck. "You never turned down a drink of good whisky in the old days, did you, Pierre? Great times then! And gosh almighty, don't it beat hell, I never suspected who you were all those years you used to sit around the store smokin' that big-bowled pipe of yourn? And you knew about the cave then?"

"Oh, Pierre Luzon, he know how to keep one secret," responded the Frenchman, smiling.

"Yes, and good for us all you kept it, old man,"

exclaimed the sheriff. "He's a-goin' to show us the cave tomorrow, Buck. There will be six in the divvy-up now, boys, for of course Pierre Luzon stands in. That's agreeable all round, fellers?"

"Sure, sure," responded the others in unison.

Tom turned to the Frenchman.

"I told you, Pierre, we'd play the game fair and square with you. Ain't that right?"

"I trust you all," replied Luzon. "I show ze cave tomorrow to my friend, Tom Baker, and you gentlemen who have been so kind to make up one purse to bring me back here from zat horrid prison."

"Guess you're about the only feller that knows where it is?" enquired Buck, cautiously.

Luzon looked at his questioner and spoke just one word: "Guadalupe."

"Does Gaudalupe know?" exclaimed Jack Rover. "I thought her long suit was the riffle where she gets her placer gold."

"Guadalupe," answered Pierre, speaking slowly, "she know ze cave, but she not know where ze treasure is buried. Ze cave her home. She live zere. Lots and lots of times she come out, and nobody ever track her when she go back. Ze outlaws they sharp-shoot from places in ze hills nobody could see. But I show you," he continued, nodding his head at Jack Rover, "I, Pierre, show you where zat riffle is. I know both where Guadalupe wash out placer gold and ze secret chamber in ze big cave where Joaquin Murietta bury him money and where ze White Wolf, Don Manuel—peace to his soul!"—Pierre Luzon crossed himself—"hide sacks and sacks of ze yellow gold. Oh, yes!"

This long speech had exhausted the old man. He dropped his head wearily.

"What you need now is a good long sleep," exclaimed Tom Baker. "Another jolt of bourbon Pierre, and then you get in between the blankets, old fellow."

"I've got your bed all ready in the next room," observed Buck.

"I guess I go to bed zen," assented Luzon.

He gulped down with relish a nightcap of the old whisky. Then Buck and Tom helped him from his chair.

"It is good to be here," murmured the Frenchman. "I grow strong again among ze mountains. I never go back—never go back to San Quentin, that one horrid prison."

"We'll nurse you like a baby," said Buck assuringly, as he led the feeble old man into the adjoining room.

Chapter XVII

The Biter Bit

ON the very night of Pierre Luzon's return, Ben Thurston was in close colloquy with his attorney, summoned specially from New York. It was not only the murder of his son that had brought about this consultation. The owner of San Antonio Rancho, while filled with fury against Dick Willoughby, was also gravely perturbed over other things. Immediately after dinner the two men shut themselves up in Thurston's office.

Thurston opened the safe and produced a little bundle of neatly-folded, legal-looking documents.

"These are the option papers," he said gruffly, as he tossed them across the table to the lawyer. "Look them over, Mr. Hawkins."

The attorney glanced through the documents in a preliminary way.

"I see the first big payment falls due on April 1st," he remarked.

"Yes, April 1st," responded Thurston, "and I was a damned fool, too, to let that Trust Company fellow inveigle me into making the date April 1st, instead of March 1st. You see," he went on, "the taxes come due on March 1st, and on this principality they amount to quite a pretty figure, I can tell you."

"How much?"

"Oh, about $18,000."

The lawyer again read the papers through, this time more carefully.

"Well, Mr. Thurston," he said, as he lighted a cigar and sat back in his chair, "I left some very important matters to come to you in answer to your imperative message. What's the work in hand?"

"Why, this option for one thing; and then, too, I want you to help me put the noose around the neck of that scoundrel who killed my son."

"We'll take one thing at a time, please," replied the attorney, speaking slowly and quietly. "So far as this option on the rancho is concerned, it seems to be quite regular. Nevertheless, five million dollars is a whole lot of money. Is there any danger of their forfeiting their option payment of $100,000?"

"Danger? Forfeiting?" ejaculated Ben Thurston. "Well, I'm not at all afraid of that. My fear now is that they may take up the option."

"Why, didn't you wish to make the sale?"

"Yes, but I am not getting money enough. The ranch is really worth ten million dollars today, in cold cash. I have recently had some San Francisco capitalists down here appraising it for me, but I had already given the option."

"I see that the agreement provides for your cattle and horses going in at the stipulated price."

"Yes, I don't know why I should have been so infernally stupid. But you see those Los Angeles fellows came over here one day in an automobile and stayed all night. We had a sort of a tiff— didn't agree very well—and I let them start away the next morning without their breakfast—rather uncivil, I'll admit. After they had gone I got to thinking matters over, and I sent a telephone message along the road to stop them and ask them to come back. They returned all right. There was one of their number, this fellow from some Title and Trust Company, who was pretty warm under the collar, and, if I do say it myself, was as peeved as hell at me. Well, he was the one who drew up the agreement, sitting here at this table. The paper looked all right to me, and so I just went ahead and signed. I know now they caught me for the $18,000 of taxes because I didn't just insist on having the option expire

March 1st, instead of April 1st. But, to be frank with you, I really didn't much mind, for at that time I was only keen to get their $100,000 for the option, never believing for a moment that they would come across with the million-dollar first payment due April 1st. You see the cattle and horses and all the stock on the ranch was a sort of sheaf of oats that I hung out in order to get them to put up their option money—just so much bait."

Mr. Hawkins shrugged his shoulders and said: "Well, Mr. Thurston, judging from this inventory before me, you certainly hung up a most generous bait."

"I didn't stop to think—that's all there is to be said. All these details hadn't been worked out into cold figures at the time I gave the option. When these men were here I just wanted to wheedle them into a bargain which would leave a cool $100,000 in my hands. I never for one moment believed they could make the million-dollar payment, although, by God, I begin to realize the danger of their doing so now."

The lawyer looked up in silent surprise. Thurston continued:

"Of course I should have had this detailed valuation made before I went into the deal. Up

to the time I read that inventory I had no real
idea of the increased value of the property and
what was on it. Oh, you may shake your head;
I'm not a good business man—never cared a
damn for business—and I know quite well I haven't
given enough attention to the ranch. You see I
have been living mostly in the East, for 'good
reasons. I don't like it here at all—I've never
felt safe in California," and he glanced nervously
at the window of the room, as if some enemy were
lurking there.

Mr. Hawkins once more reached for the inventory, and carefully examined the figures. Finally
he said: "Pardon me, Mr. Thurston, for the
observation. But you should have sent for me
before the option was signed, if you did not really
intend to carry out its terms. I find that you have
twenty-six thousand head of cattle, and you say
that the price of cattle is very high just now—
that the whole herd ought to average forty dollars
a head. This item alone makes one million and
forty thousand dollars, or, in other words, if they
exercise the option and pay you the first million
dollars, they will have forty thousand dollars
more than the payment which they make at
that time." The lawyer pencilled down the figures
while he spoke.

Ben Thurston had been listening with a gloomy look on his brow. But when he saw the figures translated into dollars he fairly bounced from his chair, walked rapidly up and down the room, and then, coming to a sudden halt, shouted: "By God, that's where they got me again. I see it all now; these fellows were a damned sight too smart for me. Well, Hawkins, you are my attorney. I don't want to go on with this deal, even if they are able to dig up the money."

The lawyer puffed at his cigar, wholly undisturbed, and then replied: "Mr. Thurston, you have already made a sale."

"No, by God, I haven't; nothing of the kind," replied Thurston. "The truth is that I should get ten million dollars for this ranch, and keep all my horses and cattle, too. I don't propose to be fleeced by that Los Angeles outfit either," he continued, running his hands through his hair. "I have it; we'll break the contract. I'll bet that option is so faulty that you can drive a load of hay right through it. Hunt up a flaw and we will send them back their option money. I don't want their $100,000 now."

"I have already carefully studied the paper," replied Hawkins, "and can find no flaw in it. It was evidently drawn by a master hand."

"Master hand be damned," thundered Thurston. "Why, the stiff wasn't even a lawyer. He was just one of the syndicate—the one I told you about a while back. He knows so cussed much about titles that the other fellows let him write the option."

"I see," replied the attorney, as a half-smile flitted over his face; "about all you seemingly had to do was to sign the option papers and count the option money. The sole hope you have now, Mr. Thurston, in my opinion, is for those Los Angeles gentlemen to let this valuable option lapse. You have only a few days to wait."

"But I haven't told you the worst yet," said Thurston sullenly, dropping again into his chair.

"What do you mean?"

"I had a long-distance telephone this morning from the First National Bank at Los Angeles saying that the million dollars due April 1st has been already paid in to my credit. But I won't touch the money—I'll be damned if I do."

"You have no choice but to accept it," said the lawyer. "It would be foolish to deceive yourself; San Antonio Rancho is sold, and with the payment just made, you, by the terms of your contract, are compelled to give immediate possession. I can only advise you to take your medicine like a man, but don't let those Los Angeles gentlemen know that you are swallowing a bitter dose." He refolded the papers, and pushed them across the table.   "Now, Mr. Thurston, if there is anything I can do to assist you in the prosecution of your son's murderer, I stand ready to do so."

Ben Thurston arose.

"We'll talk about that tomorrow. I'll hang Dick Willoughby right enough in good time. Meanwhile you tell me the rancho is sold—that I have lost my great estate for less than half its value?   Hell!   Isn't that enough for one night?"

And he stalked wrathfully out of the room, slamming the door behind him.

"He sold at the wrong price," mused the lawyer with a quiet smile.   "Perhaps he'll be trying next to hang the wrong man."

Chapter XVIII

Elusive Riches

IN the meantime the quartet at the store were making a night of it. With old Pierre Luzon peacefully asleep in the adjoining room, there were many things to speak about. Tom Baker recounted in elaborate detail his story of interviews with the governor and state officials at Sacramento, the weary and harassing delays before parole was finally granted, his own dogged determination, together with the artful pulling of political strings that had finally brought about the results desired. Then there was the trip to San Quentin, the breaking of the joyful news to Pierre Luzon in his cell, the delivery of the paroled convict into Tom's hands, and the clever solution of all further difficulties by hiring an automobile for the journey south. The narrative was all very interesting, each listener eagerly followed every word, and at the close Tom Baker's chest had expanded several inches.

"I tell you boys, there's no man alive could have done what I did. The business was in the right hands. If it hadn't been for me, you wouldn't have Pierre Luzon here tonight."

"But if Pierre Luzon hadn't written that letter," growled Buck Ashley, "you would never have started for Sacramento and San Quentin."

"Well, all's well that ends well," discreetly interposed Munson, as he raked the smouldering wood ashes together. "Gee, but its cold tonight."

Jack Rover rose and tossed another log onto the fire. In a moment a bright flame sprang up.

"The bottle's empty," observed the sheriff. "The next one's on me, Buck."

"Guess we'll charge it to syndicate account," grinned the storekeeper, whose momentary grouch seemed to have been dissipated by the cheerful blaze. "We'll have to open books, boys, and go about things in a reg'lar way," he added, as he drew the bolt of the door that communicated with the store and groped his way into the darkness beyond.

Buck needed no candle, and was soon back with another bottle of the Kentucky bourbon. Glasses were filled and clinked and pledges of brotherhood renewed.

"It's champagne we'll be drinkin' tomorrow night, Buck, old sport," exclaimed Tom, slapping his old crony on the shoulder.

"I'll long-distance Bakersfield for a case in the morning," responded Buck, genially. "By gosh, we'll be swimmin' in wine afore long, boys. First thing I've got to do is to sell out this 'ere store."

"Sell it!" cried the sheriff, contemptuously. "You can afford to give it away, Buck. We ain't a-goin' to be pikers in our old age, are we now?"

"I ain't old by a danged sight," snapped back the storekeeper, for Tom had touched a sore spot once again. "Besides, when I've got a barrel of Joaquin Murietta's gold safe in the bank, you'll see me friskin' around like a two-year-old colt," he added, his momentary surliness changing to a smile.

"And it ain't only gold, boys," said Tom Baker. "That 'ere story old Pierre told me about the grotto cavern havin' a lake of oil in it as big as a city block, sure 'nuff got me goin'. Why, we'll be able to blossom out into oil kings."

"What's that?" asked Munson.

"Why, the Frenchie told me, you know, confidential like, comin' along on our motor car that since fifty years back those bandit fellers skimmed oil from the surface of that lake and burned it in lamps down in that cavern."

"By Jove, that's interesting," replied Munson.

"We know there is oil to the west, oil to the north, and oil to the south, and it stands to reason there must be oil here as well."

"Yes," interposed Buck, "but old Ben Thurston would never allow any drillin' on his place."

"Who the hell wants oil anyhow?" exclaimed Jack Rover. "We'll have all the money we need with the buried gold and Guadalupe's placer mine."

"Yes, but oil is oil," replied the storekeeper, with a shrewd nod of his head. "They say Rockefeller has only to raise the price a quarter of a cent a gallon whenever he wants to give away another million or so to a university or a hospital."

"Well, we ain't interested in universities or hospitals," said Tom Baker. "But I agree with Buck that oil's oil, and I, for one, intend to take everything that's comin' to me. My God, we can afford to buy Ben Thurston out and do some drillin' for ourselves on San Antonio Rancho. It'll help to pass the time anyways." As he finished, he began to pour out another round of drinks.

"Help to keep you from the booze," muttered Buck, in an inaudible aside. But he drained his own glass and smacked his lips with satisfaction. "Guess I'll be gettin' another bottle, boys," he said aloud, genially.

"Oh, we've had enough," mildly protested Munson.

"Not by a jugful," replied Buck. "You and Jack ain't goin' to ride home till mornin', and there's lots of things to be talked over yet."

"Great Scott, it's already two o'clock," remarked Munson, consulting his watch.

"Then the night's still young, boys," exclaimed Tom Baker, hilariously. "Get the brew, Buck. The empty bottles will keep the tally. Come on, lieutenant, drain your glass. No heel taps in this crowd."

They had started their conversation in low tones so as not to disturb the slumbers of Pierre Luzon. But this precaution, or act of delicate consideration, had been long since forgotten. They were talking loud now, and often all together, and when Buck Ashley had returned from yet another pilgrimage to the store, none heard or noticed the door of the bedroom being cautiously pushed open by just the fraction of an inch.

All four chairs had been again drawn around the cheerful log fire.

"You were talking, Tom, of buying out Ben Thurston," remarked Jack Rover. "Then you haven't heard there's an option been given to a Los Angeles syndicate? Guess mebbe Ben

Thurston won't be the owner of the big rancho very much longer."

"And a good job, too," replied the sheriff, as he helped himself to yet another drink.

Buck Ashley shook his head incredulously. "Oh, lots of fellers have paid down money for an option, as they call it, on the Thurston property, and finally when the rub came they didn't come across and live up to their bargain, and so they just naturally lost their option money."

"I was talking to a geologist," intervened Munson, in whose mind the oil question seemed to be still uppermost, "and he says there is every indication that the Midway Oil fields, a few miles north, are not one whit better than wells that can be opened up right here."

"But what's the use," said Tom Baker, "of all the oil fields in California to us fellers if we are about to be let into the secret door of a big cavern where they've got twelve or fifteen millions of twenty-dollar gold pieces stacked up, jest awaitin' for us to take 'em." The whisky was beginning to do its work; he had already forgotten his aspirations of being an oil king.

"That's right," said Jack Rover, "and don't forget, while you're counting them twenty-dollar gold pieces, that Pierre Luzon has promised to show us the shallow riffle in the mountain stream where Guadalupe gets all that placer gold." In the cowboy's case the alcohol was making only still more fixed the one fixed idea in his brain.

"Damn this store business anyway," said Buck Ashley, inconsequentially returning to the theme that appealed to him most directly. "Do you 'spose I'm goin' to work my fingers off tying up groceries after we find old Murietta's money and the White Wolf's treasure? Not by one hell of a sight, if I know myself, and I 'low as how I do."

And at the slightly opened bedroom door old Pierre, Luzon whom they all thought to be fast asleep, was listening to every word!

"But there is one thing," cried Tom Baker, striking the table fiercely as he set down his glass, "I want you fellers to get next to yourselves now and make up your mind to."

"Wa'al, don't stop, Tom," said Rover. "Go on and tell us what you're thinking about. Get it off your chest, old man."

"It's just this way. By God, you fellers are not entitled to as much of this 'ere twelve or fifteen million dollars as I am, for I'm the feller that went to the governor and got his parole and brought Pierre back here to Tejon. Do you get me?"

Buck Ashley had straightened up and looked

at Tom Baker with an ugly scowl on his face. "It was me," he said, "got that letter from Pierre Luzon and we all throwed in, share and share alike, all five of us. And we'll cut what we find, too, whether it's one million or fifteen million, into five equal parts, or there'll be blood flowin' good and plenty."

Baker staggered to his feet, steadied himself for a moment and began to roll up his sleeves.

"There be some things," he ejaculated, "that you jest can't let wait and settle up when the deal is all closed. I know what my rights are and you fellers can't bluff me, not by a derned sight."

"Hold on, hold on, gentlemen," interposed Munson. "Let's not commence quarreling about something we are not even sure we shall ever see. Of course we hope to be escorted into the cavern by old Pierre Luzon, and we likewise hope that he'll find a hidden treasure. And by the way, Buck, this reminds me—the cut has to be into six equal parts, not five, for we owe Luzon the squarest of square deals."

"Oh, I'm not agin' that," muttered Buck. "I just didn't remember him."

"Well," resumed Munson, "why quarrel about something that is as yet nothing but a myth? It occurs to me that we should rather, individually and collectively, be exceedingly thankful that Pierre Luzon is alive, and that the White Wolf is dead, and that the one man who holds the secret has promised to show us this treasure."

"I've never believed one cussed word about the White Wolf being dead," growled Buck Ashley.

"Well, it sure was in the newspapers," said Tom Baker, turning down his sleeves and resuming his seat.

"Yes, it sure was in the newspapers," replied Buck, "and they jest seemed to settle the fact, leastways to their own satisfaction. But I've been a-thinkin' about Dick Willoughby. I don't believe he ever killed Marshall Thurston, I don't."

"Whoever did kill him," put in Jack Rover, "did it good and plenty. Put the shot right square through his heart."

"Well," said Tom Baker, reaching for more whisky, "I ain't got much to say, but what I says I stands to on this 'ere subject, and that is—"

Almost with one accord all turned at the creaking of the bedroom door, and *there* was Pierre Luzon, looking as if he had seen a ghost. His short prison-cropped hair seemed to be standing on end like bristles, and his eyes stared wildly at the four men. At last he cried out in a shrill voice that was almost a scream:

"Ze son of Ben Thurston killed! Ah, ha!" he laughed, hysterically. "Shot through ze heart! —vengeance at last begins! Ze White Wolf is not dead! He is one live man!"

The door was hastily closed with a loud bang, and the weird figure vanished like an apparition.

For a few moments the revellers sat in stupefied silence. Finally Buck Ashley said in a low voice: "Damn that whisky anyhow. It has made us talk too loud."

"Yes," remarked Tom Baker, "and also too dangnation much, I'm a-thinkin'."

Both were sober men now.

"Believe I'll have a snooze," said Jack Rover, seating himself on an old lounge in a corner of the room. But he did not lie down.

Nothing more was said for perhaps a full half hour; all were nodding or busy with their brooding thoughts.

At last Buck Ashley rose and tiptoed toward the bedroom.

"Guess I'll see if poor Pierre has gone to sleep again," he murmured.

A moment later he shouted out from the inner chamber:

"Hell, boys!—he's gone! He's given us the slip—the damned old jail-bird!"

CHAPTER XIX

The Jail Delivery

AROUND Dick Willoughby there had been woven a web of circumstantial evidence that even before his trial had convinced most people of his guilt. Only a few tried friends who absolutely refused to believe him capable of shooting down an unarmed man from ambush clung to their faith that he had had nothing to do with the slaying of young Marshall Thurston. Among the general public the only question in discussion was whether the jury were likely to find extenuating circumstances and, should the life of the prisoner come to be spared, how long would be his sentence.

Ben Thurston had lavished money with a free hand toward securing every possible piece of testimony in support of the prosecution, and before his return home even the cautious New York lawyer, Mr. Hawkins, had admitted that the case against Willoughby appeared to be conclusive. It was only a matter of a few weeks now when Thurston would be leaving the district.

Already San Antonio Rancho was in possession of the syndicate; their foreman was in charge, the stock under their control, and it was only out of consideration that the former owner was being permitted to linger a little longer in residence. But for the gloomy and morose man there seemed to be gloating satisfaction in the grim thought that before shaking off forever the dust of his old home he would first of all ensure the hanging of his son's murderer.

Among the most regular visitors at the jail were the ladies of La Siesta, and rumor now began to run around that Miss Merle Farnsworth, despite Willoughby's pleading that she should not mix her name up in the case, would offer some surprising evidence in favor of the accused man—evidence that might not exonerate Willoughby from responsibility for the deed, but perhaps would fully justify his act to the minds of the jurymen.

It was now only three days from the trial, and the whole county was agog with expectation.

That night in the small hours five masked men rode very quietly through the streets to the vicinity of the jail. All were heavily armed, and one of them was leading an extra saddle horse. The party dismounted under the shadow of some trees. One man held the horses, while his four

companions, with drawn revolvers, advanced to
the gateway. Whether it was a simple case of
cowardly yielding to threats, or whether there
had been preliminary financial greasing of locks
and bolts, aided perhaps by sympathy for the
prisoner, the fact remains that within a very few
minutes Dick Willoughby had been brought from
his cell.

"You are a free man, Mr. Willoughby," said the
leader of the masked band in a low voice. "You
will come with us."

"Who are you?" asked Dick.

"We are friends—that is enough."

"I have no wish to go," protested Dick in the
hearing of the jailers. "The jury must acquit
me—I am ready to remain here until they do
acquit me."

"Take care. The man with the money can put
the rope round your neck."

"I am not afraid."

"There is another reason. The name of a
certain young lady must not be introduced into
this case."

"I have begged her not to testify."

"But she will testify if this trial goes on—that
you know well. Now you will come with us, for
her sake if not for your own."

"Be it so then," replied Dick. "Lead the way."

Just as quietly as they had come the little band of riders rode through the silent and deserted streets. They took the southern road, and for the first few miles kept to the thoroughfare. Then, reaching a stretch of unreclaimed land, they started across country. The night was moonless and dark, but Dick knew instinctively that they were making for the mountainous country to the north of the Tejon Pass.

The leader rode a short distance ahead. Not a word was spoken. In about two hours they were among the foothills. The pace slackened, and then, as they reached a clump of oaks, a halt was called. From under the shadow of the trees a man appeared, leading two sturdy little mountain ponies. The newcomer wore no mask.

"This man will be your guide from now on," announced the leader, whose features were still concealed by the strip of black cloth tied around the lower part of his face. "I am sorry we must ask you to wear a blindfold, Mr. Willoughby. But you are among friends, and I feel sure you will help us all by your ready assent."

"I am in your hands," replied Dick, quietly.

A few minutes later he was seated on one of the ponies, his eyes securely bandaged. The saddle was a big comfortable Mexican one, and he rested his hands on the horn; for there was no bridle, only a leading rein held by the man mounted on the other pony.

"*Adios!*"

It was the leader's voice again, and now once more Dick was on the move, the nimble little pony cantering gently over the turf.

Hour succeeded hour. The sun had risen, as the blindfolded rider could tell from the warmth of the atmosphere. The canter had long since changed to a walk, and Dick knew that they had been climbing steadily, with many a turn and sometimes up precipitous slopes.

At last a strange chilliness came into the air. Dick imagined that he heard a growl, as of some savage animal. Then there came a stop, and he caught some whispered words—a woman's voice he could have sworn, speaking in some strange tongue. After a few minutes his pony started again.

But they had not gone more than a hundred yards further when his guide called out.

"Here we are, sir. I will help you to descend. Zen I take ze bandage away. You see again."

The voice had a quaint foreign accent. For a little time Willoughby remained blind. Then he began to see things, and involuntarily rubbed his eyes in amazement.

He was in a vast vaulted cavern with no visible entrance revealed by the dim light of several lanterns suspended from the roof. In the far distance a log fire was burning, and silhouetted against its ruddy glow was the figure of the aged Indian squaw, Guadalupe, with a great dog-like creature standing by her side.

"Guadalupe!" exclaimed Dick in profound surprise, turning to his guide.

This man he now saw was old, with short gray hair and a short gray beard. His face was pale, but there was a pleasant gleam in his eyes.

"Yes, Guadalupe," the guide replied. "Guadalupe, she guard ze entrance to our cave—she and ze white wolf. No one can get past ze white wolf unless Guadalupe speaks ze word."

"And who are you?"

"Oh, call me Pierre. I am Mr. Willoughby's servant. Here are fine beefsteaks ready for breakfast. Come."

"Pierre!" murmured Dick. "Pierre Luzon?"

"Zat is my name. I am Pierre Luzon."

CHAPTER XX

In the Cavern

WHEN Dick proceeded to follow Pierre Luzon he found that the ponies had already trotted away through the semi-darkness, evidently quite capable on their own account of finding their accustomed stable. Leading the way across the cavern, Pierre entered a corridor at the far end of which bright lights were burning. Soon, Dick, to his great wonderment, found himself in a comfortably, almost luxuriously furnished apartment.

There were big thick rugs on the floor, and the rock walls were completely hidden by tapestries. The dining table in the centre was set with napery, china, glass, cutlery and silverware that would have done credit to a first-class hotel. Above swung a bronze lamp of antique pattern. Another table was laden with books, newspapers and magazines. In one corner gleamed the snow-white counterpane of a massive bedstead built of oak in Old Mission style. Here and there portable oil stoves were burning, diffusing a genial warmth throughout the grotto.

(183)

Pierre watched the guest's look of bewilderment as he gazed around him.

"You will be very comfortable here," said the Frenchman. "I have orders to attend to all your wants."

"Orders, from whom?" asked Dick abruptly.

"After breakfast you will know. I have one letter for you in my pocket."

With characteristic philosophy Dick accepted the situation. The very mention of breakfast gave a keener edge to an already sharply whetted appetite. Pierre departed and presently returned with a superb sirloin steak sizzling on a hot platter. Under his arm was tucked a bottle of wine. As he set down the latter, Dick noted that it was dusty and cobwebby, as if it had emerged from some ancient cellar.

"Zis is not ze vintage of California," remarked Pierre, as he drew the cork. "It is rare old Burgundy—all ze way from my beloved France."

"*La belle* France," murmured Dick. "I spent a year there, Pierre, most of the time in Paris."

"Ah, monsieur knows France and Paris," exclaimed the old man in great delight. "Zen you speak French, too?"

"*Un peu*," laughed Dick. "*Mais je fais beaucoup de fautes, mon ami.*"

Pierre Luzon Listens at the Door and learns the White Wolf
is Not Dead—Page 147

"*Non, non, monsieur,*" cried Pierre, breaking into voluble French. "Your accent is perfect— it is delightful to hear my native language again. We shall be great friends, Mr. Willoughby. Already I am your devoted servant." He bowed deferentially, as he held Dick's chair ready for him to be seated.

"You will breakfast with me, Pierre?" asked Dick, still in his best French.

"No, no. I wait on monsieur. I shall breakfast in good time."

Pierre was not to be persuaded to take a place at the table, so Dick sat down in solitary state and was served in lordly fashion.

With the *demi-tasse* of black coffee at the close of the meal came a box of cigars—cigars fit for a prince, as Dick knew from the first fragrant whiff.

The table was now cleared and Pierre ready to withdraw. He had taken a letter from his pocket and was holding it in his hand. But Dick, warmed and fed and supremely contented, was watching the ascending rings of tobacco smoke.

"Do you know, Pierre," he said between complacent puffs, "that I was one of the bunch that helped to get you out of San Quentin?" He had lapsed into English.

"Oh, yes, I know," replied Pierre, also dropping

his French. "Ze five men who made up ze purse—I am very grateful to you all."

"Then what about the hidden treasure?"

"Ah, I was to show ze hidden treasure. But one great change come about. I made one big mistake."

"Then the story of all this gold was a frame-up, was it?" laughed Willoughby.

"No, no," protested Pierre earnestly. "Ze cave—you are here in ze cave, although you do not know ze secret hiding place. Ze treasure, it is here, too. But I can no longer show ze gold, for ze man to whom it all belong he is not dead— he is alive."

"Whom do you mean?"

"Don Manuel de Valencia—him you call ze White Wolf."

"Great guns! So he has appeared again. The newspaper stories were all wrong?"

"Zat is how I made my mistake. But I did not know until I came back to Tehachapi. Ze White Wolf is alive. It is he who has brought you here as his guest. Now you will read zis letter, and zen all things you will comprehend."

Pierre laid the missive on the damask table cloth in front of Dick. The latter fastened his eyes on it in speechless surprise. Before he recovered himself Pierre, lifting the tray of empty dishes, had noiselessly disappeared.

"Mystery upon mystery," murmured Dick as he broke the seal. The letter was a brief one, and began without any of the usual forms of personal address:

"You are in safe and honorable keeping. Have no care. Nor need you worry about your friends—they will be informed of your safety.

"Just as soon as possible the real slayer of Marshall Thurston will be revealed. You will be completely exonerated and can then return to the world, a free man. By this means a certain young lady will be spared from the gossip and the publicity which, although she has been brave enough to say it does not matter, would bring for her annoyance and pain.

"If she is dear to you, as the writer of this letter believes, you will help to shield her from vulgar curiosity by remaining quietly where you are until the proper hour for your deliverance comes. It is only necessary for you to give your word of honor to Pierre Luzon that you will make no attempt to escape or reveal your whereabouts. Your trustfulness will be rewarded—this is the solemn promise of

"DON MANUEL DE VALENCIA,
"Your friend."

Dick read and re-read the strange message. All at once he became conscious that Pierre Luzon was again standing by his chair. Their eyes met.

"Does Mr. Willoughby give ze promise required?" asked Pierre.

Dick rose to his feet and extended his hand.

"I promise, Pierre. You have my word of honor. The letter says that is enough."

"I have read ze letter before it was sealed. We all know Mr. Willoughby's word is enough—it is as good as one gold bond."

"I'd do anything for Merle Farnsworth," continued Dick, carried away by his fervid emotion. "I would die for her, if need be, to save her from one moment's pain."

"Don Manuel he know that," replied Pierre.

Dick paused and his look changed.

"How the devil does he know I love the girl?"

"Ah!" The Frenchman shrugged his shoulders and smiled. "Ah! Don Manuel he know everything. But now, I am under orders not to speak. Over there you will find ze latest newspapers, sir," he went on, pointing to the table laden with literature, "and every few days more will be brought for you—not only ze newspapers of Los Angeles and San Francisco, but also, ze newspapers of New York and London and Paris, all of which monsieur is accustomed to read."

"Great Scott, you seem to know," exclaimed Dick in a low voice.

Pierre continued placidly:

"And you play chess. There is a box of chess—échecs we call it in France, you will remember.

I too play ze game. Don Manuel and I used to
spend many hours over ze board. After I have
had my breakfast, I, Pierre Luzon, challenge you
to one game of chess."

"Be it so," laughed Dick. "But you must be
hungry, man. For heaven's sake go and eat.
We'll yarn later on. Meanwhile, I'll have a
glance through the newspapers."

Dick handled the newspapers with renewed
surprise—the very New York papers he was
accustomed to receive regularly, also the old
familiar. *Times Weekly* from London and the Paris
Figaro to which he had subscribed ever since the
old Quartier Latin days! The same with the
magazines—all his favorites were on the table.

"Well, I'll be blowed! Is it the guileless Sing
Ling whom Don Manuel has been tapping for
information? This certainly looks like home,"
and again he glanced over the table. He looked
at the titles of the books—several of the latest
novels, a volume on socialism, another on the
history of architecture.

"Seems to know my book tastes, too. I won't
be lonesome, that's certain. Well, I can't do
better than make a start with the newspapers.
I've fallen quite behind the times."

He stretched himself out on a long rattan

chair, and started with a Los Angeles daily.   He had read lazily on for nearly an hour, when there came from his lips a little cry of surprise.   Starting up into a sitting posture, Dick again perused the paragraph that had excited his special interest.

It was an announcement stating that an ideal city was about to be built in the Tehachapi valley, and that a prize of ten thousand dollars was to be awarded to the designer of the best plans for laying out such a town.   Reference was made to an advertisement on another page giving the details and the rules of the competition. To this Dick eagerly turned.

The advertisement set forth that the model city was to be located somewhere near the centre of San Antonio Rancho, that the land was traversed by the state highway, by two railroads, by two electric power lines and two oil-carrying pipe lines, also the great Owen's River aqueduct that supplied Los Angeles, some two hundred miles away, with water from the high Sierras.   It was further stated that the entire ranch was to be subdivided into small tracts, and that already hundreds of applicants were waiting to make choice of home sites just so soon as the survey work was completed and the land thrown open to selection.

The plans required, and for which the prize of ten thousand dollars was offered, were to show the finest landscape effects, the most impressive and convenient location of public buildings, the most attractive ideas for bringing into being a veritable ideal city provided with all the most modern conveniences and sanitary equipment.

"By gad, I'd like to have a shot at that," murmured Willoughby as he lay back in his chair and meditated.

After a time he picked up the London journal, and the very first thing that met his eye was the identical advertisement on the back of the cover. He rose and began to search through the week's file of the *Figaro*, and there again he found the announcement of the contest. He was too keenly excited now for more reading. He began to pace the chamber. What a clever head had planned all this world-wide publicity!

"That Los Angeles bunch of fellows are certainly great. They are evidently going into this thing right. Doubtless they are determined to build the ideal—the model—city of California. They want the best brains of all lands to help beautify the place. Gee! but I'd like to be in this contest game. But perhaps it would be presumption on my part. Yet, who knows the country better than I do? When it comes to landscape effects, I'm Johnny-on-the-spot all right. And they're in a hurry—only sixty days for the drawings. Unusual, such a short time. But I guess they're going to make the dust fly without a week's unnecessary delay. They are certainly live wires—they began by getting old Ben Thurston on the run."

He was chuckling to himself at the thought when Pierre reappeared.

"Pierre, old fellow," cried Dick, "would you be able to get me a drawing board, a box of instruments, india ink, water-colors, drawing paper, and so on?"

"What are you going to do?" asked the old man with a smile. "Do you think you are again in ze Quartier Latin, Mr. Willoughby?"

"No. But while I'm here I'm going back to the old Quartier Latin life, that's a cinch. Can you buy me that stuff?" he added, diving into his hip pocket.

But he had forgotten—he had come out of jail, and his personal possessions had been left behind.

Pierre Luzon, however, had interpreted both the gesture and the thought that had prompted it.

"You need no money here, Mr. Willoughby," he said. "My orders are to get you everything you call for. Write all you need on a piece of paper. I send a trusty messenger, and we have ze drawing paper, ze instruments, ze ink and ze paints here very soon—yes, very soon."

"Then, by thunder, I'm going to win that ten-thousand-dollar prize."

"But she is worth millions of dollars."

"What do you mean?"

"Ze young lady—she very rich young lady, Miss Merle."

Dick laughed.

"Oh, that's quite another prize, Pierre," he replied. "And if she is so very rich, as you say, why that puts her further out of my reach than ever."

Pierre nodded his head determinedly.

"If I was you, Mr. Willoughby, ze prize I would try to win is ze beautiful young lady."

When Pierre had gone, Dick again lay back in the long chair. But he was day-dreaming and love-dreaming now, wondering whether Merle Farnsworth really cared for him, whether he might dare whisper to her the story of his passionate love.

CHAPTER XXI

A Debt of Honor

PUBLIC excitement had been running high over the approaching trial of Dick Willoughby, but his delivery from jail by the masked night-riders came as the culminating climax. Mystery and romance were piling up. Despite the strength of the circumstantial evidence, the sudden fate that had overtaken the young heir to San Antonio Rancho had been shrouded with uncertainty; no witness had seen the actual doing of the murderous deed. The sensational arrest of Dick Willoughby had been followed by his still more sensational disappearance; for he seemed to have vanished from the face of the earth—he had been spirited to some place of concealment to which there was not the slightest clue, while also the identity of his rescuers remained a profound enigma.

All sorts of speculations were rife, and it was small wonder that the name of the famous bandit, Don Manuel, came to be revived. This was just the sort of audacious work the White Wolf would

have gloried in—breaking into a prison, defying
the authorities, leaving behind him a trail of
mystery and vague terror. But shrewd old-timers
pointed out that Don Manuel had never in his
whole career helped a gringo—that his hand had
been against every American, and that in his
earlier days at all events he had killed ruthlessly,
out of sheer lust for vengeance against the race
of newcomers who had despoiled him of his ancestral acres. What reason, therefore, could he have
had to help Dick Willoughby to liberty? Even
if it had been the outlaw's hand that had pulled
the trigger against the son of his hated enemy,
Ben Thurston, little would he have cared if a
score of gringos had come to their end, justly or
unjustly, as an aftermath of the tragedy.

Old Ben Thurston had discussed this very question with himself. The slaying of his only son, the
clever business deal that had called his own tricky
and dishonest bluff and lost him his principality,
the sight of his herds being driven away, the
approaching eviction from his home—all these
events crowding one upon the other had exas-
perated him beyond measure and completed the
change of the already grouchy, disgruntled man
into a veritable wild beast snapping and snarling
at everyone. Yet his mind was completely ob-

sessed by the idea that it was Dick Willoughby, and Dick Willoughby alone, who had shot his son, so there was no room in his small and obfuscated brain for any seriously renewed apprehension that his old enemy, the White Wolf, had come to life again.

Dick's escape from jail almost gave Ben Thurston a fit of apoplexy. It was the sleuth, Leach Sharkey, who alone of those around him ventured to break the news. After his first paroxysm of wrath, Thurston paced the room like a caged animal. He had begun to make a confidant of this man, his constant attendant, the protector with the handy guns in his hip pockets on whom he had come to rely night and day, the one associate who phlegmatically endured his irritable moods and abusive language.

So, in Leach Sharkey's presence, Thurston, as he walked to and fro, spoke his thoughts aloud.

"Damn all pretty faces, anyhow. First and last they have cost me a fine sum. And now it is a pretty face that has cost me my boy's life. It's hell, that's what it is. But I will have my revenge. I'll hang Dick Willoughby with my own hands if necessary—even if it is the last act of my life I'll have his neck stretched for him."

He was glaring down at the sleuth, and the pause seemed to call for some reply.

"Well, he's given us the slip for the present," Sharkey ventured. Then he caught the gathering fury in the other's eyes, and hurriedly went on: "But there is no question in the world we'll run the scoundrel down. I myself will shoot him like the dog he is the moment I lay my two eyes on him."

"Well, don't waste your breath telling me you are going to do it," growled Thurston. "Hunt him down. Take all the money you need. Get all the men you can. Search every canyon. Guard every road out of the hill country. And don't be misled by that damn fool talk about the White Wolf of which you've been telling me. That cursed outlaw is dead—dead as a herring. I ran the story of his death to earth—stood on his very grave in the potters' field at Seattle. Dick Willoughby's the outlaw now. Get him at any cost. Get him, or, by God, lose your own job, Leach Sharkey. Do you follow me?"

"Oh, I follow you," replied the sleuth, a sardonic smile still further exposing the teeth that were the most prominent feature of his face and at all times gave him a hyena-like appearance. "I'll get him, make no mistake, Mr. Thurston.

Just draw me that check, and I'll have twenty more men out on the range before morning."

At the store, Dick Willoughby's disappearance was for days the sole topic of conversation. One morning Tom Baker and Buck Ashley were gossiping together.

"What beats me," remarked the storekeeper, "is that Chester Munson wears such a spry look. He was Dick's closest chum, yet he don't seem to be one bit anxious."

"Oh, he's got the word, make no mistake," replied Tom. "Although the lieutenant is as close as wax, he knows Dick's all right, for sure. And I'm told that up at La Siesta, where Dick has his girl, you know, they're still a-playin' the pianner and the fiddle all the time. Mark my words—there's been some wireless telephone at work. Munson don't worry, his lady friends don't worry, so I begin to think we're a couple of derned old fools to fret ourselves on Dick's account."

"It's about Pierre Luzon I'm frettin' most," Buck Ashley rejoined. "To think that that damned Frenchman should have done us in the eye, got clean away and robbed us of our share of the buried treasure—that's what worries me, Tom Baker. And you'll allow now you made a mess of things by not havin' the old convict shackled to the bedpost."

"A mess of things!" cried the sheriff, rising anger in his voice and eyes. "You won't keep your mouth shut till I teach you—"

But just then there was the clatter of hoofs outside, and Tom stopped in the middle of his sentence. A moment later Munson and Jack Rover entered in a state of visible excitement. Munson carried in his arms a rotund canvas sack tied at the neck. The package was not very big, but clearly of considerable weight.

"Great Caesar," exclaimed the lieutenant, without pausing to give any greeting. "A most surprising thing has happened. When I awoke this morning I found this bag lying on my table. And what do you think it contains?" As he asked the question he dumped the sack on the counter with a heavy thud.

"You've got us guessin'," drawled Tom.

"Ten thousand, five hundred dollars in gold!" announced Munson.

"Good Lord!" ejaculated the sheriff in great surprise.

Munson went on:

"Five thousand dollars are for the French warder at San Quentin who smuggled Pierre Luzon's letter out of the prison, and the balance is for the syndicate."

"What syndicate?" gasped Buck, for the moment quite bewildered.

"The Hidden Treasure Syndicate, of course," exclaimed Jack Rover. "Pierre Luzon has sent each man back the hundred dollars he put up to get him out of the pen, and five thousand dollars extra to divide among us."

Buck and Tom sprang simultaneously to their feet.

"Hooroosh!" shouted the sheriff. "I always knew there was no yellow streak in old Pierre Luzon."

"And I always said I liked him, too," observed Buck. "But come into the parlor, boys," he went on, with a cautious look around. "Let's count the money."

"And divvy it up," added Tom eagerly. "Gosh 'lmighty, boys! I've never yet seen a thousand dollars in gold at one time outside a bank cashier's window. And to think there's that amount comin' to me right now!"

"One thousand, one hundred, pal, to be exact," laughed Jack Rover, lifting the package and following the storekeeper into the sanctum beyond the counter.

The gold was in United States twenty-dollar pieces, bearing dates which showed they had been minted more than twenty years ago.

"Some of Joaquin Murietta's loot," remarked Jack Rover, when attention had been drawn to this detail.

"No," observed Tom Baker, holding up the coin he had been examining, "Murietta wasn't alive when this 'ere gold piece came from the mint. This is some of Don Manuel's stuff."

"The White Wolf!" exclaimed Munson.

"Yes, the White Wolf," continued the sheriff. "So if the White Wolf ain't dead, as Pierre declared that night—" Tom gazed at the bedroom door as if the spectral figure might reappear— "he's honorin' the Frenchie's sight draft, that's sure."

"I see," said Munson. "He is paying the five thousand dollars old Pierre promised in his letter if he was helped to freedom and five thousand dollars besides."

"Precisely," Tom Baker replied. "But if the White Wolf is dead, as most folks say, then the Frenchie's got the key to the treasure vault, all right."

"So we've got to get him back here again, boys," murmured Buck, rubbing his hands while his eyes feasted upon the heap of gold. "I don't mind boardin' Pierre Luzon for a spell, and he can have all the bourbon he wants."

"Till he tells us where Guadalupe gets her nuggets," grinned Jack. "But you've forgotten to show 'em, Munson, the card that came with the coin."

"Oh, yes," rejoined Munson, drawing a small piece of pasteboard from his pocket. "It is brief enough. Luzon gives his countryman's family address in Marseilles where the first five thousand dollars is to be mailed. Then he writes down our five names, Dick Willoughby's first, and says the five of us are to share equally." He passed the card to Tom Baker for inspection, and went on: "Jack and I are going to ride over to Bakersfield, get the French bank draft and put Dick's money in the bank along with our own."

"Where's Dick?" asked Buck, with a quick uplift of his eyes into Munson's face.

But the latter was not to be betrayed into divulging any information that might be in his possession.

"I have not the slightest idea," he replied airily. "But I feel sure Dick's all right. He is the sort of fellow well able to look after himself. Meanwhile, Jack and I will attend to his financial interests," he added with a laugh, as he began to count the gold.

In silence the task proceeded, five thousand

dollars first being set aside, and then the balance divided into five separate heaps. When all were satisfied as to the correctness of the distribution, Munson swept the gold back into the sack, except for the two little piles allotted to Ashley and Baker. Then he securely tied the package, ready for the ride to Bakersfield.

"Buck will lock mine in his safe, boys," exclaimed Tom Baker. "Gosh me, but I'll want to look at it two or three times a day."

"Oh, I'm drivin' over to the bank myself tomorrer," declared Buck. "I've got a bit more to add to this pile."

"A few handfuls of nuggets, I suppose," laughed Rover.

"Well, I'll allow Guadalupe always pays her grocery bills. But this 'ere store ain't goin' to be a safe deposit vault, not on your derned life, with bandits around again. So you'd better arrange to come with me to town tomorrer, Tom."

"You'll need me to help you home, perhaps," grinned the sheriff. "But, I say, Munson, you ain't told us yet how this sack came to be delivered at your place."

"There's a proper mystery for you!" cried Munson. "As I said before, I found the bag this morning, lying on my dressing table. Sing Ling was the only one besides myself in the shack, and he never heard a sound all night."

"You're still in Dick's old home?" asked Buck.

"Yes, but I leave tomorrow—have notice to quit, for some surveyor chaps are coming in. I'm moving up to Mr. Robles' place. He wants me to catalog the books in his library."

"And Sing Ling?" queried Tom.

"He goes, too. You see, Mr. Robles needs a crackerjack cook, now I'll be boarding with him," Munson laughed, gaily. "You don't happen to have a porterhouse steak about the place, Buck?"

"I can heat you up a can of pork and beans."

"Nothing doing! Jack and I wouldn't spoil our appetites with such truck as that. We're going to set up a chicken dinner in Bakersfield."

"Chicken and champagne," chimed in Jack, as he swung the sack over his shoulder.

"You're beginning to get big bugs these days," called out the storekeeper as the young men left the room. "Guess, Tom," he went on, turning to the sheriff, "we could do with a jolt of Kentucky."

"Make it a bottle of bourbon," gurgled Tom, "to remind us of our absent friend."

"Dear old Pierre," murmured Buck, as he fumbled in his pocket for the key of the safe, his eyes glued all the time on the two little heaps of gold.

Chapter XXII

Underground Wonders

DICK WILLOUGHBY was in a way happy in his retreat. At first he had been inclined to regret the jail delivery—it might have been the manlier part to have faced the music and cleared his name before the whole world. But then he reflected on the uncertainties of a trial, the cases of innocent men having suffered because of damning circumstantial evidence piled up against them, the vindictiveness of Ben Thurston and the undoubted power of his money to press the criminal charge by every unscrupulous means. So Dick soon came round to the belief that he might be safer for the time being in the guardianship of the White Wolf than at the mercy of a fallible jury.

Then there was Merle Farnsworth to consider. Yes; to have brought her into a public court, to have allowed her to plead for him by telling the story of Marshall Thurston's loathsome advances —that was a thing that could never have been tolerated. The leader of the jail-breaking gang had been right; Dick owed it to Merle to save her from such a cruel ordeal.

Finally Dick's contentment over his change of quarters was completed when Pierre Luzon appeared with a superb equipment of drawing instruments and materials. There was no time to worry now over surmises as to the wisdom of this course or the other course. Work lay to his hand—work of the most absorbing and delightful kind; and with all the ambitious enthusiasm of his temperament he tackled it whole-heartedly there and then. Hour after hour, day after day, Pierre watched in contemplative silence the methodical advancement of the task to which the young architect had applied himself.

But there were frequent intervals for conversation, sometimes in French, sometimes in English, as the mood prompted. Occasionally Pierre drifted into semi-confidential reminiscences, and Willoughby soon came to know in close detail the story of Don Manuel's life—the tragedy of his sister Rosetta's death, the vow of vengeance against Ben Thurston, the early bandit days when the White Wolf counted every gringo in the land his natural enemy, the often hairbreadth escapes of the outlaw, his sublime courage and nerve in the direst emergencies.

"Don Manuel was one great man," remarked
Pierre at the close of one of these confidences—
the phrase was a favorite one with the old Frenchman. "Many and many a time he could have shot
his enemy from a distance and got away. But
Don Manuel had vowed zat he would kill him
hand to hand—zat ze villain must die with a last
malediction in his ear, and knowing zat it was he,
ze White Wolf, who in ze end had revenged his
sister's shame."

"He felt, too, didn't he, that his father had
been wronged in being driven from San Antonio
Rancho?"

"Sure—zat was another great wrong—zat was
why Don Manuel was so bitter against all ze
Americans. But he made zem pay for ze land
many and many times over." Then Pierre, as
was now his custom in Dick's presence when
speaking at any length, lapsed into French as he
continued: "But the White Wolf was a man of
high honor. He never used any of the proceeds of
his robberies for himself. True, he spent the money
to pay his band, to pay the numerous scouts and
spies whose services he secretly retained, to plan
and accomplish further hold-ups, to defy and out-
wit the authorities. But on his own needs—never
—not one dollar!"

Pierre went on to explain that after Ben Thurston had fled from California and kept away in hiding, Don Manuel had visited Spain, to claim the family estates in Valencia to which his father's death had left him the sole heir. These he had sold for many millions of dollars, and most of that money he kept in banks in London and Paris. So he was a very rich man, and had no need to rob anyone except to gratify his vengeance. Even the hoarded gold of Joaquin Murietta he had never touched. It remained intact today in the treasure vault of the cave, boxes and sacks of gold and jewels.

"Won't I be allowed to see this wonderful treasure?" asked Dick, half jesting.

"Perhaps, some day, if the White Wolf chooses to show you. But it is not for me to do that—I swore an oath of secrecy when the White Wolf trusted me—me and Felix Vasquez, who was also his confidant. But Vasquez was killed at Tulare Lake. So now only we two know the secret, and until the White Wolf himself dies my lips are sealed by the solemn oath I swore to the Virgin Mary."

The old man crossed himself devoutly.

"Then where does the White Wolf live now?"

"Ah, that is another secret. Again I would break my oath if I spoke one word."

"And Guadalupe—does she know these things?"
asked Dick in English.

"Guadalupe? Oh, no," responded Pierre,
politely adopting the change of language, "she
is just one servant, our cook—one very excellent
cook, as monsieur knows—and ze guardian of
ze cave. For ze real white wolf guards Guadalupe
—ze big animal is just like one tame dog to ze
old squaw, but with his fierce jaws he would kill
anyone who dared to approach her or come near ze
hidden entrance to zis cavern. No man can ever
find zat while ze white wolf is alive. In ze old
days he killed several men when zey dared to
follow Guadalupe."

"Then the white wolf must be very old?"

"As old as Guadalupe—as old as the Tehachapi
mountains," exclaimed Pierre, again crossing himself and thereby revealing the superstitious dread
in which he held the savage animal.

"But you can pass the white wolf, can't you?"
asked Dick.

"Never—except when Guadalupe give permission. Then ze wolf lies down and I can come out
of ze cave or enter. Ah! ze white wolf is one
terrible beast. But he never shows his teeth to
Don Manuel. Only Don Manuel can pass when
Guadalupe is not there."

"Then where is Guadalupe's riffle of gold—where is the lake of oil about which you told Tom Baker?"

"Come, I will show you zese," replied Pierre. As he rose he picked up the lantern he usually carried.

Dick jumped to his feet with alacrity and followed his guide.

They crossed the main cavern, then entered another side gallery. This had many windings and from it ran several diverging rock corridors. But Pierre led the way unfalteringly.

Fully half a mile must have been traversed when at last the Frenchman halted and swung his lantern aloft.

"Zere!" was all he said.

Dick followed the flash of the lantern, and there before him was a dark pool stretching away indefinitely into the blackness beyond. He bent down and scooped up a little of the fluid in his palm. It was a brown oil, as thin as water, and therefore capable of use without any refining process.

"Great Scott, this is wonderful!" exclaimed Dick in profound amazement.

"Very wonderful," concurred Pierre. "In zis cavern are oil and water, also gold—Guadalupe's gold. Ze gold is close to here. Come."

Pierre turned and again led the way through dark and winding corridors. At a little distance Dick became conscious of the purling of a running stream. Pierre stopped once more, but this time held the lantern close to the ground.

"Here Guadalupe come to wash out ze nuggets of gold, and since I have been in prison she buy with zem, so Mr. Baker say to me, groceries at ze store. Don Manuel, when I tell him, he very angry—she never do zat again."

"Poor old Buck Ashley!" laughed Dick. "He lost you, Pierre, and now he'll be losing his best-paying customer, too."

While speaking, he knelt and dipped his hands into the stream, bringing up some gravel into the lantern rays. But Pierre shook his head.

"You no find ze gold. Guadalupe wash many hours to get, perhaps, just one nugget. But there is heaps and heaps, if ze miners came with spades and cradles."

"Great guns, there must be the reef, too, from which the nuggets have come!" exclaimed Dick, rising erect and dropping the handful of pebbles.

"Now, we must go back," said Pierre, "for zis evening you are to be allowed to come for a ride with me down ze mountains."

"You don't say?" Dick cried, surprised and delighted.

"Yes; Don Manuel he send word today that he give permission. But you must wear ze bandage round your eyes, and you must promise to return when I give ze word."

"Don't for one moment think, old fellow, that I would leave my drawings. But where are we going tonight?"

"To La Siesta," replied Pierre.

"Hurrah!" shouted Dick. "Hurry up, Pierre! I'm mighty glad you got me those ties and things from Los Angeles. You say you can give me a hair-cut?"

"Ze old-time bandit learned to trim ze hair of his friends as well as ze pocket-books of his enemies," was the laughing answer.

CHAPTER **XXIII**

The Unexpected Visitor

MOST of the cattle had been driven off the land. The vaqueros had dispersed to the four points of the compass. Chester Munson had vacated his room in Dick Willoughby's old home, and had taken up his residence and library duties at Mr. Robles' mansion on the hill. Sing Ling had folded his tent like the Arab and silently stolen away in the same direction. A small army of surveyors had appeared on the scene and were quartered in the rancho buildings.

The only one of the old-timers who still lingered on was Ben Thurston, more gloomy and morose than ever, seldom stirring out of doors now, but conducting all his business by telephone or through the agency of the sleuth, Leach Sharkey, his only companion.

Jack Rover had pitched his camp temporarily at the store. Buck Ashley had assigned him Pierre's cot, but the cowboy had fixed it under a wide-spreading sycamore, preferring to sleep in the open rather than share the grocery-perfumed atmosphere of the store building.

Tom Baker was around most of the time.   The three men clung together with a vague sense that they had a common interest in the vast treasure which had so far eluded them, but which might any day come again within reach of their eager claws.   It afforded an endless theme of conversation, varied by talk about the passing of the rancho and all the train of changes which were bound to follow the close settlement of the valley.

One morning Jack Rover found Buck at the door of the store, with a pair of antiquated-looking field glasses at his eyes.

"Where did you get the goggles, Buck?" asked Jack.

"Oh, I rummaged 'em out of a trunk—had almost forgot I had the blamed things.   But we used to keep a sharp lookout in the old bandit days—got kinda ready for any suspicious lookin' riders on the road."   He had spoken while still peering through the binoculars, but now he turned to Jack and proffered him the glasses.   "I do wonder what 'n hell we're all comin' to anyway. This here ranch that we've bragged up as bein' the biggest in all California!   Ugh!"   The grunt was one of unspeakable disgust. "Take a look for yourself."

Jack turned the glasses in the direction Buck had been gazing, and began to adjust the focus.

"What's the matter now?" he asked.

"Matter 'nough," growled the storekeeper. "San Antonio Rancho is goin' to the dogs. Do you see them specks away out yonder in the valley? That's another band of surveyors. One feller's peekin' through a spy-glass set on a tripod; another feller goes ahead and puts up tall stakes with big figgers on 'em, and the other fellers are chainin' off the distances. This 'ere ranch 'll surely look like a checker-board blamed soon."

"Progress," said Jack, laconically.

"Progress, hell!" snapped Ashley. "These new fellers that bought the ranch have sure 'nuff driv' off all the cattle and now they're dividin' up the land. I bet they'll take the postoffice away from me—not that it pays much, for the Lord knows it don't—but it brings customers to my store."

"Well, Buck," said the cowboy, consolingly, "there are lots worse things than moving a post-office. What's to prevent your setting up the finest grocery store in the new model city the advertisements speak about?"

"That would suit me fine, wouldn't it?" cried the old storekeeper, with scathing contempt. "Goin' around in a biled shirt, and handin' out pencils and chewin' gum to the little school gals that'll be swarmin' all over the place. Not on your life, Jack! I'll be losin' both my postoffice and my store in these new-fangled times." He paused a moment, then his tone changed to one of aggressiveness. "However, they ain't built their doggoned new town yet, and it's my belief all this boom talk is just so much hot air."

"In any case you won't need to worry, Buck, after we get on the tracks of Pierre Luzon again. I intend to find the old squaw's sand-bar, or my name isn't Jack Rover."

"And I betche I'm a-goin' to find Joaquin Murietta's cache," concurred the old man with equal determination.

Just then Tom Baker slouched out of the store, where he had overheard the conversation.

"Oh, things are a-goin' to turn out all right in the end, boys, don't fret over that. And there's one thing gol-dern certain, there'll be some great things doin' in this 'ere valley once they get started on buildin' the town. The new place will just spring up like Oklahomy City, or Liberal, Kansas, or some of them big towns that had twenty thousand people livin' in 'em inside o' thirty days from the time they were surveyed and laid out."

"That seems quite impossible," commented Jack.

"Not impossible by a derned sight. My brother was at Liberal, Kansas, down there on the Rock Island, near No Man's Land, you know. The new town had been talked of and talked of for mebbe three or four months, just as this new town is bein' talked about today. Then finally the mornin' came when the new town of Liberal was to be opened up. There was to be a regular town openin', so to speak, and a sale of lots. Why, great guns, when the management of that town company rode into the station, on the early train, they found more'n ten thousand people right there campin' in covered wagons, tents and all that sorta business, just awaitin' for the auctioneerin' to start."

Tom paused to take a fresh chew of tobacco and then rambled on:

"I tell you, boys, that within thirty days there was twenty thousand people livin' in that 'ere town. Two banks were established, and one of them had one hundred and eighty-five thousand dollars in deposits, too. Oh, there's lots of people who remember the rush to Liberal, and the boomin' of Oklahomy City also. And history's fixin' to repeat itself right here on this 'ere ranch. Things will be sizzlin' when the town site is finally located and the rush starts pourin' in from Portland, Oregon, on the north, to San Diego on the south, with a few thousands from Texas and other states this side o' the Rocky Mountains. They'll sure be great doin's when the Los Angeles syndicate announce they've awarded to some feller that ten-thousand-dollar prize for the best plans for their ideal city, as they keep on callin' it."

"Munson and I were speaking about the contest and the prize," remarked Jack, "and were saying that if Dick Willoughby were only here, he'd about win, hands down. You know he was an architect once, before he came West."

"'Dick Willoughby,'" snorted Ashley, "How can he compete when he don't know anything about the blamed business? He's hid away, right enough."

"Munson knows a thing or two," remarked Tom Baker. "If he'd only speak, he could tell us where Dick is. That's my opinion."

"And there once again you're dead wrong," retorted Jack, warmly. "If Munson only knew where Dick is hiding, he would have got that very prize competition advertisement into his hands long before now. He's sore because he can't send Dick the word. Where is Dick Willoughby? By gad, it's a mystery."

"I guess you're right," said the sheriff. "That sort o' exonerates Munson from keepin' things from his partners. I think I owe it to Chester Munson to drink his health—just for ever doubtin' him. What shall it be, boys?"

And the open-air meeting adjourned.

It was the very evening of the day on which this conversation had been held in Buck Ashley's store that Dick Willoughby rode forth from the cavern blindfolded and under the guidance of Pierre Luzon. For the first hour progress was slow—round many turnings, down steep declivities, with just here and there a few miles of easier trail. But then there had been a swift canter for another hour over grass land, and now at last the riders were upon a well-made road. Dick divined that this must be the highway leading to La Siesta, but from what point of the compass they had come he had not the remotest conception.

Very soon Pierre Luzon, still riding ahead with the leading rein, came to a halt.

"Here we are. Dismount, please," he said. "You are free to remove ze bandage."

Dick looked; they were right below the knoll on which the Darlington home stood. Lights were gleaming from the windows. Dick could even hear the faint tinkle of the piano.

"I hide ze ponies here in zis little grove of trees," Pierre continued, pointing to a coppice not fifty yards from the main road. "In two hours' time, at eleven o'clock"—Pierre looked at his watch in the bright moonlight—"monsieur will return. I have your word?"

"My word as a gentleman, Pierre," exclaimed Dick, extending his hand. "So long then, old fellow. I've got to make the best use of my time."

The piano playing stopped abruptly when Willoughby, unannounced, appeared at the door of the music room.

"Dick!" exclaimed Merle delightedly, leaving the instrument and rushing toward him. If they had been alone Dick felt that right then she would have jumped into his arms. But at the distance of a few paces she halted and clasped her hands.

"How ever did you get here, Mr. Willoughby?" she asked intensely.

"I rode here," he answered, as they shook

hands. "But it is only a brief visit. Hallo, Miss Grace! I'm delighted to see you again. And you, Ches, old sport—why this is great luck to find you here! Mrs. Darlington, I'm mighty glad to see you all once more."

The whole bevy were crowding around him, shaking hands and expressing their joyful surprise.

"We knew you were safe, that was all," explained Munson.

"So you were having just the same jolly good times," laughed Dick, glancing at the piano. "I'm simply dying for some music."

"But wait a minute," exclaimed Munson, drawing a fat wad of newspaper cuttings from his pocket. "I've got to tell you about a competition you must get into—new plans for an ideal city here—"

"In the heart of the old rancho," smiled Dick, as he completed the sentence. While he spoke, he placed his arm affectionately across his chum's shoulders. "I know all about it, old man. I'm working hard on my plans—they are already more than half done."

"Bravo!" shouted Munson. "That's great news."

"But here, too, is Mr. Robles," exclaimed Dick, breaking from the group and stepping across the room. "Excuse me, senor, but I did not notice you were here till this moment."

"No excuse needed, my friend. You were better engaged"—this with a humorous sideglance at the young ladies. "But I am glad to see you looking so well."

"Where have you been, Mr. Willoughby?" asked Grace.

"That I cannot tell you," replied Dick gravely. "I have pledged my solemn word. I must leave you at eleven o'clock, returning whence I came. And meanwhile nobody must ask me a single question about my place of hiding. There now— that's all. What shall it be first, Miss Merle, a piano solo or a duet with the violin?"

"Supper, I should say," exclaimed Mrs. Darlington, as she left the room.

CHAPTER XXIV

In a Tight Corner

DICK'S after-dark visit to La Siesta was only the first of several that followed at intervals of a few days. He came and departed mysteriously, and during his brief stay every precaution was taken that no one except his few trusted friends should know of his presence. But by some means or other a whisper had reached the ear of the sleuth, Leach Sharkey, that the fugitive had been seen at the home of Mrs. Darlington.

When the news was imparted to Ben Thurston, the old man quivered from excitement.

"At La Siesta, do you tell me? Let us ride over there at once, and search the place from basement to attic."

"No, no," replied Sharkey. "I've got my scouts out. Don't you worry. We must wait till the night bird comes back. Then we'll trap him like a fat quail."

"All right. Have my automobile ready, and a bunch of well-armed fellows right here, so that we can make a rush over at a moment's notice. By God, I've been disappointed in everything else—lost my son, lost my ranch, lost my home. But I'm not going to lose that man. I'm going to get him, even if we shoot him down on sight as an outlawed fugitive from justice with a price on his head."

"We'll get him," answered Sharkey, with a grim smile. "You may count him a dead bird. I guessed he wouldn't keep away from his girl very long."

"His girl! Curse her—it was she who lured my son to his death. But I'll be avenged. If she has been harboring an outlaw, she, too, has broken the law and shall go to jail."

"Well, she no doubt thinks him innocent," suggested the sleuth.

"Innocent! All women are alike—treacherous devils at heart. I would give them the vote—yes, but the rope at the same time," he went on, growling in savage incoherence.

And Sharkey, knowing that discussion or contradiction only added fresh fuel to his vile temper, left him alone.

At last, a few nights later, a rider dashed up to Ben Thurston's house with the news that Dick Willoughby had been seen entering La Siesta, and that, following Sharkey's instructions, every avenue of escape was now guarded.

"Hurry, hurry! I've got to be in at the death," fairly screamed the old man.

Five minutes later the big seven-passenger automobile, carrying three or four armed men besides its owner and his personal guard, Leach Sharkey, was devouring the twenty miles of road that lay between the two ranch homes.

That evening the four young people were quietly chatting in the cosy corner on the interior verandah —the comfortable little nook fixed up with rugs and tapestries and oriental divans. It was summer now, and after a sultry day the night air was sweet and balmy. Willoughby was smoking a cigar in languid contentment with his surroundings, when all at once he sprang to his feet.

Tia Teresa had rushed in, frantic with excitement.

"A great big automobile is coming along the road," she cried, "and there are men watching outside the portico. Come with me," she went on, addressing Dick. "I know where your horses are hid. I can take you by a secret path through the oleanders."

Dick vaguely wondered why the duenna should know anything about his mode of coming. But there was no time to question, for just then there came the sound of voices outside.

Mrs. Darlington, pale and agitated, emerged from the drawing room.

"What has happened?" she asked breathlessly.

"I guess I'm trapped," replied Dick quietly. "No doubt it's old Thurston. There will be shooting if I resist. So there is nothing for it but to surrender."

"No, no," exclaimed Merle. "I dread that vindictive man. He must never get you in his power again. We must gain time to smuggle you out of the house. I have it. Tia Teresa—give me your mantilla and your cloak. Quick, quick!"

A first loud knocking had come on the door at the head of the portico steps. The duenna in a moment had divested herself of her loose black robe and heavy lace veil.

"Get something else to wear and meet us at the oleanders," continued Merle, taking the garments from Tia Teresa. "Put these on, Dick, and sit right there in that corner. Mr. Munson, turn off two or three of the lights. Mother, dear, control yourself. Take this book and be reading. Now, that will do. They will be here in a moment."

A second knock had been heard, and now they

knew that the door was being opened without further ceremony, for at placid La Siesta there were no bolts or bars against unwelcome visitors.

In that brief minute a wonderful transformation scene had taken place in the cosy corner. Tia Teresa had disappeared. Munson was stretched on a sofa, puffing his cigar. Merle and Grace had been playing patience during the afternoon and had left the cards in scattered confusion. Mrs. Darlington, beneath the single incandescent aglow, was quietly reading. From the darksome corner the pretended duenna surveyed this peaceful scene of domesticity.

It was Ben Thurston himself who led the way for his swarm of myrmidons.

He began without formality; his tone was coarse and rude.

"We want the outlaw, Dick Willoughby. We know he is here. So make no fuss. Deliver him over."

Mrs. Darlington had risen to her feet, and Munson, too, had sprung erect.

"What do you mean?" asked the lady with quiet dignity.

"You know darned well what I mean."

Munson stepped forward, but he played the game best by keeping himself under perfect control.

"You will speak civilly, Mr. Thurston, or leave this house. What is wanted?" he added, turning to Leach Sharkey.

"We want Dick Willoughby, of course," the sleuth replied, politely enough. "We have reason to believe he is here."

"Well, you can see for yourself whether he is here or not," said Munson, glancing around. "But if you wish to look through the house, I don't suppose Mrs. Darlington will refuse you permission."

The lady bowed her acquiescence.

"With your consent, Mrs. Darlington," Munson went on, "I'll show these gentlemen round and save you the annoyance. Come along then."

Ben Thurston had been fairly silenced by the army man's suave courtesy. He was glowering at him, dully conscious of having been suppressed.

Munson turned from the sleuth.

"Perhaps Mr. Thurston would prefer to remain with the ladies?" he asked, with a touch of smiling irony.

"I don't leave my man Sharkey," replied Thurston gruffly. "Sharkey, keep close watch on me. We'll search the place, but you stay near me all the time." Once again there was the old hunted look in his eyes as he glanced apprehensively into the courtyard.

"Then follow me," said Munson quietly.

"You have left a guard at the door of course?" asked Thurston of Sharkey.

"Oh, you just allow me to know my business," replied the detective sharply. He bowed to Mrs. Darlington and her daughters. "I am really sorry to disturb you, ladies."

"Then get the business over as soon as possible," said Munson. "Come along."

The moment the coast was clear, Merle jumped up.

"Quick! Mr. Willoughby. Follow me downstairs. I'll take you through the kitchen to the rose gardens."

It was a strange looking duenna that stalked after Merle, with a robe reaching only to the knees. But at the head of the kitchen stairway Dick discarded the now useless garments, flinging them across the balustrade.

"We must trust to our good luck now, Merle," he said.

"Never fear. It won't desert us. Hurry on."

At the clump of oleanders they found Tia Teresa, provided with another shawl. Not a moment was to be wasted in words. Merle just pressed Dick's hand by way of farewell. As he hastened away down the dark path, she, too, sped from the spot.

Perhaps fifteen minutes later Ben Thurston, going the round of the house, came to the head of the kitchen stairs. He saw the black cloak and mantilla on the balustrade.

"By God!" he cried with swift inspiration of what had happened. "We've been properly fooled! Where is that old hag of a duenna?"

Gathering the vestments in his hands he rushed through the house to the verandah. Merle was quietly seated with her mother and Grace. But there was no sign now of Tia Teresa.

Sharkey had followed close on his employer's heels. Munson came a few paces behind.

Ben Thurston glared for a moment at the vacant place where the black-robed figure had been seated. Then he turned round and, addressing Mrs. Darlington, fairly shouted:

"Where is Dick Willoughby? It was he who was wearing these damned clothes." And he flung the garments on the rug before her.

"No swearing, please," said Munson, tapping him on the shoulder.

"To hell! Who wouldn't swear? Where is the man I'm after?"

"An innocent man," exclaimed Merle, rising to her feet and proudly folding her arms.

"Looks like it—breaking jail and hiding in the hills," sneered Thurston. "He is nothing but a murderer and an outlaw. And I'm going to get him, dead or alive."

"Then catch him if you can," cried Merle, pointing toward the door that opened on the portico.

Under the girl's fearless gaze Ben Thurston wilted. Baffled, humiliated, speechless in his impotent rage, he allowed the sleuth to take him by the arm and hustle him from the scene.

CHAPTER XXV

Love and Revenge

BEYOND the oleanders a tall thick hedge of cypress favored the flight of the fugitive.

At the end of the gardens Tia Teresa took a little path that dipped into the river bed, and when they ascended again out of the hollow, Dick found himself quite close to the grove where Pierre was in hiding with the ponies.

By this time the young fellow was angry with himself for having fled so precipitately. He was full of solicitude for Merle. Why had not he remained to defend her from the brutality of that ruffian, Ben Thurston? This was the question that was now making him both ashamed and anxious.

"Hush!"

The caution came from Pierre, and showed that the Frenchman was alive to what had happened.

"I saw ze automobile rush by," he whispered. "We will ride across country, so zat it cannot follow us." He pointed in the direction he would go.

Among the Old Oaks — Page 262

"Not yet," replied Dick, determinedly. "I'm off back to the house to see that they are all safe there."

"No, no, Mr. Willoughby," protested the duenna earnestly. "You heard what Miss Merle said— she is afraid of that raging old man. Besides I know. He has vowed that he and his hired gunmen will shoot you on sight. For my little girl's sake you must not go back," she implored.

"Besides your word of honor is pledged to me," added Luzon. "You must return wiz me. I have your parole."

"Parole be hanged," muttered Dick between his teeth.

The old Frenchman laid a kindly hand on the young man's shoulder.

"No, no. Monsieur is a man of honor. And honor comes before love—always."

"If you love her," insisted Tia Teresa, "you will save yourself tonight. We will look after her. You need not worry on her account."

Dick for the moment was silenced, but unconvinced.

"Well, at all events we'll wait a bit. I don't leave this spot till I'm sure that Ben Thurston himself has cleared."

"All right," assented Pierre. "Stay where you

are, Tia Teresa. You must not be seen. Zey may be searching in ze gardens."

Even as he spoke there was the flash of a lantern among the rose bushes.

In tense silence they waited and watched. The leaden-winged minutes stole on. For a time lights flitted about, then vanished. At last came the "honk-honk" of the automobile, and a minute later the great machine with its flaring headlights swept down the roadway. They could just see that it was crowded with men. Then in a few seconds it had disappeared around the bend.

"Now we go," said Pierre.

"Just a minute longer, please," replied Dick in a firm tone. "Tia Teresa, you slip back to the house. I will stay here till you bring me word from Merle that she is safe and that all is well."

"I will soon return," said the duenna as she hurried away on her mission.

Again an interval of high-tensioned waiting. Neither Dick nor Pierre spoke a word. At last there came a rustle of the bushes from the direction of the river bed, and a moment later Tia Teresa was again by their side.

"Mr. Willoughby," she said, breathless from the speed she had made, "Miss Merle begs you to make good your escape. She is well, and happy

because you are safe. She sends this rose and"—
the old lady hesitated a moment—"her love."

"She said that?" murmured Dick, tremblingly,
as he took the white blossom and breathed its
fragrance.

"Well, does not the flower speak her love?"
replied the duenna. "Now go, go."

"Come," said Pierre, as he raised himself into
the saddle. "We shall fix the blindfold later on."

Dick furtively kissed the rose before he placed it
in the breast pocket of his coat. Then he mounted,
and, bringing his pony alongside of Pierre's, started
off at a canter across the starlit plain.

Ben Thurston did not feel inclined to sleep that
night. He paced his sitting room like an angry
bear, and kept Leach Sharkey out of bed to listen
to his growls and threatenings.

"By God, I'll have that girl shoved into jail.
Harboring an outlaw! It's a criminal offence."

"You can't do it," objected the sleuth.

"Can't do it?" shouted Thurston, halting and
glowering down upon the man who had dared to
contradict him. "You'll see damned quick if I
can't."

"Not one of us could swear that Willoughby
was there. Neither you nor I could. We never
saw him."

"He wore that disguise," thundered Thurston.

"So you think.   But thinking ain't proof—
not by a long chalk."

Thurston was now almost speechless from rage.
Half articulate words of blasphemy were upon his
stuttering lips.   But Sharkey went coolly on.

"Besides the sympathy of everyone would be
with the girl.   You can't succeed that way.   You
yourself would be covered with ridicule."

At last the torrent of curses broke forth.   ·

"Damn you, Leach Sharkey!   That's what I
pay you for, is it?   To let that scoundrel slip
through our very fingers?   And you had the nerve
to ask me for another big check this evening.
It's all a confounded plot.   You're bleeding me.
Leach is your name, and leech is your nature."

Leach Sharkey rose to his feet.   His white
teeth gleamed as his short upper lip curled in a
contemptuous smile.   He raised a threatening
finger.   It was his turn now to give free vent to
profanity.

"Stop right there, you doggoned old fool.   I
bleed you, do I?   Well, take my resignation.   All
your pay ain't worth another five minutes of your
infernal temper.   No man ever dared to browbeat
me and insult me as you have done.   And now
you may go to hell—where you belong."

The sleuth turned on his heel, and strode to the doorway. But Thurston was after him in an instant, penitent, trembling, ashen pale. He grabbed Sharkey by the coat sleeve.

"No, no, don't go, I beg of you," he whined. "I was wrong. I spoke in anger. I apologize. Good God, some one or other will get me within an hour if you leave me unprotected. I haven't a single friend—no one to stand by me." There was craven fear in his eyes as he looked timidly around. "I hear the prowling footsteps of my enemies in the night. You alone can save me, Mr. Sharkey."

"Your damned civility comes too late," replied the sleuth, as he shook the clutching hands from his shoulder.

"No, no. Don't say that. Sit down again. See, here is my check book. I'll pay you that money now—I'll double the amount—I'll never haggle with you again. Stay with me till we go East together."

Sharkey showed himself somewhat mollified. He had played his game well, for after all, cash with him was the main consideration. So smiling over the success of his bluff, he watched the unnerved coward as he tottered to his desk, dropped into a chair and drew the check with slow and painful effort, and then returned with it between his still trembling fingers.

"You'll stand by me, Mr. Sharkey, won't you?"

"Well, no more of that nonsense," was the curt reply, as the sleuth glanced at the slip of paper, then thrust it in his waistcoat pocket.

To Thurston the reconciliation brought instant relief. He drew himself up; he rubbed his hands; he even attempted a smile.

"That's a good fellow, Sharkey. You know I've always held you in high esteem. And we'll get that man yet"—the glare of vindictiveness was again in his eyes, the rasp of accustomed irritability was returning to his voice. "We'll get him, I say, even if it costs double the money I've already spent. And that devil of a girl, too—I hate her more than ever now. She'll pay for her insults tonight with her lover's life. Remember, Sharkey, no more chances. When you get the scoundrel within gunshot, it's up to you to shoot. That will be best in any case. It will save the cost of a judge and jury. You understand me?"

"I understand," nodded Sharkey. "Then, as you're speaking about doubling, Mr. Thurston, I suppose that ten-thousand-dollar reward coming to me goes up to twenty thousand."

"Yes; twenty thousand if you shoot him like a dog, and let me get away from this damned place. I have come to loathe the very name of it. Well, spread your cot now across my door. I'll try to get an hour's sleep. Good night."

And Ben Thurston disappeared into the inner room.

CHAPTER XXVI

A Date is Fixed

ON the morning after the exciting episode at La Siesta, Chester Munson was in the library of Mr. Robles' home ready for his day's duties. But he was in no mood for the routine work of cataloging and classifying the volumes on the bookshelves. Up to now the task had been one of absorbing interest, for Munson, although not a scholar, had always been fond of reading, and it was a treat to dip at times into the contents of the rare and curious works which wealth and the educated taste of a true bibliophile had accumulated.

But today the amateur librarian was thinking of other things. He was feverishly awaiting the usual morning visit of his employer, so that he might tell him the story of the previous night's happenings. At last Mr. Robles made his appearance, and gave his usual quiet greetings.

"I see you are making great progress with your work," he remarked, glancing at the pile of classified volumes resting temporarily on the library table.

"Oh, I'm getting along," replied Munson. "But I have most surprising news for you, Mr. Robles."

"Indeed?" The recluse arched his eyebrows in expectant curiosity as he took a chair beside the desk at which Munson had been seated. "Sit down, please. Let me hear the story."

"You know that I was at La Siesta yesterday evening?"

"I know that you are very often there," replied Mr. Robles, smiling. "I understand the attraction and congratulate you on your good fortune. Grace Darlington is certainly a charming young lady."

Munson flushed and bowed his acquiescence in the compliment as he said:

"It was not of her, however, that I was going to speak. I want to say to you, Mr. Robles, that Miss Farnsworth did one of the bravest and cleverest things imaginable last evening."

"Tell me about it. I am all attention."

Munson then proceeded to relate in full detail the events of the preceding evening—the surprise visit of Ben Thurston, the brutality of the man, the quick wit of Merle, the escape of Dick Willoughby, and his final message by Tia Teresa that he was safe and, in obedience to Merle's injunction, was returning to his place of hiding. During the narrative only once did the listener betray emotion; when Thurston's rude insults were repeated there came a flash into Robles' eyes, and he clenched his hands to restrain his indignation. But he interrupted with no word, and at the end spoke no comment.

Munson was a little taken aback at this silence and impassivity.

"My story does not seem to surprise you?" he remarked, with a note of interrogation.

"No," was the quiet reply, "I already knew it."

"How?" exclaimed Munson, wonderingly.

"You have forgotten, young man, that there is a private telephone between my home here and La Siesta. Mrs. Darlington has already told me about the matter. But I am pleased to have your version, and delighted more than I can tell to know that Merle proved equal to the emergency —that it was she who may be truly said to have saved Dick Willoughby." There was a ring of pride and admiration in his voice as he spoke the words.

"She's the real stuff," cried Munson, enthusiastically.

"It was well done," continued Mr. Robles, his tone taking a graver note. "For I want to warn you, Munson, as Willoughby's closest friend, that Ben Thurston or one of his hired assassins will certainly shoot on sight the instant they get the chance to do so. But by the Lord, if anything like that happens, I will hang that villain Thurston to the highest tree in Tejon for the buzzards to pick his bones." And the upraised hand, the voice vibrating with passionate determination, showed that Ricardo Robles meant just what he said.

Mr. Robles had risen to his feet. For a moment he turned his face away. Then he again spoke, but now in his customary, sedate manner.

"This morning, Mr. Munson, I leave home for a few days. Go on with your work, of course, but remember that it is quite a minor consideration. During my absence I shall rely on you to see that Ben Thurston, on any pretence of searching for Willoughby, does not cross my door."

"He shall never do that, so long as I'm here," declared the young army man, with quiet confidence.

"I don't think he will, either," replied Robles. "I have given orders for him to be shot down," he added grimly, "if he should dare to approach my gates. But I'll count on you all the same as a second guard to the sanctity of my home."

"You may count on me to the death," responded Munson, extending his hand.

"I know it, and therefore I go away on a necessary duty with an easy mind. But I have good news for you, Munson. I have instructed Sing Ling to prepare luncheon for the ladies of La Siesta every day they choose to come. So, while I prefer you to remain here on guard while I am gone, you need not be lonely. Perhaps you'll hardly wish me to come back again," he added with a smile.

"Oh, don't say that. But you're mighty kind thinking of such things at all."

"Well, you may expect our friends today about one o'clock. Now, goodbye—but not for long."

The library work proceeded but slowly during the hours that followed. Munson was all impatience now for Grace and Merle to arrive. Books were of little account, for there was none ever printed that could rival for him the charm of a certain pair of laughing blue eyes. And it was a self-confessed pseudo man-of-letters who at last rushed to the gateway to greet the fair visitors.

"Mother couldn't come," cried Grace, as she jumped from her horse and flung the bridle to a Mexican groom. "She's putting up fruit with

Tia Teresa, and I think she really believes everything would go wrong if she didn't superintend."

Munson, as he led the girls through the arched gateway, was inclined to bless both the fruit and the fallacy.

Sing Ling came across the patio with a welcoming smile.

"Dinnel all leady," he announced in tinkling syllables.

"And we're all ready, too, Sing Ling," laughed Merle, as she went up and shook the Chinaman's hand.

"Me vely glad to see you again, missie."

"I didn't know you were old friends," exclaimed Munson, in some surprise.

"Oh, didn't you? Sing Ling has been Mr. Robles' cook off and on for nearly twenty years. When Mr. Robles is abroad of course he works elsewhere. That's why you found him at San Antonio Rancho."

"But Dick told me he was his cook—had been for several years."

"With Mr. Robles' tacit consent, then," replied Merle.

The Chinaman was grinning in a vacuous sort of way, as if all the conversation was so much Greek to him.

"Sing Ling, you scamp," cried Munson, "I begin to understand now how Mr. Robles comes to know so much about Dick and myself. You've been telling tales out of school."

"Oh, no; me cookee allee time; me no go school," replied the Celestial, in guileless incomprehension.

After the dainty luncheon, Merle proposed that they should visit the watch tower. There they found the Mexican lad on duty. He had been strumming a guitar to pass the time, but at the sound of voices had sprung erect and alert. Munson noticed at a glance that the big telescope was ready trained on San Antonio Rancho.

"*Como estas, Francisco?*" asked Merle, addressing the boy in Spanish.

"*Bien, gracias, senorita,*" he replied, with a deferential bow. But he averted his glance instantly, and gazed out on the landscape.

Merle turned to Munson: "We are not allowed to converse with the servants here," she explained. "Just a word of greeting—that is all."

"I'm under similar orders," replied Munson. "Not that it much matters in my case, for I haven't your accomplishment of knowing the Spanish language."

"Oh, Grace and I speak Spanish almost as well

as English. You see, Mr. Robles, who has always
been interested in us two girls, insisted that we
should be taught his native tongue."

"And we've been all over Spain, too," interposed Grace. "Lived there a whole year. That's
where I fell in love with the violin and took my
first lessons."

"An inspiring country obviously," remarked
Munson with a flattering gesture.

"Thank you for the subtle compliment,"
laughed Grace, tossing the vagrant, wind-blown
curls from her face.

"I never come here but I love to gaze at the
view," observed Merle. "Is it not glorious—
this valley of Tehachapi?"

It was indeed a glorious scene—that noble
sweep of verdured plain, stretching north far
as the eye could reach, on the south guarded by
the rugged pass, east and west embosoming
hills twenty miles apart etching the sky with
peaks and domes and lines of beauty. For a few
moments all three visitors to the tower remained
silent and enraptured.

Grace was the one to break the spell.

"I'm going down now to the library to inspect
your work, lieutenant," she announced with a
roguish smile.

"Spare me," protested Munson. "But perhaps you would help me with some of those Spanish books," he added as an afterthought.

"Delighted! Come along." And she led the way down the winding iron staircase.

In the library the three were for the first time during the visit quite alone. Munson carefully closed the door.

"Now I've got the chance, Miss Merle," he began, "I want to compliment you on your splendid bravery last night."

"Bravery!" she laughed. "Why I was so scared I could hardly stand."

"Well, you deceived us all finely, then."

"And that Ben Thurston—what an old ruffian!" cried Grace. "But I agree with you, Mr. Munson; Merle was a hero."

"A heroine," suggested the lieutenant.

"Oh, in these days we don't make such fine sex distinctions," laughed Grace. "A real hero, that's what I call her."

"Rubbish," protested Merle. "I just did what anyone else would have done in the circumstances."

"I'm afraid men are not so ready of wit in an emergency as are women," remarked Munson.

"Just listen to that, Merle," exclaimed Grace. "I verily believe the lieutenant is a suffragette."

"A suffragist," corrected Munson, emphatically this time. "I'm hanged if I'm going to wear a petticoat even if the women are determined to don—the other things."

They all laughed merrily.

Grace turned and began examining the carefully written library cards.

"Any more news from Mr. Willoughby?" asked Merle, with a look of solicitude in her eyes.

"Nothing," replied Munson. "But I'm beginning to put two and two together," he continued. "Early every morning a horseman comes down here from the mountains and evidently brings a report of some kind to Mr. Robles. And when he rides off again Sing Ling has always ready a basket of grub, all sorts of nice things, fried chicken, spiced beef—"

"Sounds quite epicurean," interrupted Grace, tossing away the card she had been pretending to examine.

"Yes, hang it all—just the little delicacies Dick used to like."

"I never knew you fared so bountifully at San Antonio Rancho," remarked Merle with a smile.

"Oh, Dick's no candy kid, as you know well," replied Munson. "It was mostly rough and ready fare all right, but Sing Ling had a knack of adding a few dainty trifles to our meals, and it strikes me that for the purposes of this mysterious and capacious lunch basket he is trying to excel himself."

"No doubt it goes to Mr. Willoughby," said Merle. "Well, I'm real glad to know that they are making him comfortable."

"I guess, though, he'll miss his occasional visits to La Siesta. Mr. Robles says you were quite right, Miss Merle. Dick is in real danger. Those gunmen of old Thurston have orders to shoot him on sight."

"I knew it," exclaimed Merle. "Oh, I'm so thankful he got away. Even though we miss seeing him, he must never run such a risk again."

"It is all very mysterious," said Munson, in a musing tone. "And I had no idea, too, that this was such a lovely place. Mr. Robles has taken me around several times. He has the choicest dairy cattle, the finest blooded horses, rare trees and plants from every corner of the world."

"These are his hobbies," commented Merle.

"He says he wants to give me some practical lessons in estate management."

"Why?" asked Grace.

"Well," laughed Munson, "he thinks I may some day own a rancho of my own. But that will be a mighty long time."

"Who can tell?" said Merle, glancing mischievously from the lieutenant to Grace. "Even in these humdrum days soldiers have been known to come in and conquer."

Grace blushed crimson.

"Merle, how dare you?" she exclaimed, half angry, half laughing. "Next time we visit you, Mr. Munson, I'll have to bring along Tia Teresa."

"Oh, dear Aunt Teresa has a soft side for the lieutenant," retorted Merle, with merry audacity.

But Grace had recovered from her momentary confusion.

"Then I'll help you all I can, Mr. Munson, with dear Aunt Teresa," she laughingly said. "We'll send her along tomorrow instead of coming ourselves."

"Heaven forbid!" murmured the lieutenant, with pious fervor. He, too, had been looking and feeling awkward.

"So we'll say goodbye for the present," continued Grace, frankly extending her hand.

"I hope I haven't said anything to offend you," stammered Munson.

"It is perhaps what you haven't said that is the cause of trouble," laughed the irrepressible Merle.

But Grace had fled from the room, and as the others followed, Merle went on:

"I said when we left home that two would be company but three—a complication. Wasn't I right, lieutenant?"

"You are always right," murmured Munson, too bewildered to think of anything else but the obvious gallant reply.

He stood at the gateway watching the two young ladies as they cantered away. At the bend of the road Merle turned round in the saddle and waved her hand. But Grace rode steadily on.

"By jove, that's as good as telling me that I can sail in and win," he said to himself. "Thank you, Merle, little girl. Next time Grace and I are alone, my fate will be sealed."

But no one called again during Mr. Robles' absence—not even Tia Teresa.

It was toward evening a few days later when the recluse strolled into the library. Munson did not know that he had returned, and rose from his seat in some surprise.

"Still hard at work?" said Mr. Robles, as he nodded and shook hands.

"When did you get back, sir?"

"Last night. And today I have been busy with some important letters."

"Any word of Dick?"

"There is nothing new so far as I am aware."

"Mr. Robles, excuse me," said Munson earnestly. "But I'm anxious on Dick's account. You know of his whereabouts, of course?"

"I have indicated as much, although for the present I prefer to say nothing."

"Well, when is he to be restored to liberty?"

"In due time. At latest he will be free on the eleventh of October."

"Oh, that's months ahead yet. But why the eleventh of October? You excite my curiosity."

"The date is not of my choosing—it was fixed many years ago, by another than myself."

The enigmatic reply puzzled Chester Munson—not only the words themselves, but the tremor of deep emotion in the voice of Ricardo Robles as he gave them utterance.

Chapter XXVII

Among the Old Oaks

"PIERRE, now my sketches and plans are finished, how am I going to pass the time?"

It was some ten days after the affair at La Siesta, and Dick had spent the interval in close and absorbed work over his drawing board. Happy in his occupation, he had not felt the restraints of confinement.

But now that the task was completed, and the big cardboard cylinder containing the set of drawings rested on the ledge of the easel all ready to be sent away on its mission, a feeling of chafing restlessness had ensued.

"Good Lord, a fellow can't read all day," Dick went on, half in soliloquy, half addressing his companion.

"Monsieur is comfortable here?" asked the latter solicitously.

"I should say, old fellow. I was never in better quarters in all my life."

"And zere is nothing more I could get for ze table?"

"For goodness sake, don't talk like that, Pierre! In any case I don't worry about what I eat. But this is a regular Delmonico's. Guadalupe is certainly a crackerjack cook. She is even better than Sing Ling. Wherever did she learn to turn out all these little delicacies? And just my favorite dishes, too."

Pierre smiled enigmatically.

"Guadalupe very clever old squaw," he remarked.

"I would like to know her better. But she keeps out of my sight all the time."

"Guadalupe is very old. She has her fixed ideas."

"I suppose that means she does not love the Americans."

"No doubt. She prefer to be alone—alone with ze white wolf all ze time. And where the white wolf is, monsieur dare not go."

"I understand that all right," laughed Willoughby. "I strolled only once toward the log fire, and the brute showed me a set of teeth which I never wish to see again."

"Ze white wolf guard ze cave well," remarked Pierre, sententiously.

"Oh, I'm not thinking of trying to run away. You know I would never break my word.

But what the dickens am I to do all day long?"

"What do you say? Suppose we go to ze riffle and wash out some gold."

"Great Scott!" exclaimed Dick eagerly. "That's not a bad suggestion. But Don Manuel won't mind?"

"He will be very pleased—he has no use for ze gold."

"And Guadalupe?"

"Long ago she would have killed you if you had gone zere. But not now. She very old, and all her people are dead."

"And the white wolf? That confounded beast won't interfere?"

"No, no. Ze white wolf stay near Guadalupe all ze time."

"Then, by jove, it's a bully idea," cried Dick. "It gets me all right. We'll turn miners, Pierre, and we'll have a rare old sack of nuggets to divide when the time comes for me to go free. I'll be better off in the end than if I were holding down my old job at the rancho," he laughed gaily.

"I will find ze spades and ze pans to wash ze gravel. When shall we begin?"

"Well, wait now," replied Dick, glancing reflectively at the roll of drawings. "I've got to

send these plans away. I want you to get them at
once into the hands of my friend, Lieutenant
Chester Munson. He will know how to forward
them to their proper destination."

"May I suggest one zing?"

"Go ahead, Pierre. What's in your mind?"

"I venture to make one little suggestion. Why
not ask ze young lady to take ze plans to your
friend?"

"Miss Merle Farnsworth?" asked Dick in
surprise. "But how am I to do that?"

"I will promise to arrange a meeting—zat
is, if you are not afraid of Mr. Thurston and
his men."

"Afraid!" shouted Dick. "You give me the
chance to see Merle again, and old Ben Thurston
and all his sleuths may go to blazes."

"Zen I will arrange, and I zink it will please ze
young lady very much to have ze honor of taking
care of ze plans."

"You mean it will be a mighty honor for the
plans to be in her care, Pierre. But I know she
will gladly do me this service. How and when
can I see her?"

"Be ready tomorrow morning by ten o'clock. I
will take you to a quiet place among ze old oak
trees."

"Pierre, you're a regular brick," cried Dick, as he slapped the old Frenchman on the shoulder in the exuberance of his delight.

The following morning they started out for the trysting place. Dick without demur submitted to the usual precautions. He was blindfolded before mounting his pony in the great central domed cavern and it was not until a couple of hours later, after a veritable switchback ride up and down and round about in a bewildering maze, that he was permitted to remove the bandage. Dismounting, he found himself in the heart of a great oak forest, in what precise locality he could not tell, for there was nothing in sight but endless vistas of tree trunks under their thick canopy of green leaves.

Pierre touched him on the shoulder, and he followed the direction of the Frenchman's eyes. There, advancing through the sylvan twilight, was Merle Farnsworth, her hands eagerly extended, her face lighted with joy. Following at a little distance came Tia Teresa.

Dick, hastening to meet Merle, took both her hands into his, and gazed deep into her eyes.

"Oh, it's great to meet you again," he exclaimed. "And this is my first chance to thank you for having saved me the other night. My word, but you

were quick to think and to act. You cannot know
how I admired your courage and coolness."

"Nonsense, nonsense," protested Merle, in
sweet blushing confusion. "You make far too
much of the little I did."

"You saved my life," said Dick, determinedly.
"You can call that a little thing if you choose."

"No, no," she replied, earnestly. "If I really
did that, then it was truly a big thing."

"For me."

"And for all of us," she added, with face half-
averted.

"And you, too?" pressed Dick.

"Yes, for me, too," answered Merle, turning
round and frankly meeting his gaze. "I should
never have been happy again had any harm come
to you there—that night—in my very home—
without a proper effort to get you away to a place
of safety."

"God bless you, Merle, dear," exclaimed Dick,
as again he pressed her hands. He had been
carried away by his fervent emotions, but she
did not resent the familiar and endearing manner
of his address.

He would have taken her in his arms there and
then, but Merle drew back and gave a little glance
aside. Then Dick remembered Tia Teresa. To

his astonishment he found her chatting with Pierre Luzon as if they were old friends.

Dick left Merle for the moment to greet the duenna.

"And I have to thank you, too, for helping me," he said. Then he added with a laugh: "When am I to be privileged to wear that mantilla again?"

"You are not to be allowed to endanger yourself again," replied Tia Teresa. "And I warn you now. We remain here only half an hour—these are our orders."

"Whose orders?"

"Never mind. Just one half hour, that is all."

"Then I'll make the best of my time," exclaimed Dick, turning toward Merle. "I see you won't be lonely with my gallant friend, Pierre Luzon," he added with a smile.

"Oh, I knew Pierre when he was just as handsome a young fellow as yourself," retorted Tia Teresa. "But we'll excuse you, and Pierre will keep the time."

Dick led Merle down a glade of the forest, but before doing so he had unstrapped the roll of drawings from the horn of his saddle.

"What are you carrying so very carefully?" asked Merle.

"My plans for the ideal city. I told you I was going to have a try in that competition."

"I hope you'll have good luck."

"Well, I want you to help me. Will you take this package, please, to Chester Munson and ask him to send it to the proper address?"

"With the greatest of pleasure, Mr. Willoughby" —and she put forth her hands for the roll.

"No—we'll lay it down here for the present. This log will serve as a seat. See, this twisted limb makes quite a comfortable nook for you." He had halted at a fallen tree, had dropped the drawing on the turf, and was now dusting away the twigs and leaves from the seat he had chosen.

"Cannot I look at the drawings?" she asked, after settling herself cosily.

"Before handing them to Munson, if you like. But there are other things to talk about now." As he spoke he tossed his hat on the ground at her feet.

"Are you growing impatient over your confinement?" she asked.

"Impatient—it is hardly the word. I long to be out in the world again. I could never have endured the long seclusion but for my work over these drawings and my thoughts of you."

"Why me?"

"I have felt that I am doing the best for your sake as well as my own. I would not have had you subjected to the vulgar gaze of a crowded court room—not for worlds. The very thought that I have saved you from that has made me contented with my enforced idleness."

"Not idleness," she said, tapping the roll of drawings with the toe of her shoe.

"Well, no, not idleness exactly."

"And I do hope you'll win the prize," she added, looking up into his eyes.

"So do I. But perhaps you don't know what I count to be the real prize."

"Pray, what is that?"

Dick thrust a hand into the breast of his coat and brought forth a pocket book. From this he produced a little package, and opening the folds of paper disclosed the white rose which she had sent him on the night of his escape from La Siesta.

"Where did you get that?" she asked demurely.

"It is your rose—the rose you sent me."

"I did not know you were so partial to roses as to keep them after they are withered." Her voice trembled; she bravely tried to keep up the pretence of not understanding.

"It is not the gift I treasure—it is the thought
of who was the giver."

A blush stole over her beautiful face, while the
long drooping eyelashes half concealed her brown
eyes.   Dick's arms slipped around the girl's
slender waist.

"Merle, my dear, I love you.   For months past
I have known that there is no woman on earth for
me but you.   I would have spoken before, but I
have always been afraid that you could not love
me, and that talk of such a thing might terminate
a friendship that had become my greatest pleasure
in life."

For reply, placing one hand on his shoulder,
she just buried her face in his breast and gave way
to tears—tears of joy, he knew, as he kissed
her hair again and again, and then at last her
lips when she allowed him to raise her face
toward his.

"My darling," he murmured, and the kiss she
gave him back accepted and returned the words
of fond endearment.

A moment of restful bliss followed; then Merle
gently disengaged herself and rose to her feet.

"What will Tia Teresa say?" she asked, laughingly, as she glanced over her shoulder.

"I think Tia Teresa knew all about my love

long ago," replied Dick. "Yes, both she and Pierre Luzon, too."

"Then you have been wearing your heart on your sleeve."

"Or we have been surrounded by very observant people. But, I say, Merle, this reminds me of a thing I had quite forgotten for the moment." His face fell. "There is one great barrier that stands between us."

"What do you mean? You are surely too strong and purposeful a man to care for barriers."

"I never knew until the other day that you are so very rich."

"Rich!" laughed Merle. "Who ever told you such a foolish thing? While of course I have never felt poverty, don't you know that I am absolutely dependent upon Mrs. Darlington's kindness and generosity to me, her adopted daughter?"

A smile of understanding broke over Dick's face.

"You tell me that? I am so delighted," he exclaimed.

"You surely know my story well enough," continued Merle, "not to have mistaken me for an heiress. I lost both father and mother when I was a baby. Mrs. Darlington took me to her heart, and no mother could have been dearer and

sweeter than she, no sister kinder and more loving
than Grace. But I am proud to think they have
loved me for my own sake, not for any wealth I
might have owned."

"Then there is no barrier," cried Dick, as once
again he drew her to him. "Unless my poverty is
a barrier," he added. "But won't I work hard all
my life to give you every comfort you can desire!"

"Well, we'll have a good start at all events,"
said Merle, with a merry little upglance.

"How's that?"

"The ten-thousand-dollar prize for the best
plans. Have you forgotten about that already?"

"But it is not won yet."

"Oh, I have the firm presentiment that you are
going to win, Dick, dear. I am sure of it—sure!"
she repeated in a tone of conviction.

Her face was aglow and Dick caught the spirit
of her enthusiasm.

"Then I'm sure, too. And, by jove, won't we
have one grand honeymoon trip, dearest?"

CHAPTER XXVIII

The Prize Winner

DICK WILLOUGHBY'S sensational escape from La Siesta had added another thrill to the mystery surrounding the murder of Marshall Thurston. But as week succeeded week without further incident, the affair gradually faded away as a topic of conversation. All the talk now was about the coming of the new town. The fever of speculation was in the air.

"Say, boys," remarked Jack Rover one evening to his two cronies at the store, "I'm sure getting crazy about the new town. I've got a thousand bones of my own savings besides the money from old Pierre Luzon, and I'm going to invest every dangnation cent of it in town lots on opening day. You bet I'll be there mighty early in the morning when the sale starts."

"I'm sorta locoed myself," said Baker, "about them lots in the new town. Guess I'll grab off a few good corners. I look for an early rise— prices'll go up like blazes, I'm 'lowin'."

Buck Ashley snorted contemptuously. "Say,

you fellers are two dippy ones. That new town talk is a lot o' hot air, d'you hear? Jest the agitatin' work of them pesky town boomers. Won't 'mount to nothin'."

Jack Rover started a defence, but was quickly motioned to silence by old Tom Baker, who, after clearing his throat, pushed his hat back and glared at Buck Ashley.

"Buck," said he, "you're a thick-headed fool. The openin' of that town will amount to one hell of a sight, don't you fergit it. Why, that Los Angeles syndicate cuss who's a-runnin' the machine is sharper than a razor blade. Just think for one little puny moment," Tom Baker went on, enthusiastically, "of that printed notice being in every blamed newspaper in the whole country— yes, and on the other side of the Atlantic pond— offerin' ten thousand dollars for the best plans for an ideal city. Gosh all hemlock, they do say as how the mails were just chuck full of answers— architect fellers as well as them as ain't architects, a-tryin' to get their hooks on that ten-thousand-dollar prize. It was a mighty smart business notion, I'm a-tellin' you, and has boomed the town to beat the band."

"But," inquired Buck Ashley, in a sarcastic way, "who is confounded fool enough to buy lots in such a wild-cat scheme, no matter how much they advertise it? That's what I'm askin'."

"I will, for one," said Jack Rover. "As I said before, I'm going to put in my last dollar."

"As for me," chimed in Tom Baker, "I will lay my money on this 'ere proposed new town bein' the biggest town in the whole dangnation State of California outside of sea-board towns."

Just then through the gathering darkness a lone horseman rode up to the store, dismounted and came hurriedly in. It was none other than Chester Munson, flushed and excited, as he sang out a good-natured salute: "Hallo, boys. I have news for you."

As he spoke he pulled a Bakersfield daily paper from his pocket. "The new town!" he fairly shouted. "All about it, right on the front page, pictures and all. And it is Dick Willoughby who wins the ten-thousand-dollar prize!"

"That's great news, sure," cried Jack.

"It's a mighty pity Dick ain't here to celebrate," growled the sheriff.

"What's to be the name of the town?" asked Buck Ashley, in a disbelieving tone.

"Tejon, after the old fort here," replied Munson, as he pointed to the featured article with its big-type headlines and started to cull a few sentences.

"It says that the new city of Tejon, right here in the heart of a rich horticultural valley, is bound to be one of the top-notch towns of California. And the opening day is going to be immense. Next Tuesday is the date fixed. Maps and plans of the new town will be ready for distribution from the land company's office, corner Main Street and Broadway, at nine o'clock Monday morning. Let me see," he went on, looking up from the paper, "this is Wednesday. Mighty few days to wait, boys. You just ought to see the excitement in Bakersfield."

"Well, I say there ain't no such town," snapped Buck Ashley, "nor no such a company's office buildin', 'cause I was down there day before yesterday myself, right where them surveyin' fellers have been foolin' 'round for weeks, peekin' through spy-glasses at each other and measurin' off so many feet this way and so many feet that way, like a bunch o' kids playin' some game. No, siree, there's nothin' but long rows of white stakes driv in the ground. Looks to me as if they was a-gettin' ready to build a lot of hen-houses. Of course the railroad's there, and the only thing changed that I could see was a lot of side-tracks they've put in."

"Well, things have been humming the last two days," laughed Munson. "This afternoon I found all the side-tracks filled with trains of lumber, carload after carload, and not less than two or three hundred workmen, all as busy as nailers. Looked to me as if a three-ring circus were getting ready for a big show. They are already running up electric light poles and stringing the wires. Some of the men are unloading cars, some stacking up lumber, others are putting up tents, and the entire business reminded me of a hive of extremely busy bees. Go down and look for yourself, Buck, and you'll be convinced at last that the new town has arrived."

The old storekeeper had come from behind the counter, and stood leaning against a stack of boxes.

"I've been here for more'n a quarter of a century, boys," he said, in a tone of seriousness that approached to sadness, "and this old store seems like home to me. I'm some fighter and I'm some stayer. But, hell, I reckon I know when I'm licked. I guess this new town puts a crimp in me and my business, and—".

"Honk-honk; honk-honk"—it was the distant warning of an automobile that interrupted Buck's speech, and drew all four present to the doorway. There was the glare of twin headlights on the southern road.

"Some of the Los Angeles buyers, most likely," suggested the sheriff.

And so the travellers proved to be. The automobile halted at the store, but only one of the party of four or five descended., He was a bright-faced, clean-shaven man, of dapper build and faultlessly attired. In his hand was a bunch of papers.

"Mr. Buck Ashley?" he inquired.

"I'm your man," replied Buck, stepping from the doorway.

"Well, we can't stop tonight. But we wanted to say 'how-do.' I represent the Los Angeles Trust Syndicate, and these documents just arrived yesterday from Washington, D. C."

"Can't be for me, then," replied Buck, hesitating to take the proffered papers.

"But they are," replied the stranger with a laugh. "Oh, we haven't forgotten the interests of the old identities. We've had your name in mind all the time, and this is a removal order from the Government to change your postoffice over to the new town of Tejon."

Buck was speechless as his fingers closed on the documents.

"We'll hope to see you over on Tuesday morning, Mr. Ashley, so that you can secure a good

site for your new store. Now I must be going.
We have got to be in Bakersfield by eleven
o'clock."

"Honk-honk," and the automobile was gone.

"Hell, Buck, have you lost your tongue?"
cried Tom Baker, slapping the storekeeper on the
shoulder. "Don't you see what it all means?
You're goin' to shift camp, old man; you're goin'
into the new town."

"Gosh 'lmighty!" murmured Buck, at last
recovering the power of articulation. "I think
the first thing to do is to lubricate."

"A taste from the mystery keg," suggested the
sheriff, as they all crowded back into the store.

"The mystery keg? What's that?" asked
Munson.

Buck laid his hand on a small barrel at the end
of the counter.

"We call it the mystery keg," he replied,
"because we just found it yesterday mornin'
settin' at my back door. It has come to us sorta
like manna from heaven."

"And tastes like manna, too," interjected
Baker.

"It means free drinks for all this pertic'lar
bunch," continued Buck, "for there is no question
as to where the keg came from. Look at the

date on the top—1853. This 'ere barrel came out of Joaquin Murietta's wine cellar."

"You don't say?" exclaimed Munson, pressing forward eagerly to examine the little brass-hooped keg, looking bright and sound despite its antiquity.

"This whisky is sixty years old at least," Buck went on, turning the tap and filling a small pitcher.

"Tastes like it might be a hundred years older," remarked the sheriff. "Mellow as fresh drawn milk."

Buck handed Munson a pony glass of the rare old beverage.

"By jove, it is fine," said the lieutenant, judicially smacking his lips.

"Just makes my internals feel as soft and roly-poly as a ripe pomegranate," murmured Tom, as he set down his empty glass and rubbed his belt-line in a complacent way.

"Well, we'll fill up again, boys," cried Buck. "Here's to dear old Pierre Luzon, for it was sure him who sent us the mystery keg."

"And to Dick Willoughby who won the prize," cried Jack Rover.

"And to our host," added Munson in a courtly way. "To Buck Ashley, boys, the postmaster of the new city of Tejon."

"Hip, hip, hurrah!"—all four voices shouted the triple toast as the upraised glasses clinked merrily.

Buck resumed his former position, with his back against the cracker boxes.

"As I was sayin', boys, when that automobile interrupted us, I know when I'm licked. But I know, too, that the fightin' blood is still left in me, and I was a-goin' to remark that this new town sure 'nuff looks a winner. I've got plenty of lumber right in my back yard, and tomorrer mornin' I begin to have the scantlin's cut, for, by jingoes, I'll be the chap who will build the first buildin' in the new town."

"Bully for you," cried Munson.

"I say what I mean," continued Buck, his face aglow with enthusiasm, "and on Tuesday mornin' I'll buy the first town lot if I have to stand in line for forty-eight hours to get it."

"Life in the old dog yet," laughed Jack Rover.

"It's wonderful the effect of Pierre Luzon's brew," smiled the sheriff. "I think we'll just have four more spoonfuls, Buck, of that distilled nectar of sunshine. Success to the new store, old man!"

CHAPTER XXIX

The Rendezvous

SUMMER had come and gone and it was now the early days of October. The mystery of Dick Willoughby's disappearance had remained unsolved, yet it was on his plans that the new city of Tejon had been laid out, and, like the fabled palace in the Arabian Nights' tale, had sprung into being with such rapidity that men rubbed their eyes to satisfy themselves whether the transformation scene were an actuality or the baseless fabric of a dream. Within three months of the opening day auction of lots Tejon was a thriving, hustling centre of population, with whole avenues of beautiful homes, several blocks of stores on the main street, schoolhouse and other public buildings well on the way to completion.

Electricity had helped to the accomplishment of the miracle, for it had been only necessary to tap the great power cables running across the old rancho from the Kern River canyon to secure the supplies of "juice" both for lighting and traction purposes. So there was already an interurban tramway service connecting with the county seat, Bakersfield, while at night the new town was a blaze of electricity. All around country homes were going up, and ten and twenty acre holdings were being planted to fruit trees or ploughed for alfalfa.

Ben Thurston still clung to the ranch house, although it was definitely understood now between him and the new owners that Thanksgiving Day was to be the extreme limit of his occupancy. The hue and cry after Dick Willoughby had in a measure subsided, but, if the authorities had relaxed their efforts, Thurston still sought relentlessly and indefatigably for the man accused of the slaying of his son.

One night at a lonely road-house on the outskirts of Bakersfield, the sleuth, Leach Sharkey, was in close and secret conference with a bent and bowed old man. This was none other than Pierre Luzon, although his physical condition seemed to have greatly changed and he answered now to the name of José.

The two men had met a few days before on the range; Pierre had spoken of the scant living he was making from a herd of goats he pastured on the mountains, and in the course of conversation had thrown out a hint for information as to the amount of the reward that Mr. Thurston would be willing to pay if Dick Willoughby were handed over to him. Sharkey had eagerly followed the lead thus given. Hence this midnight meeting in the road-house parlor for the discussion of terms and conditions over the bottle of whisky that helps so efficaciously to dispel distrust and unloosen tongues.

More than an hour had been spent in skirmishing preliminaries, but now Leach Sharkey was congratulating himself that he had got his man fixed just right. He was running over the final arrangements so as to make sure that everything was clearly understood.

"Then Mr. Thurston and myself are to come to Comanche Point. You will take us from there to the place where we'll find Willoughby. That's the understanding, José?"

Pierre nodded in acquiescence.

"And you will bring wiz you ze reward of five tousand dollars—not gold or silver, remember, but treasury bills, for I am not strong enough now to carry a very heavy weight. Zen when you have paid me ze money, I will lead you to Mr. Willoughby."

"All right. I'm going to trust you and take my chances. But bear in mind that you don't get away with the cash until I have actually put the handcuffs on the man I'm after."

"Oh, I will not run away, Mr. Sharkey."

"By God, if you try any monkey tricks on me, I'll shoot you in your tracks. Make no mistake about that, José. And it will be hands up first to prove to me you have no gun."

"As I have promised," replied Pierre with some dignity, "I shall come unarmed. But remember, Mr. Thurston and you must be alone. If zere are any ozers I will not show myself—I will give no sign."

"Don't worry about that. We'll be alone. I need no other protection than the two guns I always carry." As he spoke, the sleuth slipped a hand to one of his hip pockets, and with a grim smile, laid a vicious-looking revolver on the table.

Luzon evinced no disquietude; he merely smiled.

"Mr. Sharkey he is ze famous man wiz ze two guns. I would take no risk wiz him. But I wish to win ze reward."

"Well, then, the reward is yours if you play the game straight. Thurston and I will be there, and you will be there unarmed. The hour?"

"Four o'clock. I will watch you come to Comanche Point all alone along ze road."

"You're certainly a cautious old duck," laughed Sharkey. "However, that's all right. Four o'clock, then. And you said Tuesday next week, didn't you?"

"Yes, Tuesday."

Sharkey glanced at a big advertisement calendar on the wall.

"That will be the eleventh of the month. Then I think everything is understood. Now I want to be off. I can just catch the last car to Tejon. Shake. You can finish that drop of whisky by yourself, old man."

They shook hands and Sharkey was gone.

The other waited for a few moments, cautiously and cunningly listening to the retreating footsteps. Then he sprang erect, transformed in an instant into a hale and vigorous man. Into his eyes there leapt a flash of joy, in his heart was a song of triumph.

"So the villain Ben Thurston will be there at Comanche Point on the very anniversary of the night, just thirty years ago, when he committed that foul crime—at the very spot where the poor little Senorita Rosetta and her unborn babe perished at his hands. Glory be to God! At last the hour of vengeance comes!"

Chapter XXX

Don Manuel Appears

A GOODLY little sack of water-worn nuggets of gold had been washed out of the subterranean stream by Pierre Luzon and Dick Willoughby. The captive had found in the work both an exciting pastime and the ease of mind that comes from the thought that his time was being spent to profitable account. So week after week he had toiled on cheerfully, setting for himself each day a full day's task. In this way also, although the want of sunshine had paled his cheeks, he had maintained his health by the regular physical exercise.

But as the appointed date of his release drew near, Dick's mining enthusiasm suffered an eclipse. The gold no longer tempted him, the eight-hour day became a burden to his soul, his whole being was possessed with feverish restlessness. He was not only filled with eager excitement at the thought of again folding Merle in his arms, but he was fired with curiosity to know what events were happening outside which would enable him

The Fight on the Cliff — Page 360

to step forth a free man, exculpated from all connection with the crime of which he had been suspected, restored to an honorable place among his fellow men.

But Pierre remained obstinately deaf to all hints for information.

"I can say nozing," was his invariable reply. Then, to divert Dick's mind, he would challenge him at chess, a game in which they had proved to be pretty equally matched, or he would produce the latest batch of newspapers.

The young fellow had read with great delight the announcement that his plans for the ideal city had been awarded the prize of ten thousand dollars. Still more welcome had been the warmly congratulatory note received from Merle at the hands of Pierre; for this letter, while it made no reference to the point, virtually sealed the pact between the two lovers that the money would provide for a glorious honeymoon trip to Europe. Dick had sent instructions to Munson to notify the Los Angeles syndicate in his name that the reward was to remain to the credit of the winner until he would come personally to Tejon to claim it, probably about the middle of October.

It wanted now only two days of the fateful date, the eleventh of that month. Dick had already gathered together his personal belongings ready for removal. He was pacing the grotto, when his eye chanced to fall upon the sack of gold.

"I forgot about that, Pierre, old fellow," he remarked. "We have to divide this spoil."

"No," replied Pierre, with quiet determination, "it is all yours, Mr. Willoughby, honestly earned, too. I have no need for any of ze gold. I have all ze money I can ever spend during ze rest of my life."

No amount of argument could shake the old Frenchman's resolution.

"Then what is to be done with the sack? By jove, I'll share it with our Hidden Treasure Syndicate. By the way, where is Jack Rover now, Pierre?"

"He is living in Buck Ashley's old store. Buck, you know, is ze postmaster at Tejon, and has a splendid store in ze new city. But Jack Rover, he just hang about ze old place."

"Well, Pierre, I've got a plan. You say it will not be until Tuesday afternoon that I leave these quarters?"

"Zat is so, and I am sorry you must still wear ze blindfold, but it will be for ze last time now."

"Oh, I'm not kicking about that. I know the

conditions under which I came here. But it will be evening when we get clear of the hills, and I won't have any particular place to go to. Next morning it will be best for me to ride right over to Bakersfield, to surrender myself and secure my formal discharge. When, did you say, am I to get the necessary documents for all this?"

"Before you depart from ze cave."

"Well, everything will fit in fine. Tomorrow you have kindly promised to take out my things. Just carry the nuggets along with you also, and leave everything in Jack's charge. But tell him that nothing must be opened or disturbed until I arrive. I'm going to give Jack Rover the surprise of his life when he sees that gold. The sack is too heavy to handle, but I guess we can make it into several packages. Jack was always crazy to find Guadalupe's sand-bar."

"So were lots of ozers," grinned Pierre. "But they have never found it yet. Even you will not be able to find it again when you are led out of zese hills wearing ze blindfold."

"I am fully aware of that, old man," laughed Dick in reply. "I suppose I couldn't discover the place again in a hundred years. But Jack's eyes will fairly pop when he sees that bunch of gold marbles. He will be mighty pleased to show the nuggets around to some of the boys who have laughed over his enthusiasm, always declaring that Guadalupe's gold simply came from some old-timer's sack of dust that had been part of Joaquin Murietta's plunder."

"Oh, no. All ze bandits get out much gold from ze riffle in zose days—Don Manuel himself had plenty."

"Well, Pierre, you just pack all my belongings to Buck Ashley's old store. And you tell Jack Rover to expect me about six o'clock the night after tomorrow—that's Tuesday. And I wish Munson to be there, too—I'll want him to accompany me to Bakersfield."

"If you write a leetle note to ze lieutenant," suggested Pierre, "I will see zat it reaches his hands. But you must say very leetle—just a few words. For nozing must be told to anyone outside until you are free."

"All right, Pierre. Here goes." And Dick seated himself at the writing table. In a very few moments he had completed his task.

"See," he said, returning to Pierre's side. "I wish you to know exactly what I have written—just a hurried scrawl." And he read aloud while the old Frenchman's eyes rested on the paper:

"On Tuesday night next, about six o'clock, meet me at Buck Ashley's old store. I shall want you to ride over to Bakersfield with me next morning, where my acquittal is assured. Give Merle the glad news.   Yours, DICK."

"Guess that's all right?" he added, as he folded the note and placed it in an envelope on which he had already inscribed the name of Lieutenant Munson.

Pierre had signified his approval with a nod, and now he carefully bestowed the letter in the pocket of his shirt.

"He will get ze letter—he will surely be zere."

"Then you say I cannot write to Merle—Miss Farnsworth, I mean?"

"I have ze strictest orders," replied Pierre. "Nozing must be told just yet. Bah! It is only two days more."

"Two mighty long days for me, old sport," said Dick, half in jest and half in sober earnest, as he sat down and began cutting at a plug of tobacco.

Most of next day Willoughby was alone. But at the regular dinner hour Pierre appeared, and announced that he had safely packed the valise and the gold in four bags to the old store, and Jack

Rover had been apprised of Dick's coming on the following night.

"He knew what was in ze sacks," laughed Pierre. "Zey were so very heavy, oh my! But I told him I would come back and shoot him like a jack-rabbit if he opened zem before you came."

"Guess it needed an old bandit like you to scare Jack Rover," replied Dick, jocularly. But he was very happy—everything was going along well—only another four-and-twenty hours now and his captivity would be at an end.

That night Dick could hardly sleep a wink, and next morning he was too restless and impatient for his approaching liberation to keep within the confines of the little grotto. In the darkness of the big central cavern he walked up and down, casting occasional glances at the distant glow of the log fire where, as he could see, both the aged squaw and the white wolf were on vigilant and ceaseless guard.

Suddenly his steps were arrested. With great surprise he gazed toward the log fire. There, with Guadalupe and the white wolf, stood the figure of a strange man, cloaked and wearing a big sombrero. All their shapes were outlined against the ruddy glow, and the monstrous beast was actually fawning at the newcomer's feet. A moment later the stranger, with a parting wave of his hand to Guadalupe, advanced toward the spot where Dick was standing. Close by was an oil lantern set in a socket of the rock wall to mark the entrance to the inner grotto.

For a minute the approaching figure had been swallowed up in the darkness, but now came the sound of his footsteps crunching on the sandy floor, and a few seconds later he appeared in the flickering radiance. Dick Willoughby had already made his inference as to the identity of the newcomer—he had been so often told that no living man but the bandit chief, Don Manuel, could pass the white wolf with impunity.

But the name Dick pronounced was quite a different one.

"Senor Ricardo Robles—it is you—*you?*"

"It is I," replied the Spaniard, quietly, as he extended his hand.

"Then you are—Don Manuel—the—"

Dick faltered and paused.

"Yes, I am Don Manuel de Valencia, the outlaw, the bandit of Tehachapi, the White Wolf, as he is commonly called. Come within, my friend. I have matters of importance to communicate."

And the visitor led the way with an ease that

showed his perfect familiarity with every opening and turning in the great subterranean series of chambers.

"I cannot remain with you very long," said Mr. Robles, when they were seated in the inner grotto, "for I have a number of things to attend to during the few hours that still remain at my disposal."

"I must not ask questions," remarked Dick, although his words belied the questioning look in his eyes.

"Oh, although I speak in confidence," Mr. Robles replied, "having learned to trust you, I shall make no secret of my contemplated movements. Tonight I hope to settle my last score"— he paused, then corrected himself—"my last piece of business in California. If all goes well, within twenty-four hours I shall be on the high seas. Never mind my exact route, but my final destination is Spain, the land of my fathers. There, perhaps, you and I may meet again."

"I hope so. I have come to be deeply interested in you, Mr. Robles."

"And I in you, young man, all the more because you are now engaged to one I hold very dear. Since her birth, Merle Farnsworth has been a— little protégée of mine." Again he had hesitated, and his voice had vibrated from emotion. But he was smiling now as he went on: "I have watched with sympathetic interest and approval the progress of your love affair."

"Through your spy-glass on the tower?" laughed Dick.

"Well, partly in that way, perhaps," replied Mr. Robles, with eyebrows humorously upraised. "You have had my quiet support from beginning to end, and now that you have won the young lady's heart, you have my most sincere congratulations. May you have long years together, and every happiness."

He had clasped Dick's hand, and placed his disengaged hand affectionately on the young man's shoulder.

"You are really very kind," said Dick, cordially responding to the hand clasp.

"Because I have counted you worthy of your great good fortune in winning such a girl as Merle. And I have taken much the same liking to your friend, Chester Munson. Have you heard the news?"

"No, but I can guess it."

"Yes, he and Grace Darlington are engaged. And to them I give my heartiest blessing just as I have given it to you and Merle. For Grace, like her adopted sister, has been always very dear to me. I have loved them both very dearly indeed all through their young lives."

"And both are devoted to you, as I happen to know," affirmed Dick with warm conviction.

"I believe it," replied Mr. Robles. His hand sought an inner pocket and drew forth a legal-looking document. "I came here not only to bid you good-bye, but more important still to place this in your possession."

"My release?" exclaimed Dick eagerly, as his fingers closed on the paper.

"Well, not exactly—but it will lead to that, never fear. It is an affidavit which has been properly sworn to before a San Francisco notary public. It briefly sets out my confession. It was I, Don Manuel de Valencia, who killed Marshall Thurston, or at least was responsible for his killing."

As he spoke the words, the outlaw drew himself proudly erect. Dick was too overwhelmed with amazement to reply.

"The young ruffian was shot partly because he deserved his fate for insulting Merle, partly because, as you cannot but know, Don Manuel, the White Wolf, had sworn a vendetta against the whole Thurston brood."

"Then Ben Thurston—is he dead, too?" gasped the listener.

"Not yet," was the grim reply. Then he paused and changed his tone.

"But I want to speak not another word about this. What happens to Ben Thurston is nothing of your concern—must be nothing of your concern. For this document here frees you from all legal entanglements, and I have no wish that you should by any chance become enmeshed again. So we dismiss Ben Thurston from our talk and from our minds. When you lodge this paper with the authorities at Bakersfield, it will be a matter only of a few formalities to secure dismissal of the charge against you. For I even put it on sworn record that your jail delivery that night was against your will."

"I have forgotten to thank you for that same delivery. I never dreamed you were my liberator, Mr. Robles."

"Because that night I was Don Manuel de Valencia. But at present I am Ricardo Robles, and in that capacity it is for me to thank you for having so chivalrously protected our dear Merle from the necessity of associating her name in any way with the death of that worthless young scoundrel. I appreciate the cheerful manner in which you have, for her sake, and let me add, for my sake, too, borne your long imprisonment here."

"I've been mighty comfortable," laughed Dick, with a glance around his luxurious quarters. "And Pierre Luzon has been a treasure—a good comrade all the time."

"Ah, yes, Pierre," exclaimed the outlaw, musingly. "Pierre is a very good fellow. He has been faithful to me for thirty long years."

"And where does he go after tonight?" asked Dick. "He cannot stay here, all alone except for Guadalupe."

"Everything is arranged. Guadalupe is accustomed to live alone. But tonight Pierre accompanies me on my long journey."

"So we may all meet again?"

"Yes, we may all meet again," responded Robles, slowly and gravely, "far, far away from the Tehachapi mountains. But now I must go," he went on in a brisk tone, "for I have to make some final preparations. You have the affidavit; see that you do not lose it on your ride down the mountains."

"You just bet I won't," replied Dick, as he held tightly to the precious document with both hands.

"Pierre will come for you here early in the afternoon. Be prepared to go with him then. As for myself, Willoughby, there is for the present only one word more to be spoken. *Adios!*"

Again they clasped hands, and a moment later Don Manuel was gone.

Chapter XXXI

Shadows of the Past

IN a little summer-house at the edge of the rose
garden of La Siesta, Tia Teresa was seated
all alone. She was awaiting the coming of
Mr. Robles to a rendezvous which he had arranged by a confidential message sent on the previous evening. It wanted some time yet of the
appointed hour, but in her state of deep emotion
and repressed excitement she had gladly sought
the solitude of this secluded corner. Deep in
thought, her mind was divided between the far-
away past and the near-impending future.

Each recurring year this day to her had always
been a sad and tragic anniversary. In the early
hours of the morning she had been to the old
Mexican cemetery on the hillside, and had be-
decked with flowers the grave marked by the
marble cross bearing the single word "Hermana,"
also the graves close by of the parents of Don
Manuel and Rosetta, the children she had nursed
and tended and fondled from infancy to early
manhood and womanhood, through twenty years

of unalloyed happiness until the gringo had come, the ancestral acres had been filched away, and dishonor and death been brought to the slumbrously peaceful home.

And from that slumbrous peace what a sudden and terrible change! On this day thirty years ago poor little Rosetta had been found done to death beneath the precipice at Comanche Point. No less done to death by the shock and shame of the pitiful story thus revealed, the aged parents of the beautiful young girl were, within a few days, sleeping their long last sleep by her side in the churchyard on the hill. A whole family blighted and withered as by the blast of some death-laden sirocco.

Then had followed the years of terror during which Don Manuel, the White Wolf, the dreaded outlaw, had wreaked his vengeance on the whole race of gringos. She had never seen him all through that time, although at intervals money had reached her by Pierre Luzon's trusted hand, enabling her to maintain herself in the little Mexican village near the old fort of Tejon. At last had come the fight when the band of outlaws had been finally dispersed, Pierre Luzon wounded and dragged away to serve the rest of his days in prison, Don Manuel vanished like a wraith in the mist, gone where no man could tell.

But through the years that succeeded, Tia Teresa had known that he lived—had known in her heart of hearts that he would live until the vendetta he had sworn against Ben Thurston would be accomplished. The remittances that arrived from time to time, first from Spain, then from England, needed no signature to show that they were from her young master of former years and that he still held his faithful old nurse in affectionate remembrance. And at last had come the crowning surprise of all.

Tia Teresa had been bidden to come to Los Angeles by a letter which bore a strange signature, but the handwriting of which she had immediately recognized. And there, in a fine home beneath the foothills that skirt the city to the north, she had found Don Manuel again, much older in manner than by lapse of years—quiet, reserved, tinged with a sadness of which she knew the cause, but happy withal, for he was married to a beautiful English girl and had a little baby daughter. And as nurse to this child Tia Teresa, to her great joy, was promptly installed.

Thus again she had become the trusted servant in Don Manuel's home, the only one around him possessing his full confidence and knowing the secret story of his past. For, amid these changed surroundings, his name was Ricardo Robles, his standing that of a Spaniard or Mexican of wealth, of scholarly tastes, and devoted to the seclusion of his home with its spacious surrounding gardens.

Their next door neighbors were an English family named Darlington, Mrs. Darlington and Mrs. Robles having been life-long friends. And here, too, was another tiny child in the home, likewise a daughter.

Seated in the summer-house, Tia Teresa was going over in her mind the whole chain of happenings—the new era that had dawned and had brought the hope of restored and abiding happiness for Don Manuel. But it had been fated not so to be. Within a year his young wife had died, his child was motherless, he himself, if not alone in the world, was broken-hearted. For a spell he had fits of brooding, then all of a sudden he had sold the home that could only henceforth be for him a place of saddening memories.

His daughter Merle, taking her English mother's maiden name of Farnsworth, was transferred to the loving care of Mrs. Darlington. Thus had it come about that Grace Darlington and Merle Farnsworth had been brought up as sisters, with

Tia Teresa their nurse, and in later years their devoted attendant.

Ricardo Robles had resolved to travel, but Tia Teresa had quickly divined that the vendetta was again in his heart. For no other reason could he have decided on masking the paternity of his infant daughter by giving her the maternal name. And from Tia Teresa Don Manuel had no secret to conceal. "Yes." He had sworn he would hunt Ben Thurston through Europe, and it was to protect the future life of his child from any association with future consequences of the blood feud that he had handed her over to his friends under their solemn promise that, as Merle grew up, she should never know anything more than that both her parents had died.

So once again Don Manuel had gone his way and disappeared. Some years later the Darlington home had been transferred to England, where Mr. Darlington had fallen heir to some ancestral estates. Again, after a lapse of years, another change had occurred—Mr. Darlington dying, and Mrs. Darlington being left a widow in the big, now gloomy, English country-house, with Grace and Merle approaching young womanhood, and all of them, Tia Teresa included, longing again for the sunshine of California.

Intermittently during those years in England, Ricardo Robles had visited his friends, but the secret about his real relationship to Merle had always been preserved. Both daughters in the home had been brought up alike to regard him simply as a dear and valued friend, whose comings brought much happiness to their lives in the shape of gifts which preserved fond memories during his prolonged spells of absence.

And while the little family was still plunged in deep sorrow for the death of Mr. Darlington, Mr. Robles had reappeared as the messenger of great joy. For he brought the news that the beautiful rancho of La Siesta, lying in mid-California, among the foothills of the Tejon Valley, had been purchased for the express purpose that the widow and children should make it their future place of abode. In this way had come about the return to the land which each and all already loved best and regarded as truly "home."

"Five years ago!" murmured Tia Teresa pensively. And they had been all so happy here, the young girls growing up with every accomplishment money and the best governesses could bestow, Don Manuel not far away watching the progress and developing beauty of his daughter, always hovering near for acts of helpful kindness.

Five years of placid enjoyment, of unbroken tranquility, till all of a sudden the old enemy had returned and all the rankling wounds of the old vendetta had been reopened!

In the Spanish soul of Tia Teresa there was bitter hate still, and fierce joy even now that the hour of retribution was approaching—that at last after all those years her little Rosetta would be avenged. Yet time had had some mellowing influences, for in her musings now she experienced a vague sense of uneasiness for possible consequences that in former times had never for a moment been tolerated. The true spirit of the vendetta had always been in her very blood—strike when you can, without thought of what may happen next.

But now she was thinking of coming happenings —of sorrow perhaps for Merle, of the undoubted danger for Don Manuel himself.

And while thus she conned the chances, her head bent in deep meditation, her eyes half closed, Ricardo Robles, approaching with noiseless step, stood by her side and laid an affectionate hand upon her shoulder.

"I have come, Tia Teresa," he said simply, as he sat down at the edge of the little rustic table.

Chapter XXXII

Forebodings

"FOR this last hour, Don Manuel," she said, placing a hand on his, "I have been going over all the long story of the past, from the days when you were a little boy and Rosetta was suckled at my bosom. Why should I not have loved her?" asked the old duenna almost fiercely. "Why should I not love her still?" she added, in a lower tone, as she bowed her head and covered her eyes with her disengaged hand. "There is love that can never die, Don Manuel."

"Nor should we wish it otherwise," he said gently, caressing the hand extended toward him. "And this very night our undying love for dear little Rosetta will be proved—tonight at last she will be avenged."

With a start Tia Teresa sat erect.

"Then it is all arranged?" she asked breathlessly.

"Yes, all finally arranged," was his quiet rejoinder. "We meet this evening on Comanche Point—the place where I have always vowed he should answer for his crime. And you remember what day this is?"

"I remember—can I ever forget?—the very day we found her dead beneath the cliff."

"The very day, Tia Teresa. So my vengeance will be complete. Before now I could have shot him a dozen times. But he would never have known that his death was by my hand. Tonight, however, he will know. And he will realize that the vendetta is the law of God—an eye for an eye, a tooth for a tooth; his life, so precious to himself, for hers so dear to us in the happy old-time days."

"But you, Don Manuel?" she asked fearfully.

"It does not matter much about me," he answered. "But all the same I have come to speak a little in regard to myself. Tonight Ben Thurston assuredly will die, and should I perish with him, the story of the vendetta cannot fail to be revived and the identity of the recluse, Ricardo Robles, with Don Manuel, the outlaw, will be established. This will come as a great shock to all my dear friends at La Siesta—to Mrs. Darlington as well as to Grace and Merle. But this counts for little—the name of Don Manuel is just as honorable a name as that of Robles. And you can tell them further that all the loot I ever took from the gringos lies today untouched in Joaquin Murietta's cave. I sullied my hands with none of it. I was made rich by the sale of, my ancestral estates in Spain. And that wealth the law cannot confiscate, for I have been only its trustee during all those years. Everything I possess has been vested from the first in the names of Merle Farnsworth and Grace Darlington."

"Grace as well?" mumured Tia Teresa, enquiringly.

"Certainly, for I love both the girls dearly; there is ample to divide between them, and by ranking them together I guard Merle from the thought that I was anything more to her than to Grace. To both alike I was just a deeply attached friend." He paused a moment, then regarded Tia Teresa fixedly. "For my little girl must never know that her father was an outlaw, with a price on his head; yes, with blood on his hands, if it is only the blood of the worthless Thurston breed."

"That is no stain—it is an honor—it is a duty that you owed," exclaimed the duenna with fervency, her hands clenched against her bosom as she spoke.

"You understand—we understand the vendetta, you and I, Tia Teresa. But the Americanos do not understand. And I have brought up my little girl as an American, for her own happiness I long ago realized. So she would never understand. When she comes to know that her old friend Ricardo Robles was Don Manuel de Valencia as well, she will breathe a gentle prayer of rest for his soul. But she will not be distressed by the knowledge that her father was the bandit and outlaw—she will not have to face the cruel world with that stigma attached to her name. For that I have contrived, for that I have suffered the dumb agony of childlessness all these years."

"And that, in God's name," exclaimed Tia Teresa, "is part of the price Ben Thurston, thrice accursed, has to pay."

"And tonight will pay," responded Don Manuel, determinedly. "But I speak of all this just to put you on your guard. It will be necessary for me to say something to Mrs. Darlington as well. I have brought for her the papers that will establish the rights of Merle and Grace to all I leave behind." As he spoke he touched his coat where the shape of a packet in an inner pocket showed.

"Your will?"

"No. As I have explained, I require no will. The property is theirs already. And I do not need to tell you, my dear Tia Teresa, my beloved friend, that you, too, have not been forgotten."

As he spoke he raised her hand and pressed it reverently to his lips.

"Don't speak like that, Don Manuel," she protested.

"I know that all I owe to you can never be repaid," he continued, humbly, gratefully—"the devoted life-service for me and for Rosetta and our beloved parents as well."

Again he kissed her hand, and this time she accepted the seal of his high-souled and chivalrous regard. There were tears in her eyes now.

"But, Don Manuel, you need not die tonight. Death for him—that is right. But why for you?"

"Perhaps not for me—most certainly," he replied with a little, reassuring smile. "Oh, do not imagine that I deliberately court death for tonight. On the contrary, I have all my plans carefully laid. An automobile is ready for the road, and I have a yacht waiting for me at a quiet spot on the coast, and if all is well, by tomorrow's dawn Pierre and I will be on the ocean. No one around here except at La Siesta will miss Ricardo Robles, and if the name of Don Manuel is associated with the death of Ben Thurston, only once more will the White Wolf have strangely disappeared just as he used to do in the old times."

He was laughing, not loudly, but just with care-free, almost joyous triumph, as he rose to say good-bye.

"Then, Tia Teresa, if events work out just as I have planned, we may all meet again, somewhere, somehow—I cannot say more at present. For I shall be happy to see my little girl happy in her married love, and later on I shall close my eyes contentedly when I can feel assured that nothing from the past will ever emerge to spoil her life or bring to her distress of mind."

Tia Teresa, too, had arisen.

"God grant it may be so," she fervently exclaimed. "But somehow my mind misgives me. Today I am softened as I have never been before. Even for the sake of our dear Rosetta in Heaven I feel inclined to plead with you to let Thurston go his way and the vendetta be forgotten." And she clung to his arm imploringly.

"Never!" cried Don Manuel, putting her gently but resolutely aside. "That can never be, Tia Teresa. You know it. A vow sworn over my wronged and murdered sister's grave, over the graves of my parents as well, must be fulfilled. To break it at the very moment when it is in my power to give it fulfillment would be the act of a coward—a sacrilege that could never be atoned.

No more words like that. I must not even listen."

She was sobbing as she dropped back into her chair. Her silence was the confession that she was powerless to argue against the unwritten law of the vendetta.

"So I kiss you good-bye for the present, Tia Teresa." He suited the action to the word, and, stooping, saluted her first on one cheek, then on the other. "Be your old brave and resolute self again. Where shall I find Mrs. Darlington?"

"Alone in her boudoir. This is her day for correspondence," replied the duenna, resolutely striving to repress her tears.

"Then I'll leave you here. Let your best wishes go with me."

Almost lightly he touched her hand and was gone, disappearing among the roses.

Tia Teresa bowed her head across her folded arms. She was thinking not of the past now, but solely of the future.

"How would it all end?"

Chapter XXXIII

Old Friends

"I AM glad to find you alone," spoke Mr. Robles, as he advanced into the subdued light of Mrs. Darlington's boudoir.

She was seated at her escritoire. Around her were letters lying open for answer, others sealed and ready for the mail, also sundry books of account which indicated that the chatelaine of La Siesta was a business woman who paid attention to the running of her household and the management of her estate.

"Always so pleased to see you," she replied, as she rose to give her visitor welcome.

"Pray, keep your seat, Mrs. Darlington. You form an attractive picture—the lady who is not too much of a lady to neglect her correspondence and her business affairs. And it is about some business matters that I have come to talk with you this evening."

She smiled pleasedly over the compliment paid in the old-fashioned courtly style of the true Spanish grandee. She herself always suggested the old-time, old-world lady of fashion—one belonging to the old lace and sweet lavender era that has so nearly passed away.

"Business matters?" echoed Mrs. Darlington. "That sounds quite serious. We have had no cause to talk business for years and years. La Siesta has certainly justified its name."

"But even the most pleasant siesta must in time come to an end," he replied with a grave smile. "There are things in this world that must be accomplished—calls of duty that interfere sadly with continuous repose. I am leaving tonight on a journey—perhaps a long journey," he added slowly and thoughtfully.

"Oh, going abroad? The wanderlust again? That's too bad. We shall all miss you so much." She spoke the words with real concern in her tone and in her eyes.

"Not exactly the wanderlust," he responded. "But there is a certain task I must perform. And it takes me away—far away from your delightful La Siesta."

"And for a long time?"

"That will be decided by events. I shall write you a long letter when once I am on the ocean. Meanwhile there are certain documents I wish to leave in your charge, my good kind friend."

He drew the packet from the breast pocket of his coat. "They are important papers, and I wish them to be locked in your safe."

"Under seal, I see," she remarked, indicating the big circle of wax that closed the cover.

"Yes, sealed with my signet," he answered, touching the ring on his finger. "But all the same I wish you to know the nature of their contents. That is why I have sought this little private talk."

Silently she settled herself to listen, and he went on:

"You are aware that many years ago I sold out all my interests in Spain—lands and flocks and mines. Well, except for the money I used in building and furnishing my home, I invested the whole amount so realized in British Government bonds. But not in my own name. They stand in the names of Merle Farnsworth and Grace Darlington."

Mrs. Darlington showed some surprise.

"Merle, of course. But why Grace, Mr. Robles? I need not tell you that she is already well provided for."

"That I fully understand. But I preferred it so. To me both children were very dear, and have always continued to be very dear. There was more than a sufficiency to divide. I wished them to share my patrimony, even though the one might have a greater claim on me than the other. But it was precisely, to guard against such a thought occurring to the mind of any outsider that I have treated Merle and Grace exactly alike. The secret that Merle is my daughter is known only to you and Tia Teresa and me, and, as I have always wished, it must be kept from Merle herself and from all others—now, more than ever," he added after a little pause.

"I have never sought to pry into this mystery," replied Mrs. Darlington. "You had valid reasons for it, I well understood. But I was glad for the wee baby's sake to take her to my heart—the child of the dearest friend of my girlhood days. And it was nice, too, for her to have her mother's maiden name—Merle Farnsworth. So, from the very first, I loved her just as much as my own baby, Grace."

"That I know," said Robles, gratefully touching her hand. "I can never adequately thank you for the mother love you have so generously bestowed on my child. And I have always been grateful, too, for the chivalrous manner in which you have never sought to have me explain my actions in this matter—my virtual separation from the daughter whom, while hiding our relationship, I have loved all through her young life with passionate devotion."

Mr. Robles was deeply moved. He bowed his head and covered his eyes with his hand. In sympathy, Mrs. Darlington also was greatly affected.

"You have been the best of fathers to Merle," she said in a trembling voice, "even though Merle little dreams of what she really means to your life. But oh, Mr. Robles, how often have I not pitied you when I have seen you restraining in her presence the natural impulses of your heart!"

"It was my duty," he replied, regaining his composure by stern self-command and sitting erect again. "My bounden duty to her," he added, resolutely. "So, as you have so kindly done before, we shall leave that subject alone. You call it a mystery. Be it so. Just let it abide a mystery to the end. Now, Mrs. Darlington," he went on in a changed tone, "please lock up these papers. If I ever want them again I shall come to you. But if anything should happen to me, the seal is to be broken. You are my trustee. But there is no troublesome will to prove and execute. As I have already indicated, all the property I die possessed of, all the property that is inalienably and rightfully mine, including my home on the hill

—everything is already apportioned between Merle and Grace, and stands in their names by a deed that dates back almost to their days of infancy."

"It is unheard-of generosity," protested Mrs. Darlington. "I mean so far as Grace is concerned."

"Not another word, I beg of you. I have already given valid reasons besides those of affection and gratitude. Now, Mrs. Darlington, let me see you lock up these documents, and my mind will be at rest."

Without further speech she took the packet of papers from his hand, crossed the room, and, standing before a safe inset into the wall and already open, deposited the papers in a little drawer. Then she swung back the safe door, and the click of the combination as she turned the knob told that her visitor's wishes had been fully complied with. Slowly she returned to her seat at the desk.

"Thank you," said Mr. Robles, pressing her hand.

"Then I am not to ask why you are leaving us tonight?" enquired Mrs. Darlington.

"Please not. I just came to you, as I have many times done before, to speak the little word—*Adios*. And it has always been spoken brightly between us, my dear friend. For have I not returned again and again like the proverbial bad penny?" he continued with a smile.

"And so it will be yet again, I hope," she replied. "Bad pennies of your kind, Mr. Robles, are better than minted gold. And you must think of the young people. Engagements should not be too long. Everything is settled so far as Dick and Merle are concerned—with your full approval?"

"With my fullest approval, and to my great joy and peace of mind."

"Well, and you know, too, that it is just the same old story as regards Chester Munson and my little girl."

"Munson has so informed me. He wanted my congratulations on his good fortune. Chester Munson is certainly a fine fellow, and Grace could have made no better choice for the bestowal of her love. Again I am filled with happiness at the turn events have taken."

"But if there are to be wedding bells for four, their peal will not be so joyous if you are absent, my dear Mr. Robles."

"I shall try to be present," he replied, with a little wistful smile. "Who knows? Wouldn't it be fine if the wedding bells were to ring in Spain?"

"No, no, my friend. You forget that all four are

young Americans. The honeymoons in Spain, if you like. But the weddings in California, please."

"So be it," he answered. "Then if I cannot get back for the wedding bells, we may have a family reunion during the honeymoons." He laughed almost gaily as he rose. "Now, where are our young Americans? I wish to say good-bye to them, too."

"Where Dick Willoughby is, I cannot say. But he is safe—you still assure me of his safety, Mr. Robles?"

"Assuredly. And I have good news for our dear Merle. Tomorrow Willoughby will be free, with every suspicion removed from his name."

"Oh, that will be glad tidings indeed for Merle— for both the girls."

"Then let us take the news to them. Where shall we find them?"

"As usual, I fancy, in their favorite cosy corner. And Mr. Munson is here, too. He is to have luncheon with us. He said you had given him a day off from his onerous library duties."

"Quite correct. I told him I would meet him here, for I have a message for him as well. Come then, let us join the young people."

Again, like the courtly hidalgo, he presented a hand to his hostess and led her from the room.

CHAPTER XXXIV

Heart Searchings

AS Mrs. Darlington had anticipated, the trio of young Americans were discovered in the cosy corner. Grace and Munson were engaged in a tête-à-tête that was obviously very delightful to themselves, while Merle at a discreet distance was busily engaged in watering the pot plants and flowers. She was the first to sound a note of warning.

"Here comes mother, and Mr. Robles, also, I do declare."

The young lovers started a little apart, and Grace in a moment was demurely busy over a bit of sewing that had been resting undisturbed in her lap during the previous half hour.

Merle advanced toward Mr. Robles.

"This is delightful," she exclaimed, as she warmly shook hands. "You will stay to luncheon, of course."

"No, my dear. This is to be only a brief visit, I am sorry to say."

Grace had also come forward, and he saluted

her in his usual quiet, kindly manner. But for Munson he had a word of sly banter.

"Better than drilling a squad or cataloguing musty old books," he remarked, bestowing a significant side glance in Grace's direction.

"Infinitely better," replied the ex-soldier and amateur librarian, with frank and unabashed satisfaction.

Mr. Robles took a seat close to Merle.

"I came to bring you two pieces of news," he said, taking her hand, yet addressing his words to all the company. "First and foremost, by tomorrow the charge against Dick Willoughby will be withdrawn, and he will be a free man."

"Oh, that is good news indeed," cried Merle, fairly hugging its bearer.

"Then they have at last discovered the murderer of young Thurston?" enquired Munson in a tone of eager satisfaction.

"Yes, or rather he has discovered himself, I believe. Oh, you need not ask me for the name. It will only be made public when Willoughby formally claims his liberty."

"I am so thankful," murmured Grace. "But of course Dick's complete exoneration was bound to come."

"And I am the bearer of a special message to you, Mr. Munson. I have not read it. But it was given to me as the one most likely to get it promptly into your hands."

Speaking thus, he passed over to Munson the hasty scrawl that Dick had written in the cavern and entrusted to Pierre Luzon for delivery.

Munson ripped open the envelope, first scanned the contents, then read aloud:

"On Tuesday night next, about six o'clock, meet me at Buck Ashley's old store. I shall want you to ride over to Bakersfield with me next morning, where my acquittal is assured. Give Merle the glad news.   Yours, DICK."

"That I have already been privileged to do," said Mr. Robles, as he smiled down on the young girl by his side. Their eyes met, and a look of grave earnestness came into Merle's.

"And the second item of news, Mr. Robles?" she asked, in a low tone. "I hope it is also gladsome tidings."

"Oh, it is of comparative unimportance," he answered. "Simply that I am going away on a long journey, and may not see all you happy young people again for quite awhile."

Merle's face fell. "I am so sorry," she murmured, a note of real feeling in the softly-spoken words.

"As you grow older you will realize that the world is full of partings, Merle," he answered.

"But why should there be partings among us?" she protested. "Now that Dick is free, there is not a shadow on all our happiness. And we do so wish you to share it, Mr. Robles. It will not be just the same if you are gone."

"It is very kind of you to think like that."

"That's just how we all think," interjected Grace.

"But when duty calls, one must needs answer," replied Robles. "Right there is an end to all argument."

"And where are you going this time, Mr. Robles?" enquired Merle.

"On a long journey—as far as Europe, I hope. But my plans are not quite certain, except that I start tonight. However, I shall be in correspondence with Mrs. Darlington, and I trust that when you young people come to make that contemplated foreign tour, your footsteps will be turned in my direction. Meanwhile you have, all of you, as you already know, my warmest congratulations and heartiest good wishes."

As he spoke, Mr. Robles rose. His manner indicated that he wished no further questioning. After a comprehensive glance around, he advanced, first of all, to Munson and extended his hand.

"Mr. Munson, you will receive a letter tomorrow that contains an offer for you to continue your work in my library, which I hope will prove acceptable, at least for the present. Grace, my dear, I take the liberty of an old friend." And he kissed her brow. "With your mother I already have had a good long talk," he continued, as he pressed Mrs. Darlington's hand and looked into her eyes. "And now, Merle, dear, I am going to ask you to gather me some roses in your garden. I want them for a particular purpose, and, as you know, there are no roses like those of La Siesta."

Merle was standing eager and happy to do his bidding—privileged to have the chance of conferring such a little service on her dear old friend, her friend from the earliest childhood days of her remembrance. With impulsive good-nature, Grace was ready to help as well. But a quiet look from her mother restrained her, and Merle and Mr. Robles passed from the verandah, hand in hand.

For nearly an hour they wandered among the rose bushes, picking the choicest blooms, talking a little on many things, silent at times, but both happy in each other's companionship. At last Mr. Robles looked at his watch. The hour of parting had come.

Merle had deftly tied the roses in a bunch, and now she placed them in his hands.

"A bouquet from me—from your little friend Merle," she murmured, with a wistful attempt at a smile.

"From my dear little friend, Merle," he replied, gravely repeating her words as he looked down into her upraised face. It was a beautiful face, in its fresh youthfulness, its eager joy of living, the sublime unconsciousness of self that reveals the spotless soul. For an instant their eyes met.

During that brief spell Robles' whole being trembled. His arms moved as if to enfold the sweet girl to his breast. But with a mighty effort he controlled himself, and he simply kissed her on the brow, just as he had done to Grace in the cosy corner.

"God bless you, Merle, my dear," he murmured as he turned away with a final wave of his hand.

In a moment he was gone from her view. But the girl's gaze remained fixed—still directed down the avenue of trees along which the figure of her life-long friend had disappeared. There was a look of dazed wonderment in her eyes.

"Oh, can it be so—could it be so?" she faltered, as she raised a hand to hold back the tears.

An hour later Robles was in the little Mexican

churchyard, scattering the rose blooms gathered by his daughter Merle on the graves of the dead relatives whose names she would never know as such. Already there were the flowers that Tia Teresa had that morning brought—a garland of white arum lilies around the cross that marked the sleeping place of Rosetta, wreaths of rich red carnations on the tombstone inscribed with the father's and the mother's names.

And now on the turf beneath the memorials Don Manuel, with lingering fingers, dropped the roses here and there, as if to rest with their beauty and their fragrance on the forms of his beloved dead. The last bloom fluttered to the ground. Then, standing erect, hands upraised, no words uttered, but with the unspoken words none the less reverberating through his very soul, he vowed once again the vendetta which he had sworn on the identical spot thirty long years before.

When he turned to leave the tiny hamlet of the dead, a wonderful transformation had come over his countenance. The placid calm was gone; the fierce fire of implacable hatred and unswervable resolve burned in his eyes. He had bidden adieu to all the softer things in this life. His sole concern now was with the enemy whom he had marked down for death that night.

CHAPTER XXXV

At Comanche Point

BEN THURSTON, during the afternoon, seated in his big armchair, had first nodded over a newspaper and then dropped off to sleep. He was awakened by a touch on the shoulder—rudely awakened, for he jumped to his feet, and in a dazed way glared at the disturber.

"Excuse me," apologized Leach Sharkey, "but I want to remind you that this is the afternoon when we are to meet that old Portugee I told you about."

"I need no reminder," was the gruff reply. "I am ready to start when you are. By the way, what's the fellow's name?"

"José, he said. He claims to know every nook and corner in the range. Has lived in the mountains for many years; keeps goats and bees, and shoots a mountain lion occasionally, earning the bounty as well as getting the skin."

"Shoots," echoed Thurston, somewhat nervously.

"Oh, that was in his younger days mostly, I fancy. Today he is a tottering old man who couldn't hold a rifle straight if he tried. But he's well acquainted with the mountains, that's the main thing. He tells me he has known where Dick Willoughby is hiding since the very day after he broke jail."

"Then why didn't he come to me?"

"Because he knew nothing about the reward. But at our very first chance meeting among the hills I very soon made five thousand dollars look mighty good to him. By gad, you should have seen his eyes pop and his hands tremble."

"It is a fortune for such a man."

"That's what got him. He has been supplying Willoughby with goats' milk, but is paid only two bits a quart. So he grabbed at my bait like a hungry coyote. You have the money ready, I suppose? Treasury bills—that's what he stipulated for, because he's too frail to hump a sack of gold around."

"The money is in that wallet on my desk. You had better carry it."

Sharkey stepped across the room and shoved a fat leather wallet into the breast pocket of his coat.

"So frail, is he?" Thurston went on, musingly. "Well, I needn't take a gun."

Sharkey smiled. He knew Ben Thurston's timidity in even handling a revolver, and the man's abject reliance on his armed bodyguard.

"Not the slightest necessity," assented the sleuth. "I've always got my brace of bulldogs ready;" and the professional gunman, touching the broad leather belt to which his holsters were attached, grinned complacently.

"And nó danger to be feared from Willoughby himself, you said?"

"None whatever. In fact, he don't have a gun, José declares. So he only sneaks out after dark for a constitutional. The old fellow will take us to the spot where we can grab him by the neck."

"That sounds like business," replied Thurston, rubbing his hands. "And shoot him down, Sharkey, if he runs."

"He won't give us the slip this time—you can bet dollars to doughnuts on that. But of course he's got to have the chance of hands-up before I fire. Killing is killing, and I prefer the handcuffs. There is really less trouble in the long run."

"Well, perhaps I, too, would prefer to see him hanged," murmured Thurston, with gloating satisfaction. "But don't forget that we must get him this afternoon, dead or alive. I'm sick of this life of watching and waiting."

"The end's in sight at last."

"Then we'll go back East—after I have had my revenge. It will be sweeter to me after all the trouble we've encountered. And by God, we'll drag that Farnsworth girl, too, through the mire. Hell to all of them! I've never had anyone but enemies around me here."

While speaking, Thurston reached for his overcoat thrown across the back of a chair.

"All right, we'll start," said Sharkey. "I'll go and get the horses ready."

It was about half past three o'clock when the riders reached the base of the mountain barrier not far from the entrance to Tejon Pass.

"We've got to make it on foot now," remarked Sharkey, as he swung himself from the saddle. "I'll tether the horses to this manzanita."

Thurston dismounted, and while his companion led the animals under the trees, he gazed aloft at the precipice beetling in front of them.

"Damn it, I wish you had chosen any other place than Comanche Point," he exclaimed irritably.

"We had to come to the spot where we can find our man," replied Sharkey complacently. "It is on the ridge above that Willoughby has his place of hiding. Come along, we have a good stiff climb before us."

He led the way up the first slope of the winding trail and Ben Thurston followed, reluctantly now, half doubting the wisdom of his having left his home for such an adventure.

Meanwhile there had been two other riders on the range that afternoon, mounted on little hill ponies. The one man was blindfolded; the other rode in advance and guided the second pony by a leading rein. It had been the usual experience to which Dick Willoughby had now become accustomed—hour after hour along winding, maze-like trails. At last the call had come to dismount, and the bandage had been removed from Dick's eyes. He saw that he was in a little box-like nook in the mountains.

"You will remain here," said Pierre Luzon, "until I whistle for you—you know my signal. Zen you will lead ze ponies along zis path. When you come to me, I will put you on ze road for home, and we will say good-bye."

"I suppose I may smoke," laughed Dick, philosophically. The day of surprises had left him dulled to any further wonderment.

"Sure, smoke," replied Pierre. "But remember ze forest regulations," he added with a chuckle, "and do not set ze brush on fire."

"Oh, I'm no green tenderfoot," laughed

Willoughby, as he drew his briar-root from his pocket. "And it's quite a balmy afternoon for October."

He sat down and propped his back against a moss-grown rock.

"You must not stir from here," continued Pierre. "Remember I have to find you again."

"Guess I've learned to obey orders. I'm quite comfortable where I am." And Dick started contentedly smoking.

Pierre, following the little path to which he had drawn Dick's attention, pushed through the brushwood and disappeared.

Just ten minutes later Pierre Luzon stood on Comanche Point and gazed down the trail leading up from the pass below.

"Zey are coming, zey are coming!" he exclaimed eagerly to himself, with finger outpointed in the direction of the two climbers on foot half way up the ascent. Then he slipped back into the shadow of a clump of stunted pines that grew close to the cliff.

Fifteen minutes or so passed. Then the heads of Ben Thurston and Leach Sharkey showed above the final steep ascent that led directly on to the projecting spur known as Comanche Point. Thurston was breathing hard after the difficult climb.

"Here we are at last," remarked Sharkey cheerfully, as he glanced around.

Even as he spoke, a tottering figure came forth from among the pines. A few minutes before, Pierre Luzon had been erect and vigorous and nimble on his feet, but now he seemed to be indeed a frail and bowed old man.

"I have come," he said, as he approached the figures on the cliff.

"Hands up, then," cried the sleuth, half laughing. "You remember, I said I would search you for a gun."

"I have no gun," Pierre answered, as he halted and elevated his arms.

Sharkey advanced and, without taking the trouble to draw either of his own weapons, ran his fingers with the quick touch of experience over the old man's clothes.

"I knew you were on the square, José," said the bodyguard, quickly satisfied. "Well, I've brought the mazuma."

He drew from his pocket the fat wallet, opening it for a moment to display the wads of greenbacks. Then he put it back again.

"Now where is our man?"

"He is down here, just a little distance," replied Pierre, in a cautious whisper. "I am not strong enough to hold him. But you come. Ze boss, he can remain here for ze present."

Ben Thurston had turned away and was looking down into the valley.

"We'll be back in a short time," called out Sharkey.

But Thurston, if he had heard, made no reply.

"Now show the way, old fellow," continued the sleuth, addressing his guide.

A moment later Ben Thurston was alone.

Alone on Comanche Point—gazing over the broad sweep of lands that had been his princely heritage, but which he had now lost forever! The valley lay beneath him, bathed in the mellow evening sunshine. But his eyes were riveted on a single spot. And what a transformation scene for the erstwhile cattle king—this new city with its checkerboard of streets and all around it new homes amid plots of young fruit trees and meadows of alfalfa!

The whole picture was one of fascinating beauty—the city itself the finishing touch that gave it human interest. But in Ben Thurston's soul there was nothing but bitterness and disgust. He had kept on complaining that he had been unscrupulously plundered by the Los Angeles syndicate, and with the realization now of what enterprise and enlightened progress could achieve, he began to feel that he had been mercilessly stripped of what was rightfully his. Greed and envy and vain regrets were all commingled in his surge of envenomed thoughts. But avarice predominated.

"Good God, to think I parted with the rancho at a beggarly acreage price, when I might have been selling town lots today. There will be a dozen other towns springing up to follow this one."

In his agony he groaned aloud and covered his eyes with his hands to shut out the hateful sight.

Just at that moment the sound of a twig crackling underfoot smote his ear. He turned round; into his face stole an ashen look of terror as he watched an approaching figure wrapped in a Spanish cloak and crowned by a broad-brimmed sombrero. His haggard eyes asked: "Is it man or ghost?" He would have screamed aloud, but found himself voiceless from fear.

At last the figure stood before him with proudly folded arms.

"The White Wolf!" gasped Thurston, in a faint whisper.

"Yes, Don Manuel de Valencia—the White Wolf, as you choose to call him. And now at last, Ben Thurston, we meet face to face, and alone—after thirty long years, and without a woman's tears this time to save you!"

Ben Thurston sank to the ground, a huddled heap, trembling in every limb.

CHAPTER XXXVI

Outwitted

PIERRE LUZON led Leach Sharkey along
the trail. Beyond Comanche Point it
dipped again owing to the contour of the
mountain, then at a distance of about fifty yards,
took a sharp turn round an abrupt face of rock.

"Where the hell are you taking me?" asked the
sleuth, as they approached this bend.

"Only a little further," replied the guide, in a
feeble quavering voice as he glanced over his
shoulder.

The men were only a few paces apart. In the
shadow cast by the cliff, Pierre's pallid face with
its stubbly white beard looked like that of a veritable ancient, and his bent form and tottering
steps completed the picture. The sleuth smiled
at his momentary discomposure.

Around the turn, however, Pierre grabbed at a
revolver lying ready to his hand on a ledge of
rock, and when Sharkey followed, it was to find a
hale and stalwart man, erect, alert, with the flash
of conscious power in his eyes.

"Hands up!" cried Pierre, in a voice of stern command. Leach Sharkey was standing three short steps away and was looking now into the muzzle of a big automatic pistol. Over his countenance there stole a sickly smile. But he knew the rules of the game too well to attempt any resistance. His hands went slowly above his head until both arms were fully extended.

"You've got the drop on me all right, José," he murmured, in self-apology.

"Face the rock," came the next curt order— the very tone was reminiscent of old bandit days.

Sharkey obeyed in silence, and in a trice both his guns were withdrawn from their holsters and flung among the brushwood.

"You go ahead now," said Pierre, stepping aside to let the other pass. "You can drop your hands, but if you cry out or attempt to run, zen you are one dead man."

The discomfited sleuth meekly complied, although there was now a black scowl on his face as he stepped on ahead. In all his professional career, Leach Sharkey had never before fallen so ignominiously into a trap like this.

Not a word was spoken while a distance of some two hundred yards was being traversed. Then Pierre called out the one word: "Halt!"

Sharkey did not dare even to look round. He stood still as a piece of statuary.

"You sit on zat stone over zere," continued Pierre, "and do not rise until I give you permission. Now we will proceed to business."

Sharkey sat down as ordered.

"Hell, you can have your five thousand dollars right enough," he said, pulling the wallet from his pocket.

"No, my friend. I did not bring you here to rob you. I am out on parole, and I never break my word. I am Pierre Luzon!" He spoke the name with triumphant pride.

"Good God!" exclaimed Sharkey, in dumfounded surprise. "You belonged to the White Wolf's gang?"

"I belong now to ze gang. Ze White Wolf is alive!"

Leach Sharkey had looked sick before, but a ghastly grey pallor came into his face now.

"Then he has got hold of Ben Thurston—at last?" he faltered.

"Yes, at last," replied Pierre, with a grim smile of joy. "Don Manuel and Ben Thurston are alone on Comanche Point just now. Zey will settle old scores—zat is zeir affair. Now, I attend to my affair."

Sharkey looked up enquiringly, but said no more.

"Leach Sharkey," continued the old French-man, "you are one strong man. You will now take ze handcuffs from your pocket—I know you carry zem—and drop zem over your shoulder. Zere, zat is right. I am glad you obey wizout giving me any further trouble. Now, you will hold out your hands, behind your back—you know exactly how."

Yes, Leach Sharkey knew exactly how. And he also knew what the business end of a big revolver meant, with the forefinger of a daring bandit like Pierre Luzon on the trigger. He was handcuffed and helpless right enough in very short order. For the first time in his life the man who had so often slipped the bracelets on others, found the bracelets around his own wrists.

"Next I want ze key of ze handcuffs," Pierre resumed. "Which pocket, please?"

Sharkey, with a downward thrust of his chin, indicated the waistcoat pocket.

"Zank you," said Pierre, as he thrust in his fingers and produced the key. "Now, we will throw zis zing away"—as he spoke it went whizzing through the air—"and when you get home to ze rancho, ze blacksmith zere will set you free."

"Oh, I'm going home, am I?" said the sleuth, considerably reassured.

"Yes, Pierre Luzon no longer rob or kill or break ze law. He keep his word of honor always. And I promised to bring Dick Willoughby to you tonight. Now I shall be true to zat promise, too."

And through his teeth he blew a shrill whistle.

At the sound Dick Willoughby started up, and shook the ashes from his pipe. Following Pierre's instructions, he led the two ponies along the little trail through the chaparral. Within five minutes he emerged on a broader trail, right at the spot where the Frenchman was standing.

"Hello, Pierre!" Then Dick's eyes fell on Leach Sharkey, and at the very first glance he saw the shackled hands. "But what's the meaning of all this?" he asked in bewildered surprise.

"It means zat you will take zis man down ze mountains. He came to arrest you, but you can tell him now zat you are one free man. You can show him ze paper which proves it was not you, but Don Manuel, who is responsible for ze death of young Thurston."

"Great Caesar!" muttered the sleuth, "I thought that from the first, but the old fool would not listen to me."

"Mr. Sharkey," said Dick, "you and I have no quarrel. What Pierre says is true—I have a sworn affidavit in my pocket, fixing the responsibility for that unhappy affair where it belongs."

"I believe you, Mr. Willoughby," replied the sleuth. "I'm glad you are innocent, but I was only doing my duty in trying to arrest the man charged with the crime."

"I understand all that. I bear you no ill will."

"And I'd shake hands if it were not for these damned bracelets," continued Sharkey.

"Pierre, there is no need of handcuffs," said Dick, turning to the Frenchman. "Set him free. We will go peaceably home together."

"No, no," replied Pierre, determinedly. "Leach Sharkey, he is one giant in strength. He will go home as he is. Besides, I have trown ze key away." And he laughed aloud.

Sharkey nodded in helpless admission of his sorry plight.

"Too bad," murmured Dick.

"And now," continued Pierre, "zere is no time to be lost. We will help zis man onto your pony, and you will ride my pony and hold ze leading rein."

"But he can't ride with his hands behind his back like that," objected Dick.

"Oh, yes, he can," grinned Pierre. "Ze good horseman ride wid his knees, and most of ze road you can be by his side and hold him on. And it is ze only way, for ze key, as I have said, is gone."

"I suppose we've got to accept the situation," said Dick, with a glance at Sharkey's lugubrious countenance. The man of strength was obviously crestfallen at his almost ridiculous plight of power-lessness.

Pierre resumed his instructions. "You will not go back to Comanche Point, but will take ze mule trail down into ze valley. You know it, Mr. Willoughby—it is about one mile furzer on."

"I know it," replied Dick.

"You will leave Mr. Sharkey at the rancho and zen ride to ze place where your friends are waiting for you. Now, zat is all. I must go. We have already said our *adios*, my dear young friend."

Dick grasped the proffered hand and warmly pressed it.

"Good-bye, Pierre. I can never thank you enough for all you have done for me. Good-bye."

Leach Sharkey was assisted into the saddle, and the horsemen started on their way.

"Good-bye," shouted back Dick Willoughby, yet once again.

"*Adios!*"

And as the two figures disappeared around a bend, the Frenchman uttered a deep sigh. "A splendid young fellow! I wonder shall we ever meet again!"—this was the thought in his mind as for just a moment he stood in an attitude of deep dejection.

Then swinging around, he started back at a run for Comanche Point.

Chapter XXXVII

The Dawn of Comprehension

ALL through the afternoon at La Siesta, Merle was in a meditative mood. After luncheon Mrs. Darlington had returned to her letter-writing and her book-keeping. Munson and Grace had departed for a walk through the pine woods, after vain but not too strenuous endeavors to get Merle to accompany them. Left to her own resources she had retired to the drawing room, had tried to interest herself at the piano, but after a little while had given up the attempt; and, coiled in a big chair, had surrendered herself to a "big think," as she mentally termed it.

In that momentary searching of the eyes between her and Mr. Robles just before their parting in the rose garden, there had come a flash of revelation to her soul. She had divined a yearning in his gaze that was surely more than the affection of an old and devoted friend. There was passionate tenderness that belied the gentle yet almost perfunctory kiss on the brow that he had finally bestowed at parting. Nor had she failed to notice the restraint which the strong man had imposed upon himself. And strangely enough, her own momentary impulse had been to throw her arms around his neck and kiss him, just as a fond daughter might have kissed a father at such an emotional moment—on the eve of a long journey, the whither unrevealed, the return all so uncertain.

She recalled, too, their previous conversation while she was gathering the roses—his words of kindly wisdom, his little bits of advice that now seemed to be weighted by more than mere friendly interest in her future happiness. Then her mind traveled back slowly, step by step, all the way to childhood days—a long vista marked by his comings and his goings, his prolonged absences, his unexpected but always welcome reappearances, his numberless acts of thoughtful kindness. Once she had been seriously ill, when a little girl, and the memory of that illness had ever been the memory of his face hovering over her cot, night and day, till the crisis had been passed and she had been on the way to assured convalescence.

There had always been an air of mystery about Mr. Robles, but she had never sought to penetrate it, instinctively recognizing that there had been some great sorrow in his life, and almost unconsciously accepting the affectionate regard he had lavished on Grace and herself as some sort of consolation for him in his loneliness. She knew that Grace was only her sister in name, but none the less Grace was to her a real sister, just as Mrs. Darlington was a real mother—the only mother she had ever known. Weaving together now the threads of memory, she became conscious of the mystery in her own life. There was assuredly some fuller story than the story she had been told in the past and had always tacitly accepted— that her parents had been neighbors and dear friends of Mrs. Darlington in the long ago, and when they had died, the baby girl left behind had been bequeathed to her motherly care.

At this stage in her ruminations Merle sat bolt upright in her chair. The shadows of evening were beginning to close around her, but the dawn of revelation was in her heart.

Would Mrs. Darlington still be alone in her boudoir? Merle answered the unspoken thought by stealing from the room.

Yes, Mrs. Darlington was at her writing table, lighted now by candles on each side which, covered by little red shades, only dimly illuminated the apartment. Merle flitted in without her coming being observed.

Mrs. Darlington was no longer writing—her

elbows were resting on the table and both hands were covering her eyes in an attitude of deep thought, perhaps of sleep, as Merle for a moment imagined when she had noiselessly gained her side.

"Mother dear," she said softly, laying a hand on her shoulder.

"You here, my child?" exclaimed Mrs. Darlington.   There was no trace of slumber in her eyes.

"Yes, and I want to have a little talk with you—all alone," said Merle, as she dropped into a chair, the very chair which Mr. Robles had previously occupied.

The look of vague sadness and anxiety in Mrs. Darlington's face deepened.

"What about, dear?" she asked.

Merle's mind had been made up, and she came to the issue with point-blank abruptness.

"Is Mr. Robles my father?"

The startled look on the other's face was almost in itself an admission of the truth—Mrs. Darlington had been caught off her guard.   But she made a desperate attempt to parry the question.

"What makes you fancy such a thing?" she faltered.

"Because there is certainty in my heart," replied

Away on the Honeymoon Trail—Page 387

Merle bravely. "It came to me first when he bade me good-bye in the garden. And now I see it in your face."

The young girl dropped on her knees, and, an arm around her mother's waist, gazed up imploringly.

Eyes met eyes. Falsehood was impossible in either case. Mrs. Darlington stooped and folded the kneeling girl in a fond embrace. Both were weeping now. No word had been spoken, but Merle knew that she had correctly divined.

It was a few minutes before there was sufficient self-control for the conversation to be resumed. But then, Merle still kneeling by her side, Mrs. Darlington spoke:

"I had promised to keep this secret, dear," she began, fondling the girl's tresses. "But you have gained your knowledge apart from me, so I cannot be held to have betrayed my trust. Yes, Mr. Robles is your father—your loving and devoted father. Your real name is his—Merle Robles you should always have been called."

"And why not?" asked Merle. "Oh, I am proud and overjoyed to think of him as my father."

"Because he has some important reason to have the world think otherwise. I know you will believe me, dear Merle, when I say I do not know that reason. He is too grand and honorable a man for me to have ever pressed for an explanation. I just accepted you as a gift from his hands—his child and the child of my girlhood chum, named Merle, as you know, like yourself."

"So, if I have solved one mystery, there is still another mystery beyond," murmured Merle.

She rose, seated herself, and remained silent for a moment, her hands locked across her knees, her brows knit in thought.

"But why distress your heart over unknown things?" said Mrs. Darlington. "As you have learned by your today's experience, mysteries solve themselves in due time."

"Yes," replied Merle, "but somehow I feel that this is the due time that I should know everything—for my dear father's sake," she added, "not for my own. Oh, mother, you should have seen his face of anguish just before he parted from me this afternoon. It was revealed to me only for an instant. But now I feel sure that something terrible is going to happen—to him."

She was sobbing again, as she flung her arms impulsively around Mrs. Darlington's neck and sat in her lap, just as if once again she had become a little child.

"Oh, mother mine—I shall always call you

mother mine, for you have been a dear, sweet, kind mother to me ever since I can remember. But don't you see that today I have also found a father whom I deeply love? Nothing must happen to him."

"Why should anything happen to him?"

"I do not know. Where is Tia Teresa?"

The question came with startling suddenness as Merle started up with another ray of illumination in her mind.

"I haven't seen her since morning," replied Mrs. Darlington.

"Nor have I," said Merle, standing erect, wiping away the traces of her tears, and with a few pats adjusting her rumpled hair. "That is very strange."

"No. I happen to know that this day, the eleventh of October, is always a sad anniversary for Tia Teresa—the death of some dear friend who lies buried in the little Mexican cemetery on the hill. She has always refused to tell me the story. But early this morning she went, as usual, to place flowers upon the grave."

"Flowers—for a grave!" exclaimed Merle. She was thinking of the roses she had gathered that afternoon for Mr. Robles—for her father— because he specially wanted the most beautiful blooms. But she did not give her thought to Mrs. Darlington.

"It is all so strange," continued Merle. Then her air of decisiveness returned. "I'll go and see if Tia Teresa is in her room."

Mrs. Darlington was gravely perturbed at this persistency. Oh, if only the mysteries of the past could be left alone, the joys of the present accepted for themselves! Probing into trouble cannot but lead to further trouble—that, for her, had been the secret of contentment. But she was powerless to intervene. Merle had already departed on her mission of enquiry.

Chapter XXXVIII

Exit Leach Sharkey

THE ponies were jogging down the trail, Leach Sharkey uncomfortably lurching in his saddle when some sudden bend or dip was encountered, Dick Willoughby good-humoredly holding him on when such emergencies rendered the service advisable if an ignominious fall were to be avoided. There was a song of joy in Dick's heart—liberty was at hand; he was riding down from the hills to join his loved one again. But there was sullen brooding in the soul of the outwitted sleuth—growing more sullen with every mile traversed, with every kindness rendered, with the very realization of his own ridiculous predicament and the contrast of his companion's light-hearted happiness.

At last they reached the foot of the trail, leading on to the road that crossed the plain. At the distance of a few miles the Rancho San Antonio showed amid its clustering shade and orchard trees.

"Let us dismount for a bit," suggested Sharkey. "I feel all in—dead beat and tired."

"But how will I get you on to your horse again?" replied Dick, a trifle dubiously.

"Oh, we'll manage that. Please help me down."

Dick sprang to the ground, dropped the reins over his pony's head, and soon had Leach Sharkey on *terra firma*.

"You're no light weight to handle," he laughed. "By the way, Sharkey, I forgot to ask: Where's your boss this afternoon?"

Sharkey eyed Dick curiously.

"You don't know?"

"Why should I know? It's quite a time since I met the gentleman."

"You are aware who Pierre Luzon is?"

"Certainly. Pierre has come to be quite a friend of mine. He's a good fellow all right."

There was a moment's pause. Dick was rolling a cigarette, Sharkey furtively watching every expression on his face.

"Well, the Frenchie played me a dirty trick when he threw that key away," remarked the sleuth, rattling the handcuffs behind his back.

"I guess Pierre was resolved to take no chances," replied Dick, grinning through the tobacco smoke as he surveyed the helpless body-guard. "He only needed a pair of hobbles to complete the job."

A muttered curse came from Sharkey's lips—
but this was an aside. For Dick he had an insinu-
ating smile.

"You might get these blamed handcuffs off all
right, Willoughby. Look at that big boulder
there. If I set my hands across it, you might hammer through the chain. Or if you have a pistol,
that might do the trick."

"No, I've got no pistol," Dick replied.

He did not notice the gleam of satisfaction in
Sharkey's eyes—the wolfish smile at the corners
of his wolf-like teeth. At the moment he was
looking around for a convenient stone that might
serve as a hammer.

"But I think I might break that chain all right
with this," he went on, as he stooped and picked
up a heavy, sharp-edged fragment of granite from
the rock-strewn ground. "Come along, then.
Set your wrists just here. At least, we can try."

The trial succeeded—the slender steel strain
stretched across the boulder soon yielded to the
succession of battering blows.

Sharkey flung his great big brawny arms aloft.
He was still wearing the bracelets, but his hands
were free.

"Feels better, don't it?" said Dick, with a
sympathetic smile.

"A damned sight better," roared the sleuth, as he turned quickly round. "Now, young man, you are my prisoner. I arrest you for jail-breaking. There's my star. I don't say hands up, for I know you haven't a gun."

As he spoke, Sharkey opened his coat so that the official badge might be displayed.

Dick in his amazement stepped back, just one pace. Sharkey advanced, his high hands outstretched.

"Make no trouble, now. You know I am only doing my duty."

"Duty be hanged," cried Dick, as with a swift uppercut he caught his would-be captor on the jaw. Sharkey staggered, and Dick, with a right-arm swing, banged him on the temple, bowling him over like a ninepin.

Sharkey was soon on his hands and knees; then dazed and tottering, he got onto his feet again. But Dick was watchfully waiting, and with sharp jabs, right and left, sent him down once more. The sleuth lay motionless now.

Like a flash Dick grabbed the riata hanging from the saddle-horn of his pony, and without a moment's loss of time had its coils around the arms and chest of the prostrate man, roping him like a thrown steer with all the skill of the trained cowboy. In a brief minute the knots were tied, and with the final clove-hitch the fallen Samson was turned over on his back. Sharkey's eyes opened, glaring dully at his conqueror.

"You contemptible hound!" exclaimed Dick, as he tossed the loose end of the lariat from him. "By God, I've seen a few low-down things done in my lifetime, but this is certainly the limit. I suppose you would have betrayed me for the sake of the reward, even though you know now for certain that I was wrongfully arrested at the start. You damned Judas! You deserve to be hanged like a horse-thief, Leach Sharkey—that's about your proper finish."

And Dick in his righteous indignation glanced around as if in search of a convenient tree for the operation.

"I'll give no further trouble," mumbled Sharkey.

"It will be my particular care that you don't," replied Dick. "Get up, you hulking brute." And grabbing the coils of the riata, he fairly lifted Sharkey to his feet.

"Now, I wouldn't shame the pony by putting you on his back again. Follow me."

Picking up the free end of the rope, and gathering the leading rein of Sharkey's horse into the same hand, Willoughby vaulted into his saddle.

"Come along," he called out, turning round as the riata came taut. And thus, a dozen paces behind, the sleuth, discomfited again a second time that day, and humiliated worse than ever, followed perforce in his victor's trail.

Perhaps half a mile of the open road was thus traversed, Dick speaking not another word, but looking round occasionally and giving an energetic yank at the rope whenever there was evidence of laggard steps. Sharkey stumbled along, his chin buried in his breast, his eyes half-closed to conceal their dumb, vicious glare of concentrated but impotent fury.

They had now reached a gate; Dick dismounted and threw it open, pointing the way for Sharkey to take.

"It's about five miles to the rancho," he said. "I don't know how you'll get through the other gates, but I reckon you can crawl under them, like the snake you've proved yourself to be. Now, off you go," and with the words he looped the loose end of the riata around the victim's shoulders. "That's a better necktie than you deserve, Leach Sharkey. If it was any one but myself, you would be helped to a start by a few vigorous kicks behind."

The sleuth shambled through the gateway, with

shamed, averted face. With a click the gate was closed. For just a few minutes Dick watched the figure moving away through the now gathering dusk. Then he laid a hand on his saddle-horn.

"I hope it's the last I'll see of that animal," he murmured to himself, as he sprang lightly into the saddle. And at a canter he started along the road, the led pony, after a few heel-kicks as if in joy at being relieved of its burden, soon dropping into the swinging stride.

Chapter XXXIX

The Fight on the Cliff

FOR a few moments Don Manuel contemplated the cowering figure of Ben Thurston in contemptuous silence. His end was accomplished; his enemy was in his power; like the cat with the mouse just a few inches from its paw, he could strike at any moment. He spoke now with measured calm.

"Do you remember what day this is? The eleventh of October."

He paused for a reply. Thurston's lips were parted but remained dumb. Don Manuel resumed:

"Thirty years ago this very night—here at this very spot, you brutally killed my poor little sister, Rosetta."

Thurston shrank back. His lips moved, but no sound came.

"Oh, attempt no denial," continued Don Manuel, for the moment clenching a menacing fist over him. "You cannot forget the tell-tale button which you snatched from my hand to hide

(356)

the proof.   Nor have I forgotten the lash of your quirt that drew blood from my cheek"—and he wiped his face with the tips of his fingers as if to rub away the memory of the deadly insult—"the very day on which I buried my dear father and mother," he added, in a voice vibrant with emotion.

He bowed his head; there was another brief period of silence.   Then he recovered himself and went on:

"The deaths of my beloved parents are just as much on your head, Ben Thurston, as the death of the guileless, innocent, young girl whom you betrayed, and then with coward hands pushed over this cliff, mangling her body on the rocks . below.   My vengeance has been slow in coming, but after all, I am glad of the delay.   For all through these years you have not only suffered the agony of constant fear, but I have lived to see you landless, bereft of the broad rich acres which belonged to my father and were never rightfully yours."

"That's not so—my claim was established in the law courts."   Thurston managed to articulate the words.   The sound of his voice seemed to restore some little measure of courage, for he sat up, and leaning an elbow on a rock, adjusted himself in a more comfortable position. But he did not seek to gain his feet—the bandit's figure still towered over him.

"Law courts—your American law courts!" exclaimed Don Manuel, with ineffable scorn. "You know you bribed the judge who gave the decision. Dare you deny it?"

Thurston ventured no denial—his dropped jaw proclaimed his consciousness of guilt.

"Nothing was too base for you," Don Manuel proceeded. "You robbed, despoiled, destroyed my home. But now at last your hour has come. I have waited patiently for this hour. On many an occasion, Ben Thurston, I could have shot you dead from a distance. But I have waited—waited —waited for the time when you would know that it was I, the White Wolf, who was sending you to your doom just as I have already sent your ruffian son to his."

"So it was really you—who murdered my boy?" stammered Thurston.

"Don't call it murder—it was righteous retribution for both him and you. Oh, I can tell you something tonight, for a secret does not pass from a dead man's lips."

The victim so confidently doomed, shuddered. Don Manuel continued:

"Merle Farnsworth is my daughter; your vile and debauched son dared to insult her, and so he died—rightly died. Yes, at my hands—I take full responsibility. And I am glad to tell you this before you follow him out of the world. To-night, Ben Thurston, you go over this cliff—you die the death you gave to my sister."

As he spoke, Don Manuel cast loose his Spanish cloak, and dropped both it and his sombrero to the ground.

Thurston at last staggered to his feet.

"So get ready now to fight for your life," Don Manuel resumed, folding his arms across his breast as he surveyed his victim.

"But I am unarmed," cried Thurston, pointing to the revolver at the other's belt. His outstretched hand trembled, his voice was a terrified shriek.

"Then I, too, shall be unarmed," replied Don Manuel, as he unbuckled his belt and tossed it lightly from him. "Come along, then—it is man to man with naked hands." His tone now was one of concentrated passion and hate, and he advanced with arms extended for an enfolding embrace.

Now did Ben Thurston realize that his only chance for life lay in his superior weight, possibly his superior strength.   At the thought, craven fear changed of a sudden to the courage of desperation, and like a wild cat he leaped at the throat of his adversary.

Then began a terrible struggle—two strong men writhing in each other's grip like savage beasts. Soon their clothes were torn, their bodies begrimed with sweat and mud, their faces and naked arms bespattered with blood, for Ben Thurston's nose had been broken in one of the first falls. Thurston, besides his extra pounds, had also the advantage of being younger by a few years. But Don Manuel was in better physical condition and his muscles were like bands of steel. So it was pretty much of a level match in this grim fight to the death.

As they tugged at each other, as each attempted to bear the other down or trip and throw him, as at times each tried in their locked embrace to crush in his adversary's ribs and squeeze the last breath out of his body, as they milled round and round, swayed and fell and rolled over and then for a moment regained a kneeling or an upright position—both men realized that it was the one who could last the longest with whom the mastery would rest.

Pierre Luzon, running up the trail, came to the

edge of the open space where the desperate contest was in progress. But the onlooker did not attempt to interfere—he had had his orders; he just crouched and watched the swaying, writhing figures.

For an hour or more the fight proceeded, at times fast and furious, with breathing spells to follow, during which grips were tenaciously maintained. Points of advantage alternated now to the one side, now to the other, but after each succeeding tussle both combatants were exhausted without victory being pronounced for either. Every vestige of clothing above the belt line had long since been torn away, and they were sweating like lathered horses.

The milling and wrestling had gradually grown weaker, and it was clear now that the final test of endurance could not be much longer delayed. Yet again Don Manuel renewed the attack, and had forced Thurston to his knees, when the latter by a supreme effort raised himself again, and then by sheer weight pressed his opponent back a pace or two. But just at this moment Thurston's strength seemed to give out, for he dropped down sideways, dragging his enemy after him.

Then Pierre Luzon saw the object of the manoeuvre. Thurston had gained the spot where

Don Manuel's discarded pistol belt was lying, and now he was reaching out with a disengaged hand to grab the gun.

The Frenchman darted forward.

"Keep out of this," cried Don Manuel, peremptorily, although he was breathing hard.

"Look out! Your gun!" screamed Pierre, as he seized Thurston's wrist in a vice-like grip.

Just an instant too late, however, for Thurston's fingers had already closed round the weapon and it went off with a bang.

Pierre dropped to his knees. It was he who had received the bullet—through one of his lungs. But he had wrested the pistol from the treacherous villain's grasp and now it fell, still smoking, to the ground.

The wounded man coughed a great mouthful of crimson blood on to the slab of rock. Then he recovered himself and raised his head. Thurston and Don Manuel, even in their weakened state, were fighting more desperately than ever, blinded by hate to every sense of danger, and Pierre was just in time to see them slip on some loosened stones and then, still locked in the death clench, go rolling over the edge of the precipice.

"*Mon Dieu! Mon Dieu!*" murmured the Frenchman. He staggered to his feet and without waiting turned and started down the steep trail, stumbling like a drunken man.

At the foot of the zig-zag pathway he gazed helplessly around. He would have pushed his way through the brushwood to seek his beloved chief. Dead! He must be dead. No one could have dropped that sheer three hundred feet onto the cruel jagged rocks below and live. Yet, who knows? A tree might have broken the fall—Don Manuel might still be alive.

Pierre, however, was incapable of further effort. His limbs trembled beneath him, and again he was spitting blood.

All of a sudden he spied the two horses tethered under the manzanita tree. He tottered toward them, untied the first one he reached, and with difficulty pulled himself up into the saddle.

To reach Dick Willoughby and get help— that was the thought in the reeling brain of Pierre Luzon as with a final effort, leaning forward over the saddle, he turned his steed in the direction of Buck Ashley's old store, and urged it to a canter.

Chapter XL

Revelation

MERLE paused at the foot of the stairway leading up to one of the towers where Tia Teresa had her room. She deliberated for a moment, consulted the tiny watch on her wrist, then turned to retrace her footsteps.

"There will be plenty of time," she murmured to herself. "I shall be best able to manage Tia Teresa when I know still more than I do now."

She repaired to her own room and put on her automobile cloak, cap, and veil. Without telling anyone of her plan, she left the house, went to the garage, selected a runabout that was specially her own, and was soon speeding along the highway in the direction of the cluster of hills amid which the little Mexican cemetery was nestled.

She had been there just once before, several years ago, and she knew that her machine would have no difficulty in ascending the trail. Within less than an hour, indeed, she was at her destination.

In the grey evening twilight the place looked very dismal and desolate. The tiny adobe chapel in one corner was falling into ruins because of disuse and neglect. A tall rank growth of weeds overran most of the graves. But there were two that showed marks of loving attention, and toward these Merle advanced. Here she found the fresh wreaths around the headstones, and her own roses scattered on the turf.

"Hermana"—she read the single word on the white marble cross adorned with spotless arum lilies. "Sister," Merle murmured, translating the word.

Then she turned to the big gravestone close at hand, and moved the wreaths of red carnations so that she might read the words inscribed. From these she soon knew that this was the family burial place of the de Valencias—that here rested the former owners of the San Antonio Rancho, the beloved parents of two children, Manuel and Rosetta.

"Manuel," "Rosetta"—she repeated the names. The latter awakened no memory, but when she filled out the former to "Don Manuel de Valencia," she instantly recalled the old-time bandit of whom she had heard many a tale.

"The White Wolf," she murmured eagerly.

"Yes, yes. His father once owned the rancho, and that was the cause of the deadly feud—the Vendetta of the Hills. But I thought all that was forgotten. Yet here are the beautiful fresh flowers."

Seating herself on a flat monument near by, Merle pondered, piecing things together. "Sister" —the cross must mark the grave of the girl Rosetta, and have been erected by her brother, Don Manuel. Then whose hand had strewn the roses? Mr. Robles! In a flash she knew that Mr. Robles was Don Manuel.

And her father, too! The further thought came with such suddenness, with such absolute conviction of certainty, that for a moment she felt appalled. Her father the notorious robber chief, the desperado on whose head a price had been set, the outlaw who had defied the whole state of California to arrest him. Somehow she felt no shame—Don Manuel de Valencia had been a sort of heroic knight-errant in all the stories she had heard—his hand only against the rich, his heart always for the poor and oppressed, his attitude toward the intrusive gringos quite justified by the sharp practice whereby he had been robbed of his patrimonial acres. It was this very story of wrong which had been one of the reasons that

had from the first predisposed the household at
La Siesta to despise the Thurston family at the
Rancho San Antonio.

Then from thinking of Don Manuel, Merle's
mind passed to Ricardo Robles—the courteous,
dignified, generous, lovable man she had known
all her life, the very man whom she had rejoiced
that day to call her own father. Don Manuel
could be judged only by this standard, and her
heart went out again to Mr. Robles, whatever
the name which he had formerly worn.

The shadows were closing around her, the night
air bit sharply, and Merle arose. Two or three
of the rose blooms had fallen beyond the lines of
white stones that marked the graves. Merle
advanced, and picking these up gently, placed
them on the breasts of the sleeping dead. Her own
kith and kin! Now she realized how she came
to have brown eyes and raven tresses—the blood
of Spain was in her veins. With this thought
throbbing in her heart, she left the cemetery and
hurried away for home.

Tia Teresa was the only Roman Catholic at
La Siesta, a devout member of the faith of her
fathers and of her childhood days with which
no one around her had ever sought to interfere.
Her room was her private chapel, a curtained

recess at one end being fitted up with a crucifix, a small altar, and a *prie-dieu*.

Here Tia Teresa was kneeling and praying, the only light in the apartment coming from the altar candles, when Merle softly tiptoed in, still wearing her automobile cloak. She hesitated to advance, and momentarily turned to withdraw. But Tia Teresa had seen her, and by a gesture had bidden her to remain. For a few moments the old duenna's lips continued to move, then she told another bead on her rosary, arose from her knees, crossed herself devoutly, and with a final prostration before the crucifix, terminated her devotional exercises.

"What brought you here, my child?" she asked, approaching Merle.

"Why are you engaged in prayer tonight?" asked Merle, answering question with question.

"You know I often pray," replied Tia Teresa. "You have seen me many, many times."

"Yes, but not at this hour, when you are always with my mother."

"She will be wondering where I am. I had better go to her now."

"No," rejoined Merle. "I wish to speak to you. Come here, Tia Teresa; sit down by my side, and treat me once again as the little girl of the long ago whom you used to pet and fondle."

"That's very easily done," responded Tia Teresa, with a pleased smile, seating herself on the low sofa close to Merle. "Come to my heart, my darling, as in the long ago."

And the duenna drew the girl to her loving, protecting bosom. She noticed now that Merle was trembling under the influence of some deep emotion.

"What is wrong with you, my dear?" she asked anxiously.

"I have learned many things today, Tia Teresa," replied Merle, taking her old nurse's hands and softly stroking them. "First, that Mr. Robles is my father"—the duenna started, but Merle went quietly on—"and that he is really Don Manuel de Valencia, the famous outlaw."

"Whoever told you that?" fairly gasped Tia Teresa.

"No one. I found everything out for myself. After I had looked into Mr. Robles' eyes at our parting this afternoon, I knew the truth. It was impossible for mother to deny it, but it is not she who has told me anything. I have just returned from the little Mexican cemetery on the hillside where Mr. Robles, my father, had taken the flowers for which he asked me."

"And you saw his flowers—and my flowers, too?" faltered the duenna, realizing now how Merle had gleaned her knowledge.

"Yes; I inferred that the wreaths were yours, and of course I knew that the scattered roses were from my father. He is Don Manuel. But I want you to tell me a little about Rosetta." It was Merle now who put her arms around Tia Teresa and drew her affectionately to her.

"You have always loved me, you know, my dear," the girl went on coaxingly. "Now I understand why you were so deeply attached to Mr. Robles, for you told me once that you had nursed Don Manuel. And that is why I have been, perhaps, just a little closer to you than Grace"— the pressure of Tia Teresa's arms told that Merle had correctly divined—"because I was of the blood of your old master. But why has there been all this secrecy toward me?"

"Don Manuel's name could not be revealed— he had been outlawed."

"And Rosetta—tell me about Rosetta?"

"She was the real cause of the feud between Mr. Thurston and Don Manuel."

The duenna had spoken the words before she had realized how much they told. With unfaltering intuition Merle guessed their meaning.

"You mean to tell me that Thurston wronged Rosetta—betrayed her?"

Tia Teresa nodded assent—she was too deeply agitated to speak another word.

"And this day—the eleventh of October—the day when you decorate her grave?" enquired Merle, in a tone and with a look that compelled an answer.

"Is the day she was found dead on the rocks below Comanche Point," replied Tia Teresa.

At the same moment the duenna started to her feet. A wonderful and terrible transition came over her usually placid countenance. Her eyes fairly blazed with mingled fury and hatred. Her fists were clenched by her side. Her whole frame trembled.

"Murdered by Ben Thurston!" she added, the words hissing like hot lava from her lips.

"Murdered?" cried Merle, incredulously. She too, had risen.

"Yes, pushed over the cliff by his coward hands. His torn coat, one of the buttons between her dead fingers, proclaimed his guilt before God and man. But there was no justice in the land in those days— the days when the gringos broke up our Spanish homes. Now you know everything—that was the real reason of the Vendetta of the Hills."

Tia Teresa was calm again—it was Merle who was deeply agitated, too deeply agitated for a moment to speak.

The duenna went on triumphantly. "But the vendetta once sworn will always be fulfilled. Tonight at Comanche Point—"

Then she stopped short, as she saw the look of terror and horror on Merle's pale face.

"Tonight?" queried the young girl tremulously. "They meet tonight? Then that is where Mr. Robles is going—that is why he bade us all that sad good-bye? My father, oh, my dear father!"

And dropping down again on the sofa, she burst into a passion of weeping.

Tia Teresa sought to soothe her. But Merle was not to be comforted. Yet while she sobbed she was thinking, for suddenly she rose again and dashed away her tears.

"At what hour tonight?" she asked.

"I do not know," answered the duenna.

"Then he is in danger—perhaps at this very moment he is in danger. Don Manuel's life—my father's life is worth a hundred lives of such a man as Ben Thurston. Quick, quick, Teresa. Get your mantilla and cloak. My runabout is in readiness. There, let me help you."

Merle was speaking with swift insistence.

"Where are you going?" whispered Tia Teresa, as the girl's fingers were buttoning her cloak.

"To Comanche Point. We may not be too late to save him."

A minute later the two women had stolen down the narrow stairway of the tower and were speeding through the gathering darkness of the night.

Chapter XLI

Beneath the Precipice

WILLOUGHBY had found his friends Munson and Jack Rover at Buck Ashley's old store, eagerly awaiting his coming, with a fine supper sizzling on the cook stove, prepared in Jack's finest professional cowboy style.

"We've got to feed you up a bit, I reckon," grinned Jack, as he slipped the Gargantuan slab of beef-steak from the griller on to the big hot dish waiting for its reception.

"And some potatoes, too," he went on, "not forgetting the fried onions that beat all your new-fangled sauces to a frazzle."

Dick was nothing loth to fall to. He had been too excited to do more than taste the midday meal that Pierre Luzon had prepared for him in the cavern. It had been a long hard day, and now he was hungry as a wolf. In ordinary circumstances he had no objection to fried onions, but, with delicate regard for possible contingencies, he left to the others a monopoly over this item in the bill-of-fare.

There were so many things to talk about that it was a difficult matter to know where to begin. But at the close of the meal Jack Rover solved the question by sweeping the supper things from the table, and emptying thereon the contents of one of the bags of gold.

"Good old Guadalupe!" exclaimed the delighted cowboy, as he patted the nuggets with a loving hand. "I always told you that the ancient squaw had a real gold mine. I guess we'll be able to stake out our claims tomorrow, eh, Dick, my boy?"

"I'm afraid not," smiled Willoughby. "The fact is that, although I helped to wash out that gold, I have not the faintest idea where the riffle is up among the hills."

Jack's face fell. There was a moment of disappointed silence, and just then there came the sound of a faint tapping at the outer door.

"What's that?" asked Munson. The faces of all three showed that they had heard simultaneously.

Dick rose, crossed over, and threw the door wide open.

"My God, who's this?" he asked, as he stooped over the figure lying prone across the steps. "Pierre, Pierre!" he added, as he turned over the face.   "It's Pierre Luzon, boys, and desperately wounded!"

The others were pressed together in the doorway.

"Looks as if he had crawled here on his hands and knees," remarked Munson.

"There's his horse out among the chaparral," exclaimed Jack, pointing to the shadowy form of the animal from which the wounded man had obviously tumbled.

"Stand clear," cried Dick, gathering up Pierre in his arms.   "He has fainted, but is still alive."

And Dick, carrying the senseless form, passed into the bedroom beyond the living room, and there laid poor old Pierre on the very cot which he had occupied once before—on the eventful night when Tom Baker had brought the paroled convict from San Quentin.

A few drops of whisky brought the wounded man back to consciousness.   Dick leaned over him and caught the faintly whispered words. Pierre was speaking in the French of his childhood days.

"He is dead—he is dead!   At last Rosetta is avenged!"

Dick motioned his companions to silence.   He bent down close to the dying bandit.

"Who is dead, Pierre?   Ben Thurston?"

"Yes, yes. Ben Thurston. Glory be to God! Don Manuel is avenged!"

"And how did you come to be shot, Pierre? Where is Don Manuel?"

"Dead—dead, too!" The wounded man this time cried out the words and struggled to sit up. His eyes opened wide, and fastened themselves on Dick. His voice again dropped to a whisper; he was speaking lucidly now. "But perhaps he lives. Who knows? Go and save him, Dick— Don Manuel—go, go."

Exhausted, Pierre sank back on the pillow. His eyes closed. The death rattle was in his throat.

"Where is he—where shall I find Don Manuel?"

Dick uttered the words close to Pierre's ear. He alone caught the faint answer. Pierre Luzon was dead.

"He's gone, Chester," said Dick, standing erect.

Munson stooped, put his ear to Pierre's breast, then pressed apart one pair of the eyelids.

"Yes, it's all over," he said solemnly, as he folded the coverlet over the already marble-like face.

In stricken silence the three men passed to the outer room, shutting the door softly behind them.

"What's happened?" asked Jack Rover, "I couldn't catch his bloomin' lingo."

"Something terrible. There has evidently been

a fight to the death on Comanche Point between Ben Thurston and Don Manuel. Looks as if both of them had gone over the cliff in the struggle."

"Gee!" muttered the cowboy.

Dick remained just a moment in deep thought. His plan of action was promptly decided on.

"Munson, old man, you saddle my pony, and ride to Tejon for help. Jack, you remain here with the body."

"And with the nuggets," remarked the cowboy drily.

Dick paid no heed to the interruption. He continued:

"I'll take the horse outside, and ride back to Comanche Point. That's the best we can do, and the main thing is to do it quickly. Pass me that flask of whisky—it may come in handy. I'm off now, boys. You'll find me at the cliff. Bring a doctor, Ches. So long!"

The moon had now risen, and while Dick was galloping toward Comanche Point from the one direction, the runabout, with Merle at the wheel and Tia Teresa by her side, was speeding from the other end of the valley toward the same destination. The horseman was the first to arrive.

Willoughby had no need to search long beneath the precipice. A loud, continuous cry of lamenta-

tion guided him to the spot.   There, wailing over
the corpse of Don Manuel, was the old Indian
squaw, Guadalupe.   Even in death the two bodies
were locked in each other's embrace, and Dick
noted with horror that Ben Thurston's teeth were
buried in the flesh of his enemy's shoulder.
Guadalupe was in the act of trying to separate
the dead men when Dick intervened.

Great heavens, what a withered, aged face was
raised toward his own! It was the first time he
had ever seen Guadalupe unveiled and at close
quarters. Her cheeks were wrinkled into a
hundred folds; her eyes were sunken in deep
cavernous hollows. When he touched her, she
rose and, jabbering furiously for all the world
like an angry ape, reviled him with curses, her
meaning unmistakable, although she spoke in some
strange Indian tongue.

Just then Dick caught the distant chug-chug
of the automobile. He looked up the valley,
wondering who might be passing at that hour
of night. This was not the main highway;
nobody ever came to Comanche Point after
dark. Some intervening spur of the foothills
dulled the sound; all was still and silent.

He became conscious that Guadalupe's fury had
spent itself, and turned round. The squaw was

gone.   His eyes searched the scrub; at one place he saw the twigs bending, and he even fancied he could detect the outline of the white wolf gliding away through the brushwood.   But that was all.

Again the sound of the automobile smote his ears;   louder now, and only a few hundred yards away he beheld the headlights sweeping toward the spot where he stood.   He resolved to intercept the vehicle and stepped across the belt of chaparral that intervened between him and the roadway. Gaining the thoroughfare, he called aloud and the machine slowed down.

But what was his utter amazement when Merle jumped from the runabout.   To her there could be no more surprises on this night of surprises.

"Dick," she exclaimed, as she accepted his embrace almost as a matter of course.

"How do you come to be here, Merle, my darling?" he asked, holding her in his arms.

"Something terrible is going to happen.   I have come to try to prevent it.   Have you seen Don Manuel?"

"Don Manuel!"   He repeated the name in great surprise.

"Mr. Robles is Don Manuel," she gasped by way of explanation.

"I am aware.   He told me so today."

"Well, where is he now?   And his enemy, Mr. Thurston?"

Dick still had an arm on her shoulder. She was gazing up into his face, her voice trembling with emotion as she breathlessly plied him with her questions.

"You have come too late, dearest," Willoughby gently replied.

"Dead!" she exclaimed.

"Both are dead. They fought and rolled over the precipice. I have just found their bodies lying in the chaparral back there."

Merle leaned forward, sobbing on his breast.

"Take me to him, take me to him," she cried.

"No, Merle, my dear. It is better not. You must go home. Tia Teresa," he added, addressing the duenna who had drawn near, "she must go home. Munson has gone to Tejon for help. There will be people arriving here very soon now."

"He is really dead—Don Manuel?" asked Tia Teresa in a voice of awed sadness.

"There can be nothing but the one answer," replied Dick. "Don Manuel has passed on."

"Take me to him," moaned Merle.

"No, no, Merle. This is no sight for you."

"But, Dick, Dick, don't you know one other thing?" she pleaded, raising her tearful eyes.

"What other thing?"

"Don Manuel—was my father—my dear, dear father."

Again Willoughby was overwhelmed with amazement.

"Your father?" he murmured.

"Yes, I only came to know it today. So, Dick, dear, even though he is dead, let me kiss him now, let me kneel by his side and tell him that I loved him, and will always love and revere his memory. Let me watch by him until the others come."

Dick drew the sobbing girl close to him. His eyes sought those of Tia Teresa. He shook his head, telling the duenna in an unmistakable way that Merle must be taken home—that she must not be shocked by the gruesome spectacle hidden in the chaparral.

Even as their eyes met, the faint throb of an automobile was heard, and glancing across the plain Dick saw the far-away headlights twinkling like twin stars. With a gesture he directed Tia Teresa's attention to the coming help.

"I shall watch by our beloved dead one," said the duenna. "My place is by his side. Come, dearie," she went on, placing an arm around Merle's waist. "Mr. Willoughby will drive you back to La Siesta, and I shall see that your father's body is taken to his home. There we shall pay all honor to the dead."

Together they led Merle, unresisting now, to the runabout. Dick got in beside her, and took the wheel.

"They will be here very soon now," he said to Tia Teresa. "Mr. Munson will give you all the help you require. I'll look after Merle."

He backed the machine, turned, and the little red light swept up the roadway into the distance. From across the valley the headlights of a big automobile were now glaring like flashing suns in the soft moonlight.

It was the hands of Tia Teresa that separated the bodies. That of Ben Thurston she flung from her as if it had been carrion for the buzzards and coyotes. Then she knelt down and stroked with loving hand the brow of Don Manuel. On the dead face was a look of ineffable calm.

"Manuel, my Manuel, the little child I nursed! My beautiful, brave Manuel!"

Thus lamenting, she awaited the coming of Munson and his friends.

Chapter XLII

Wedding Bells

A FULL year had passed, and the good people of Tejon had at last ceased to speak daily about Dick Willoughby's exciting adventures, Ben Thurston's inglorious death, and the romantic and now indubitable ending of the famous outlaw, Don Manuel.

Both the victims of the desperate fight on Comanche Point had been laid to rest—Don Manuel, in the little Mission churchyard above the hill, side by side with the beloved sister of his youthful days, whose betrayal and death he had at last avenged, although at the cost of his own life; Ben Thurston, in the modern cemetery beside his son, the poor weak youth in whom the once sturdy family of pioneers had sunk to final decadency. Pierre Luzon, the brave and chivalrous old Frenchman, slept near the grave of the chief he had served so loyally, and, according to the old-time bandit code of ethics, so nobly and so well. In the God's acres where all feuds pass to oblivion there was perfect peace.

Sing Ling had unobtrusively departed for China, a wealthy man, as the bank manager at Bakersfield could have told, no doubt destined to become a leading magnate in the Flowery Land. Guadalupe was never seen again; the aged squaw had probably died in her secret cave. The white wolf, too, had perished; a cowboy riding the range had been attracted by some buzzards flying and circling round and round far up on the mountain side, and on making his way to the indicated spot, had found the animal's carcass picked almost to the bones. The old days were forever gone.

But in the beautiful city of Tejon a glorious era of happiness was in progress. Christmas-tide had come round again, and had been made gay with a tournament of roses, and then with the dawning of the New Year had followed a round of festivities in honor of the double wedding of Dick Willoughby and Merle Farnsworth, Chester Munson and Grace Darlington.

In no place was there more sincere and hilarious rejoicing than in the back parlor of Buck Ashley's fine new store, where the mystery keg, sacredly reserved for this great occasion, was once more on tap and the postmaster, assisted by Tom Baker and Jack Rover, dispensed hospitality to a few chosen friends. But all good things come to an end, and it was with a regretful sigh that the sheriff squeezed out the last few drops from the tilted keg and sipped for the last time "the blessed nectar" that had served to keep green the memory of "dear old Pierre."

The marriage ceremonies had been performed in a fine little church that sheltered all denominations in the new town, and amidst a shower of rice and old shoes the happy couples had departed for the wedding breakfast at La Siesta.

To Merle the day was one of blissful joy, but of tender regrets as well. During the quiet afternoon hours she and Dick had conversed about their dear old friend, Mr. Robles—the gallant and chivalrous Don Manuel—the beloved father whose identity as such was known only to their own two selves besides Mrs. Darlington and Tia Teresa.

And now the hour of departure on the honeymoon trail had come. The idea of a trip to Europe had been abandoned for the present. The young couples were going up among the Canadian Rockies, by divergent routes which would meet a little later on, and all were full of enthusiasm at the thought of seeing the mighty mountains in their wintry grandeur.

Mrs. Darlington accompanied the young people to the railway station, but Tia Teresa was too deeply affected to trust herself away from home. Merle had kissed her a tender good-bye in the apartment in the tower, and, despite the joyful promise that they would soon meet again, had left the old duenna in prayerful tears before her little altar.

At last they were pulling out from the depot, where the church crowd of the morning had re-assembled in full force, with fresh supplies of good-luck munitions.

Thus, like a disbanding company of players, the actors in this tale of California, pass into history. The olden days of bandits are no more, while the hatred of the gringo is only a tradition. The broad acres of the San Antonio Rancho no longer lie comparatively fallow in Nature's pasture, but are tilled by the thrifty plowman as he labors afield with fullest confidence of a bountiful reward. Meanwhile, the mountains that look down upon the beauteous valley guard their secret well. But searching eyes will yet, undoubtedly, sometime, somewhere, rediscover the mysterious cavern with its hoarded millions of loot, stored by the rapacious hands of Joaquin Murietta, the White Wolf, and their brigand bands, its lake of oil from which outlaws fed their lamps, and its subterranean river from whose shallow riffles Guadalupe, and Dick Willoughby also, gathered a wealth of golden spoil.

THE END